Blank
Canvas
I0714784

Blank Canvas

ARTIST DUET – BOOK ONE

PERSEPHONE AUTUMN

BETWEEN WORDS PUBLISHING LLC

Blank Canvas

Copyright © 2022 by Persephone Autumn

www.persephoneautumn.com

All rights reserved.

No part of this book may be reproduced in any form or by any electronic or mechanical means, including photocopying, information storage and retrieval systems, without written permission from the author except for the use of brief quotations in a book review.

This book is a work of fiction. Names, characters, establishments, organizations, and incidents are either products of the author's imagination or are used fictitiously to give a sense of authenticity. Any resemblance to actual events, places, or persons, living or dead, is entirely coincidental.

If you're reading this book and did not purchase it, or it was not purchased for your use only, then it was pirated illegally. Please purchase a copy of your own and respect the hard work of this author.

ISBN: 978-1-951477-28-8 (Ebook)

ISBN: 978-1-951477-29-5 (Paperback)

Editor: Ellie McLove | My Brother's Editor

Proofreader: Rosa Sharon | My Brother's Editor

Cover Design: Kat Savage | Kat Savage Designs

Books by Persephone Autumn

Bay Area Duet Series

Click Duet

Through the Lens

Time Exposure

Inked Duet

Fine Line

Love Buzz

Insomniac Duet

Restless Night

A Love So Bright

Artist Duet

Blank Canvas

Abstract Passion

Devotion Series

Distorted Devotion

Undying Devotion

Beloved Devotion

Darkest Devotion

<u>**Standalone Romance Novels**</u>

Depths Awakened

Sweet Tooth

Transcendental

<u>**Poetry Collections**</u>

Ink Veins

Broken Metronome

Slipping From Existence

<u>PUBLISHED UNDER P. AUTUMN</u>

<u>**Standalone Horror Novels**</u>

By Dawn

For those who have been broken by people and circumstances beyond your control. For those who decided to take a leap and be selfish for the first time.

PROLOGUE
DEVLYN

Four Years Ago

"We should break up."

I rear my head back as if Kelsey slapped me. Did I hear her correctly?

The crowd continues to cheer and dance as high-volume music plays around us. A tassel smacks my cheek as another graduate from our senior class squeezes through the throng of bodies.

Leaning in, I speak next to Kelsey's ear. "Sorry, didn't hear you over the noise." At least I don't think I heard her. "What'd you say?"

Kelsey takes my hand and guides us through hundreds of our classmates and their families. Her hand in mine feels different, colder, less comforting. Nothing like the girl I've known the past three years. The abrupt change has me queasy and unsettled.

Once we reach the outskirts, she stops and spins to

face me. The downturn of her lips is an instant red flag. A warning sign telling me I didn't mishear what she said a moment ago. But I refuse to believe it. Not until I hear the words clearly from her lips and the reason why.

"Devlyn, I'm sorry." Her bottom lip juts out as her eyes droop at the corners.

She's sorry? You have got to be kidding me. Her *sorry* appears a little too forced, a little too practiced.

Kelsey and I have been practically inseparable since Andrew Bishop's "We survived freshman year" party three years ago. It wasn't an instant love connection, but she carried herself unlike other high school girls. More mature and less catty. She had this air about her; a strength I gravitated toward. Plus, she made me laugh. A lot.

We had hung out all summer. By the time sophomore year started, Kelsey Martin was officially my girlfriend. Not a single day passed where I doubted our relationship or its backbone. We were solid. Practically attached at the hip. In love.

Or so I thought.

"You're sorry?" The words leave my lips harsher than intended, but I don't regret the severity of my tone. Not when the girl who has owned my heart for three years says she wants to break up. I glance off to the side, too stunned to see anything. When I return my gaze, every soft line of her face—the ones I drew from memory with pencil and charcoal—blur into a blob of unpleasant colors. "Doesn't seem like you're sorry," I choke out.

A hand grazes my forearm and I yank it from her grip.

Her head falls forward as she sniffles. "Please don't hate me." Sadness laces her voice and makes me question reality. Makes me question the reason behind this sudden change.

"How did you expect me to feel?" I shiver, cross my arms over my chest and hug myself. "Did you expect me to be okay with this?" I close my eyes, take a deep breath, and open them on the exhale. "You gave no indications. We see each other every day and you've never said or shown you're unhappy."

"I'm not," she says quickly.

Our eyes meet and I shake my head. "Then why?" I want to touch her. Want to reach out, wrap my arms around her, and mold her to my frame.

But I won't. Never again. Doing so only muddles the water more.

She stares off toward the crowd, laughs without humor then meets my doubtful eyes. "Graduation day," she murmurs. "Today should be one of the happiest days of our non-adult lives." I nod but keep my lips sealed. Right now, I don't trust my voice or the words I might spew. "Last night, as I got everything ready for today, it blindsided me."

My brows pinch at the middle. "What did?"

Kelsey waves a hand toward the massive gathering, as if I should automatically know the storm of thoughts brewing in her head. "This!" She points to random people, then waves a hand at the room. "Graduation. The end. And not just the end of high school, but the start of what follows."

This isn't hot off the press news. Most of our senior year was spent in assemblies discussing what would happen this year and what it all meant. Most of junior and senior year was packed with college discussions and plans for after high school. Kelsey and I had discussed all this at length with each other. Us taking different paths after high school wasn't anything new. And we talked, on more than one occasion, about our relationship post high school.

Our conversations never revolved around breaking up. Of course our relationship would be different, but we planned to stick it out.

Yes, hundreds of miles would separate us—Kelsey starts Florida State in the fall while I start at Ringling. Less than a day's drive away, our plan was to spend as many weekends and breaks together as possible. We had it all mapped out.

Or so I thought. Obviously, unbeknownst to me, those plans flew out the window.

"And?" I drag out the single-word question. "We talked about this."

She shakes her head, not wanting to hear what I have to say. "No, Dev. We talked about our fantasy life, post high school." Her eyes close a beat, then meet mine. Another shiver racks my body at the coldness in her eyes, the stiffness in her posture. "Reality check, we aren't kids anymore. Even if we met in the middle, seeing each other on off days would be exhausting. Both of us will get behind in our studies. It's just too hard."

She averts her eyes to the senior class twenty feet from us. Her spine straightens as she wipes all emotion from her face. Bile rises in my throat as I take in this new side of her. A side I have never seen. A side that makes me sick to my stomach.

How long has this part of her existed? How long has splitting up been on her mind? I refuse to ask because I fear learning the truth. That she has considered the idea of breaking up for much longer than a day or two.

"Breaking up is for the best," she says without looking my way. "We should get to experience college and this new phase of our lives. Make new friends. See the world… without fear of hurting each other."

All I hear is… *I want to have fun and be open to new experiences without being tied down. Better to break up now than cheat on my boyfriend and feel guilty.*

I won't throw the words in her face, but I am no fool. Well, maybe I *am* a fool. A heartbroken idiot who believed the girl he loved would want to be with him for years to come. A naive guy who thought his girl cared for him as much as he did her.

What the fuck is wrong with me?

What boy believes he found his soul mate at fifteen? Trusting boys with moldable hearts, that is who.

Kelsey continues on her tirade of why our breakup is for the best, but I don't hear a word she says. Her voice is white noise in my ears. The words scrambled and vacant and pointless. When I don't respond to something she said, she pats my shoulder, mouths something else, then walks off.

Week-long seconds pass as I stand in the same place and stare at the fuzzy basketball championship banners over the collapsed bleachers. A warm hand settles on my shoulder, a perfume I have known since childhood fills my nose. My mom says something beside me, her voice saccharine and insincere yet firm. A woman not to be crossed. I have no clue what she said, but I nod.

I exit the gymnasium with my parents, thankful when Dad's arm hooks around my shoulders, and walk to the car. Our drive to the restaurant is a blur. Graduation dinner goes by in a haze of disbelief. With each passing minute, a black vignette clouds my periphery. Blankets my vision. The thumping organ in my rib cage beats with less enthusiasm. And it doesn't take long before the pericardium around my heart shrinks. Withers. Splinters into thousands of jagged pieces and stabs the vital organ it holds.

With each new wave of darkness, I make a new vow.

I will never let anyone in again. Never let someone close enough to ruin me with such severity. And never will I give another my heart. The agony in the fallout isn't worth the risk. No one is worth this endless heartache.

Then, I give in. Let pain and darkness swallow me into the abyss. Let my world go numb.

ONE

SHELLY

I LOVE PINK. MUCH OF MY WARDROBE CONSISTS OF various shades of the hue. But seeing this much—balloons, streamers, cake, clothes, drinks—has me nauseous.

Another round of oohs and awes fills the room as Cora opens another gift and holds up an infant-sized black dress with tiny pink hearts. Then she pulls out a pair of black Mary Jane's, small enough to fit in her palm, and her eyes glaze over.

The smile on my face is genuine. The joy in my heart is real.

I am happy for my best friend and her husband, Gavin. They deserve nothing *but* happiness and love after the journey their relationship has endured. I never pictured them as parents, but since finding out Cora was pregnant, they smile more than ever before.

Truly, I am happy for them.

The last two and a half years have been a whirlwind. For everyone in our circle. Everyone except me.

My best friend since forever—the woman we are here to celebrate joining motherhood soon—reunited with the love of her life. Gavin. Their reunion tipped the first domino.

Watching Cora and Gavin come back together and fall in love all over again, was magical. Like something from one of the romance novels on my bookshelf. I sat front and center with popcorn in hand. Consoled my friend when she needed someone to listen and give advice. Offered my shoulder when she needed to cry. But deep down, anyone who knew them before knew their relationship would stand the test of time. After more than a decade apart, their love was timeless. Genuine. The real deal.

"Oomph." Cora sets down the gift bag, shifts on the couch, and rubs her growing belly.

Elizabeth, more affectionately called Mom by more than just Cora, rises from her seat in the living room and wanders down the hall. Not a minute later, she strolls back in with an office chair lumbar pillow and offers it to Cora.

"Might make you more comfortable."

"Thanks, Mom." She tucks the cushion behind her, leans back, and sighs. "She has been so active the last week. I swear she's rearranging my organs in there." Cora laughs and we all join in.

My eyes drift around the room. Take in the small group of women gathered to celebrate the impending arrival of Cora and Gavin's bundle of joy. So much love resides in our close-knit circle, and I am blessed to have these women in my life. Women who will drop whatever they are doing to help one another. Friendship and family like ours cannot be bought. It brews over time and strengthens with each passing day.

Cora continues to rub her belly, then sucks in a breath. "She kicked." A pained smile lights up her face as her gaze shifts from one person to the next, until she reaches me, her best friend. Cora is the one person I know better than anyone else walking the earth, and vice versa. "Come here, Auntie Shell. Check out Miss Clara's latest dance moves. Something tells me she'll be our karaoke choreographer one day."

I laugh and shake my head as I cross the room and plop down beside Cora. "I have a feeling this little girl will change us all." Looking over at Autumn, whose belly has just started to round as well, I smile. "Just as Clementine did."

I lay my hand on Cora's belly and she guides me to where baby Clara kicks. The second her little foot punts my hand, tears pool in my eyes. Feeling this sweet girl stretch her limbs warms my heart. She will be loved and spoiled, not by just her parents, but by us all. Especially me.

Cora sucks in a breath and looks to me for confirmation. "Did you feel that?" I nod but don't answer, too scared my voice will be sandpaper. "Girl is one tough cookie. She'll exit the womb kicking her legs."

Elizabeth and Autumn laugh. Of the small group of

women in attendance, only two have experienced pregnancy and childbirth. Elizabeth, of course, and Autumn. Gavin's mom didn't fly out for the shower but will be in town a while once Clara joins the world. Erin, Penny, Peyton, and I sit in silent awe. Motherhood has never been big on my radar, but I don't discount the idea. If the right person came into my life and our relationship became serious enough to travel down that path, the possibility of motherhood would be given merit.

But motherhood, let alone love, is such a distant reality in my life. Not intentionally. I love the idea of finding the one and falling in love. I love knowing, one day, I will have someone special at my side.

If anyone listens to my inner ramblings, go ahead and send him my way. Please.

"Can't wait to meet her," I say, then look to Autumn. "And your new addition too."

Little Clara settles and Cora resumes opening gifts. We play strange baby shower games for hours. Tasting jars of baby food while blindfolded and trying to guess the flavor —which is disgusting, in case you were unaware. Guessing the number of candies in a baby bottle. Speed changing diapers on dolls while someone covers our eyes. Each game is equally fun and weird, and the laughter never lets up.

Once the games are done, we scope out the massive buffet of food.

Peyton—my soon-to-be sister-in-law—told her mom about the baby shower and Tracy insisted on catering the day. No complaints here. I file into line near the end, pick up a pink paper plate with "It's a girl!" swirled in the center, and pile food onto my plate.

Being that it is Cora's day, Tracy got a list of her favorite foods and things she steered away from while pregnant. Needless to say, much of the buffet has Asian flavors. A variety of vegetable sushi, rice noodle dishes, and spring rolls. But there are also macaroni and cheese balls, lettuce wraps, muffin-sized fruit tarts, and large trays with fresh vegetables, fruit, cheese, crackers, and dips.

Tracy is awesome in the kitchen and made enough to feed three times the people present. She also made two dozen chocolate cupcakes with white-and-pink frosting. No doubt we will all leave with tons of leftovers. Again, no complaints.

With Micah and Peyton's wedding only three weeks away, I am eager to see what Tracy makes for her only daughter's reception.

Another nail in my love life coffin… my brother is getting married. To the woman who crushed on him in high school. Who also happens to be the woman he bullied in high school. The entirety of their relationship leaves me baffled.

When Micah and Peyton started hanging out as acquaintances-slash-friends, I never expected it to go anywhere. Their history was a hot mess. Not only had my big brother been her high school bully, Micah had been burned by his one and only serious relationship. And Peyton was far from interested in finding love after past losses. As a romantic couple, they were wobbly and jagged. Destined to fall apart.

But they found a way to grow beyond the horrible parts of their past. Developed an irrefutable friendship. Then slowly, they fell in love. Their love story was rocky, but neither of them gave up. What they felt for each other superseded every obstacle thrown their way.

Is there anyone in my life I *don't* envy? *Someone send help. Please.*

All I want is to find *the one*. Have a boundless love that captivates me from the start. A love that makes you forget anything and anyone else exists. A love that consumes every molecule of air you breathe. That owns every beat of your heart. A love you would crumble without.

That's not asking for too much, right? Wanting someone to look at me like I am the reason they breathe isn't asking too much. Wanting someone to take hold of my hand and never let go isn't asking too much. Not from where I stand. My friends have that type of love. It's only fair I have it too.

Sure, my notion of love and romance and happily ever afters are skewed by the countless romance novels I read. So what? There is nothing wrong with a woman knowing what she wants. There is nothing wrong with setting emotional expectations. There is nothing wrong with wanting immeasurable love.

Could I have dated half the county by now? Sure. Plenty of men have flirted and let me know they were interested. And who knows, maybe I would have found *the one* had I put myself out there more. Of the men I flirted with and casually dated, my *the-one* alarm never rang. Not once was there a whirl in my belly. No instinctual voice to tell me *give this one a chance.*

Does this make me pathetic? Not in my eyes. Does this make me a sad excuse? Depends who you ask. But I would rather be single than exist in an unhappy relationship. I'd rather be single and sad than tied to a person and dismal. Period.

Most of the men I dated were nice. Gentleman. Never pushy or angry I didn't give it up—which shocked me more than expected. The men in my everyday life—family and friends—are mixed bags in this department. That is, until they got hit by Cupid's arrow and settled down. My brother was the worst of them all, but only because of how things went down with his ex. Can't say I blame him.

Out of the inner circle, the original group—Cora, Micah, Jonas, Erin, and me—I never expected to be one of the last standing solo. The woman who preaches love and fate is one of the last to find it herself.

Erin has been dating on and off, but stays too focused on work for a relationship to stick. Leading a solo life doesn't bother her. At least she gets out there and makes an effort, which is more than I can say for myself.

"You okay?" Cora parks in the chair next to me and wraps an arm around my shoulders. "You're quiet all of a sudden. Which is not you."

I twist in my seat and smile at my best friend. Neither of our lives has been perfect. The years she and Gavin were apart were harsh and painful—for her and those of us who cared for either or both of them. All the nights I spent hugging my best friend and shushing her cries were tough. At the time, I didn't understand her heartache. How losing Gavin caused her to cry for days and weeks and months. Couldn't comprehend how her soul ripped in two at the loss of him.

And I still can't.

Not because I have a cold heart or am numb to emotion. Simply put, I have yet to experience an all-encompassing love. A love that owns every piece of you. I also don't know what it feels like to lose something so profound. To have your heart torn in two.

Instead of moping at her baby shower—one of the most joyous moments in her life—I should be giddy. The excited aunt showering my most loyal and lovable friend with pink frilly outfits and pacifiers and boxes of diapers. I should be hyping the party, not bringing it down.

Unfortunately, the small cynical part of me refuses to relinquish my selfishness. Refuses to spread false joy.

I take her hand in mine and meet her sincere, bright gaze. "I'll be okay. Just in a funk."

"Say no more." A very pregnant Cora hobbles out of her chair and tugs me upright. Before I admonish her, she hugs me tight to her body—a challenge in and of itself. My arms wind around her frame as I bite the inside of my cheek to halt the threatening tears. "I love you, Shell," she whispers in my ear. "No matter what, you can always come to me with whatever. You know that, right?"

Biting my cheek harder, I nod. "Yeah," I choke out. "I know."

She leans back enough to look me in the eye. Swipes

my hair from my cheek. Studies my glassy irises. Tips up the corners of her lips slightly. "Whenever you want to talk, I'm here. Always. Doesn't matter what time or what it's about, I'm here."

I nod again. "Okay." I swipe beneath my eyes and sniffle. "But not today. Today is about you and"—I rub her belly—"Miss Clara."

Cora narrows her eyes for a split second, then drops her gaze to her swollen belly and rubs large circles. "Can't wait for us all to meet her, Shell. Pregnancy has been the most astonishing and uncomfortable experience." We laugh. "But I wouldn't trade a second of it." Cora lifts her gaze and locks me in place. "One day, you'll know too."

"Yeah, okay," I scoff. "Procreation requires a deposit, if you catch my drift. And no one's stopped by the bank."

Cora snort-laughs and braces herself on my shoulder as a hand holds her belly. "Oh my god, Shell. Finances have never sounded so dirty." She laughs harder, then stops abruptly. "Shit. I gotta pee."

I giggle to myself as my best friend waddles down the hallway as fast as her feet and belly will allow. What an interesting sight.

The rest of the shower goes by with more food, baby talk, and laughter. I smile and laugh at all the right times. I am happy for my friend. Happy that the stars in her life have finally aligned. Happy she and Gavin reconnected and rediscovered their love.

In many ways, their love story gives me hope. Tells me all things are possible.

Now, I need to *believe* it.

If romance novels have taught me anything, it is that love happens when you least expect it. Not all love is explosive. Not all love hits hard and fast. But... love happens for us all. In one way or another. I just need to practice patience while I wait for mine to show.

No matter how long it takes.

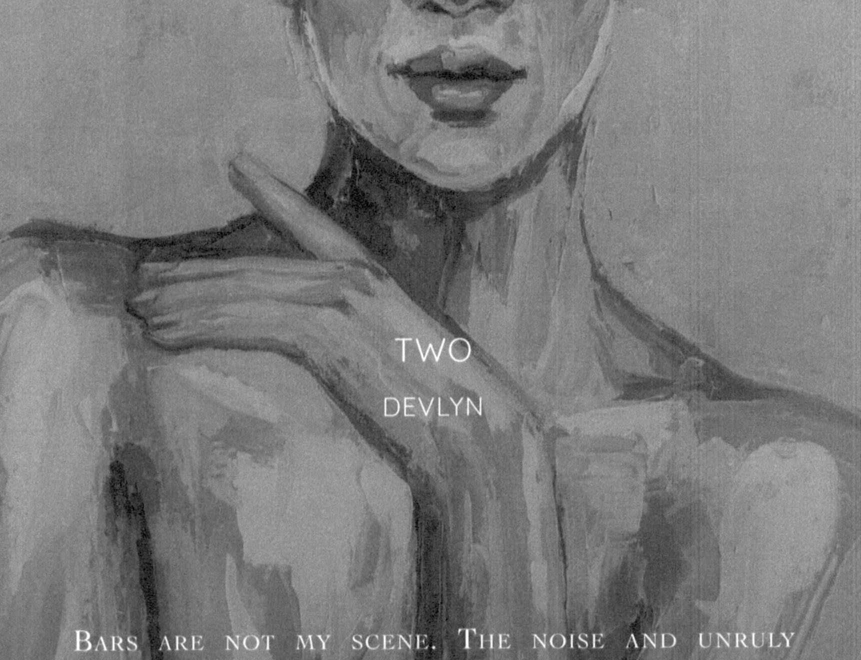

TWO

DEVLYN

BARS ARE NOT MY SCENE. THE NOISE AND UNRULY behavior make my skin crawl. Hundreds of desperate people vying for attention. Countless others drowning their sorrows and problems with a temporary numbing agent. The occasional few just here for food and a laugh with friends.

Like me.

I wouldn't be sitting at this high top if not for the guy across the table. Chet Yarborough. The man who got me through some rough days at Ringling. Days I avoid thinking of at all costs. Chet graduated with his Bachelor of Fine Arts spring of last year and moved to New York a month later to pursue his career. Since arriving in the Big Apple, his name has splashed the artist headlines a few times. In our world, having your name in the headlines is a big deal—no matter how big or small the media outlet.

When Chet called last week and said he would be in town, I jumped on the chance to hang with him. Even if that means sitting in a bar and shirking away from swaying bodies. It isn't often I leave the house or my studio. Not without a reason. Some might call me a hermit. I don't really care. There is no point in wasting gas or time or money if my leaving serves no purpose.

Chet dunks an onion ring in an odd but tasty barbecue-ranch sauce. Before it reaches his lips, he asks, "How've things been? Tell me what's new."

Before I get the chance to avoid and spin the question back to him, he shoves the onion ring in his mouth. If I say nothing, the empty time while he chews will be awkward. Not that I care about uncomfortable situations —life is full of discomfiture. I just go with the flow.

But Chet is the opposite. A rarity among our kind. The extraverted artist. The guy who paints and sculpts and draws for others more than himself. A people pleaser artist with a chatty disposition.

"Not much, man. Graduation was a few months back. Still doing my own thing—side projects, special requests, and whatnot—like before. Staying busy. What about you? How's New York?"

He finishes chewing and washes it down with a swig of beer. "New York is its own world. Bustling and alive and nothing like Florida. Like all places, it has its ups and downs, but I love the energy. It inspires me in ways I never expected."

New York is arguably one of the best places for the arts, in all forms. I never picture myself in places like New York or San Francisco, Los Angeles, or Miami. They are fantastic cities, hands down. Artist friendly and more welcoming than most. But the constant crowds, people in my space and nonstop business make me queasy. Bad enough I already live in one of the most populous areas of Florida. No need to up the ante and suffocate myself.

"That's great, man. I hope to move away too. But somewhere less crowded. Somewhere I can sit outside with an easel, a blank canvas and my brushes, and get lost without interruption."

Chet nods and then stares off into the crowd. Zoning out and getting lost in the idea. "Sounds nice," he mutters.

More than nice, actually.

Before either of us gets in another word, a man's voice booms from the far wall. "Good evening, ladies and gents. Welcome to another night of glory and excellent renditions. Also known as karaoke night."

The night went from a three out of ten to a five with this announcement. I don't necessarily love karaoke, but at least it may simmer down the crowd nearby. Have fewer people in my personal bubble for the rest of our time here.

A server arrives at our table, offers refills, and asks if we need anything else. With Chet more than happy to talk all night, I order something more substantial than an appetizer. She scribbles down my turkey burger and fries, our drink refills, and Chet's buffalo wings on a small notepad, then wanders back to the bar.

An older man steps up onto the karaoke stage and the crowd roars to life with wolf whistles and rapturous applause. Obviously, he is karaoke famous in this place. A local favorite.

I study the man as he takes the stage. Old enough to easily be my grandfather, the man sports attire of someone half his age or younger. His vibrance captivates and holds your attention. For a beat, I picture him in a swirl of blues and reds and whites on canvas. The wrinkled lines of his face a testimony of a life well lived.

Across the dining area, a voice screams above all the rest and steals the spotlight momentarily. "We love you, Karaoke Grandpa."

The old man blows kisses to the masses. "I love you too, sugar."

I scan the sea of excited bargoers in search of the woman who called out to him. Not sure why, but I need to put a face to the voice. I crane my neck and survey hundreds of men and women, looking for the one face excited to see this man grace the stage and microphone.

And then I land on her.

Familiar and not in the same breath. Sun-kissed golden skin. Dark, twinkling irises fanned by long lashes and accentuated with bold brows. Thrill on her naturally pouty lips and at the corners of her eyes. A slim yet prom-inent nose. Thick, dark-blonde waves swing from her ponytail; the occasional stubborn lock grazes her cheek, but she doesn't swipe it away.

Where do I know her from?

I dig through my mental archive and search for her face. Run the contours of her cheekbones and lips and nose against my mental database. Scour all the places I frequent and the jobs I have done. And it doesn't take long before I get a hit. Before her familiarity becomes crystal clear.

Last year. The mural I painted outside Petal and Vine Florist before fall semester. The woman more vibrant and spectacular than all the blooming buds in the shop. The woman I spent hours sneaking glances at, only to get small snippets of her profile or the way her hair glowed in the sunlight. The woman whose name I never learned because our paths barely crossed.

No matter how many peeps I got of her partial profile, I wanted more.

I had never spent so much time on such a simple project. Never purposely dragged out my art to spend more time in someone's presence. I may not know her name, but the fading memory of her had been a muse for much of my art this past year.

How odd I didn't recognize her right away. Must be the lighting or this place; both so very different from the flower shop.

Fingers snap in front of my face and I jerk back. My eyes snap to Chet and his shit-eating grin. I don't crumble under his scrutiny. Nor do I feel shame or guilt. Instead, I stare back with a look that asks why he got all snappy.

"Who is she?"

I shrug. "Don't know." Not a lie. We never shared a conversation. Far as I know, she has no clue who I am either. "Looks like someone I've met but can't place." Half-truth. But that is all I plan to give Chet. Last thing I need is a long list of intrusive questions I have no answers to.

He glances over his shoulder at her profile; too long for my liking. I bite my tongue, stow the possessiveness simmering in my veins, and wait for him to break his stare. Thank goodness, for his sake, I don't wait long.

"You should talk to her." I raise my brows at his suggestion. He shakes his head and laughs. "I have no intention of hooking up with anyone while I'm home. Not my style. You, on the other hand, will be around. And she has obviously caught your eye."

You have no idea.

I pick up my water and sip it to avoid responding for a moment. Before I set the cup down, the server comes to the rescue. She deposits red plastic baskets lined with red-and-white-checkered paper beneath our food. Soon as she steps away, I pluck my burger from the basket and take a monstrous bite.

The entire time we eat, neither of us says a word. I pretend to listen and focus on the crowd favorites. Chet appears to enjoy the entertainment.

While he does, I sneak the occasional glance at my anonymous muse. Take in her smile. The brightness with a hint of shadow. A touch of shade not all eyes would detect.

But I see them all. The light, the dark, the spectrum in between.

There is something beautiful about capturing all the facets of another person. Without words, without touch. Just what the naked eye sees. Translated through the mind of another. An unspoken truth sketched in graphite, scrawled in charcoal or stroked in oils.

Nothing speaks louder than the voice of art. A transcription of one's mind interpreted differently by another.

Five karaoke performances later, I eat the last of my fries. The server deposits our bills on the table and we pay. Chet has long since moved on from provoking me to talk to the woman. Hallelujah.

"How long are you in town?" I ask as we step into the balmy, late-September air.

"Few more days. If my folks don't shackle me to the house, maybe we can hang again before I go."

Neither of us is an idiot. Chet will spend half his time with his parents and the other half catching up with other friends, but I nod anyway.

"Sounds great, man. Let me know."

One backslapping bro hug later, we go our separate ways. I hop into my car, exit the lot, and speed down the road. My fingers twitch with the need to be in my studio. To bring the golden-haired beauty to life on paper or canvas.

Her image had faded in my mind's eye. Not much, but enough. Tonight, though… I did all I could to memorize every angle of her supple skin and flushed cheeks. The way her locks escaped from the elastic and framed her face. How her cheeks rippled near the corners of her lips as she pushed them upward. The subtle arch of each brow as it highlighted her already ethereal appearance.

I park in the driveway, jump out, and stop myself from running inside. Not that I care what the neighbors think. Surely, they already find me peculiar. They wouldn't be wrong, but I own my awkward nature. All artists are quirky in their own way.

I kick my shoes off at the door, weave through the house, and take the stairs two at a time. The closer I get to my studio, the stronger my pulse pounds. Scents of the earth filter through my nose—the fibrous sixty-pound sketch paper, the metallic tinge of graphite, the pungent, piney odor of turpentine. I inhale deeply as I step through the studio. Breathe in the smells so familiar and comforting.

Snatching a sketchbook from the long table along the wall, I go to the drafting table, sit down on the stool, and pick up my pencils on the side table. With ease, I sift through the sketchpad to the first blank page and run my palm down the endless possibilities.

Closing my eyes, I see her again. Beauty. Charm. Abundance. Sharp and soft angles. And a hint of melancholy.

That small dash of despair calls out to me. Begs me to bring it to life and set it free. Spill the hurt onto paper and release it from her soul.

I press the tip of the pencil to the paper and begin. In a matter of minutes, I already have the rough contours of her heart-shaped face and jaw definition. Hunching over the table, I shift the pad this way and that, over and over. I zone out. Let the art pull me in. Possess me and flow through my fingertips. With each line drawn, each stroke of a softer or harder lead, each brush of the pad of my finger to shade, I breathe easier.

It isn't purely about bringing her to life with my

fingers and a set of tools. It is about connection. A connection so foreign, yet so intimate. A connection I crave, yet don't know how to manifest.

This woman wakes up the lost pieces of my soul. Stirs the biochemistry in my brain and paints it with color. Draws me into her orbit and locks me in with her gravity.

The scary part?

I want to stay there. In her bubble. In the one place I don't have to imagine the twinkle in her dark, mysterious eyes. Or the subtle pout of her bottom lip. Or the sadness that emphasizes her stellar smile.

I want to stay in her bubble and never leave. Exist in her space and breathe her air. Stand at her side and lace my fingers with hers.

But I won't. I can't.

Being in anyone's bubble isn't in the stars.

Not for me. Not ever.

THREE

SHELLY

No place I'd rather be than right here.

Petal and Vine wasn't always my dream job, but I consider myself lucky to have this place. In a world full of craziness and uncertainty, standing in the middle of this florist shop gives me purpose and eases the stress in my life. Working here started off as an accident, but I don't regret a day I walk through these doors.

Early junior year of high school, my aspirations lie in interior design. For homes and businesses alike. As far back as I recall, I had an eye for design and flow and symmetry. Oftentimes, I rearranged my bedroom when the air felt stagnant. Rearranged my clothes in the dresser and closet. Hung posters and photos in new places. In change, I discovered new life. Energy invisible to the naked eye, yet it made the hairs on my arm vibrate with intention.

On a Friday girls' night, years ago at Cora's house, her mom interrupted our hundredth *Lord of the Rings* marathon. I didn't mind, though. That girl and that movie —cue eye roll. Anyway… Elizabeth asked if we would help her at the shop the next day. She had a huge wedding order to fulfill and her employee called out sick. Like the good daughter and daughter's friend, we obliged.

That was the day I learned to love all things floral related. It wasn't only the natural perfume that woke me up, but also the way I could create something beautiful. How something so small and simple could bring a smile to someone's face. Improve someone's day with a gift. A single bloom or three dozen.

Working at Petal and Vine has been a long journey. I have worked here half my life. Literally. This career, this life, has gifted me so much over the years. Stress. Tears. Days when I wanted to throw in the towel. But also joy. Courage. Strength.

Most of all, opportunity.

In little more than a year, my name will appear as the owner of Petal and Vine. In a year, I will own a business. Elizabeth and I have gone over all the fine print little by little, so neither of us is overwhelmed by the transition. But this step is huge—for us both—and thrilling.

"Got another online order," Elizabeth says as she steps up to the arrangement table.

I wiggle a dahlia between a fern stem and baby's breath, then look at Elizabeth across the table. Without question, Cora is a younger, spitting image of her mother. Working with Elizabeth has been like working side by side with my best friend. With my family. Within the walls of Petal and Vine, it feels like home. Warm and comfortable and welcoming. Over the years, Elizabeth has transitioned from mother figure to boss to coworker to friend. But she instantly snaps back into mom mode when any of us needs that side of her. I count my lucky stars to have such a wonderful woman in my life.

No offense to my own mother. Nicole Reed is a lovely woman. Strong and brilliant and thoughtful. I wouldn't be who I am today without her. She and Dad raised my brother and me in a loving environment. Taught us to go after our dreams and never give up.

But as of recent, Mom has been a bit overbearing. Intrusive and suffocating. The incessant probing started before Micah and Peyton became official. Questions about relationships and love. And babies. God, has it been agonizing. No one would ever accuse me of being anti-baby, but the pressure Mom puts on us for grandchildren has me double-locking the chastity belt.

Which is why it is a blessing to have two mother figures in my life. Elizabeth balances out the crazy Mom puts on my shoulders. Gives me another person to express what has me bogged down when I feel Mom may go off the rails.

"Great!" I survey the full vases in the cooler behind her. All orders waiting to be delivered or picked up today and tomorrow. "Business has been picking up steam. Not sure if it's the ads or word of mouth. Whatever it is, I'm here for it." Majority of our orders are online, but we have regular foot traffic as well.

I get back to work on the current arrangement and Elizabeth starts the online order. Setting it in the cooler when I finish, I stare at the abundance of lavender, yellow, and white rose bouquets, boutonnieres, table arrangements, and more. All for one momentous occasion.

Tomorrow, my brother is getting married. Never thought I would see the day. With his track record, I sure as hell thought I'd marry before him. But life had other plans and I am so happy for him. Thrilled he found love.

Micah and Peyton have come a long way since high school. A year and a half ago, when I'd learned Micah had started hanging out with Peyton, Cora and I jogged his memory of who she was and what he'd done to her. I had never seen my brother so petrified in his life. Horrified by the ghosts of his past. Ghosts he created. He did anything and everything to right his wrongs, stepped up and became a better man, and Peyton forgave all his past transgressions.

Every time I see the two of them together, their dopey, lovesick eyes, I know love can overcome every obstacle. And if *they* can defeat history with love, all things are possible.

Which means I, too, will find love one day. I only hope it happens before a full head of gray hair and a dozen cats.

"Is everything set for the wedding tomorrow?" I ask, although I know the answer. We finished the last of the arrangements before close yesterday. But the stress of my brother's impending nuptials makes me ask anyway. Last thing I want is to forget an arrangement and throw the whole day off.

Elizabeth steps up to my side, places a hand on my

shoulder, and strokes her thumb back and forth. "Yes. Never thought I'd see this day."

I turn to face her. "What do you mean?"

She shakes her head and laughs. "I remember all the stories Cora shared. *Shelly's brother is gross. He's always staring at girls and licking his lips*," she says in a mocking tone.

I tip my head back and laugh.

Cora and I have been friends since elementary school. It wasn't odd for our families to hang out together on weekends to appease us. Which also meant my annoying brother was around. Two years wasn't a major age difference, but it was enough to steer me away from him before entering middle school. Rumors of my brother kissing most of the girls in middle school before my first year there spread faster than STDs. It was nothing compared to the year before he and Peyton became an item. I have no intention of walking down that dirty alley again.

"He was gross." I laugh harder and Elizabeth joins in. "But I'm glad he and Peyton found each other. It was questionable for a bit, but they came out stronger on the other side. She makes him a better man."

Elizabeth pats my shoulder. "Agreed." She goes back to the table and continues the online order.

Rounding the table, I clean up my mess and put the pruning tools back in place. I start for the small office in the back corner of the store when Elizabeth speaks up.

"Oh, I almost forgot." I turn around and give her my full attention. "Patty from my book club asked about floral arrangement classes. What do you think?"

Petal and Vine has had more business in the last two years than the previous five years combined. We aren't hurting for business or income. But as a small business owner, it is always wise to have other sources of revenue. Anything could happen to taper off orders. Supply shortages, economic changes, clients unhappy with the ownership transition. The last one seems less than likely considering we hide nothing from our clients, especially those that have been loyal from the beginning.

"Classes are a wonderful idea. Floral arrangement, buying for the seasons, how to maintain planted and trimmed flowers. The possibilities are endless."

"Excellent. The ladies will be thrilled." A smile brightens Elizabeth's face.

"I'll do some research, come up with a list of classes to offer and when, price them reasonably yet still be competitive with the market."

A list forms in my mind of all the options we could offer. Different skill levels. Showing attendees how to artfully decorate their space with one bundle of flowers. Ways to use flowers for special occasions such as birthdays, anniversaries, holidays, and gatherings.

I smile and spin to face the office. I don't make it three steps before Elizabeth stops me again.

"Also…" I pivot on my back foot and meet her gaze. "Remember when we had the mural done last year?"

What an odd question, but I roll with it. "Yes, of course." I don't add anything else, unsure what to say.

"I spoke with the artist last week. He'll be by in a couple weeks to do some touch-ups on the mural and add a thicker layer of sealant. To help prevent fading from the elements."

Oh. My. God. Ohmygod.

A thin layer of perspiration blankets my skin. At the rate it seeps from my pores, I will undoubtedly look like I walked in the rain without an umbrella in no time. My heart does this bizarre somersault in my rib cage before bounding into fifth gear. Then my stomach flip-flops beneath my diaphragm.

Is it hot in here?

Will Elizabeth be weirded out if I stand in the walk-in cooler for the next half hour? Probably not. We go in there so frequently, she won't bat an eye. But if she sees me without a jacket, she will ask questions.

"And since he'll be here," she continues as if I am not having an existential crisis, "I asked him to paint a mural on the west wall inside the shop." Her gaze shifts to the wall she references. "When the morning sun hits it, it'll feel like we're in a meadow."

Elizabeth's eyes light up as she envisions said meadow-like mural. Meanwhile, I seem to have forgotten how my lungs operate. *Inhale through the nose, hold it, exhale through the mouth.* Is it too much to ask my heart to settle? *Jesus.*

The Artist—that is what I call him since he never introduced himself and I was too chickenshit to ask his name—consumed too much of my free time last year. Not to mention my dreams for months after. Elizabeth hired him to paint the mural on the outer east wall. The entire time he was here—twenty days to be exact—I made up every possible reason to step near the small east window panes, just to sneak a peek at him. When I ordered lunch, I asked if he wanted anything… just to hear his voice.

We didn't exchange many words in those twenty days, we barely looked at one another, but there was just something about him. Not a physical feature, per se—although, he was easy on the eyes. But he had this zeal. A vibrancy that radiated off him. Anytime my eyes landed on him, anytime I stood within ten feet of him, my brain shut down. My motor skills went on vacation. Every outgoing function I possessed hid in the shadows.

I don't know what it is about *the artist*, but he feels familiar. Not in the sense that I had seen him at the grocery store every Wednesday after work. No, his familiarity resonates deeper. Rooted in layers of past lives. Memories of a time lived lifetimes before this one.

And now, he will be here again. Adding more to the flowery garden scene on the outside of our building. Creating an indoor meadow for all to admire, for me to admire, every day.

"Sounds lovely." I clear my now dry throat. "Can't wait to see the outcome. It'll be beautiful, I'm sure."

Before Elizabeth reads too much into my suddenly scratchy voice, I turn on my heel and pick up the pace as I head for the office. Once inside, I close the door behind me, lean against the grain, close my eyes, and take deep breaths.

Get it together, Reed. He's just a guy. I repeat the words until they turn into Scrabble squares in my head. *He's just a guy.*

Out of nowhere, a new voice whispers in my mental

ear. *Keep telling yourself that. He isn't just some guy, and you know it. Why else would you be freaking out?*

"Ugh!"

I stomp over to the desk, wake the computer up, and sort through emails to distract myself. It works… for a little while. But it isn't long before my mind drifts back to the man with floppy brown-and-golden hair. To the way his body moved with the art. How *he* was as much the art as the brushes and paint and strokes.

A year has passed since he was here. A year since I have seen him in person. Yet, the image of him is quite predominant when I close my eyes. Tall and lean, his jeans and T-shirts loose on his frame. His quiet demeanor as he focused on the art. The soft timbre of his voice faded long ago, but just the thought of hearing it again forms a bubble of anticipation beneath my breastbone.

I drop my head in my hands and sigh. "God, I'm hopeless," I mumble into the empty office.

Hopeless or not, *the artist* will be here in two weeks. Time to prepare myself to not look the fool. On the outside, at least. The mess brewing inside me will undoubtedly magnify between now and his arrival.

Where are you, inner zen master? Because I definitely need to locate my inner calm. Stat.

FOUR

DEVLYN

Get out of the car. It's just a job.

The same nine words cycle my mind for the sixth time. Yet I remain glued to the driver's seat. My grip tightens on the steering wheel as I stare at the flower shop through a trellis of jasmine, beyond the three-foot wooden fence. One breath. Then another. My fingers loosen and I unbuckle the seat belt.

Get out of the car. It's just a job.

I open the car door and get hit with more than a dozen floral fragrances. The exterior of Petal and Vine is unlike any other florist shop in the area. Similar to a small business outdoor nursery, except the plants outside are for visual appeal, not purchase. The shop has an old-world feel. An impression of simpler times and forgotten contentment.

Walking under the jasmine-woven lattice, my sneakers crunch the gravel as I come to a halt. Clusters of flowers greet me with their version of good morning. Butterscotch yellow and boysenberry purple. Blush and fuchsia pinks. Apricot and tiger orange. Sage and rosemary green and several shades between. Bushes and vines decorate the earth and the store with foreign strategy. The gravel path weaves between the plants for visitors to see and smell and touch. Bright and subtle. Sweet and pungent. Smooth and prickly. The occasional bench or chair along the way, parked beneath tall crepe myrtle and oak trees, so one can enjoy more time with the blossoms.

Past the blooms and slithering greenery is the shop. The exposed cinder block on the east wall is slathered in layers of paint. An image of another garden beyond this one. Cobblestone frames the cinder block and gives the feeling you are stepping through realms, into the place where only flowers and plants exist. The color hasn't faded much, but the paint isn't as bold as it was last year. To the right of the cobblestone, two tall windows with wide black borders frame glass-paneled French doors. Black lacquered wood rests above the windows and doors with *Petal and Vine* written in white script.

It's just a job.

Taking a deep breath, I start for the doors. Brush my fingers over soft rose petals and wispy grass shrubs along the way. Turn the knob and step inside, a blast of cool air hitting my skin. The shop is the equivalent of a three-bedroom, single-story home, minus several walls. Dried lavender hangs in twined bundles from the ceiling. Before I take in more of the shop, a voice calls out.

"Devlyn." Elizabeth steps around a rack of flower bins, wipes her hands on an apron at her waist and offers one to shake. "Good to see you again."

"You as well, Ms. Davies."

A smile lights up her face as a hand rests over her heart. "Please, call me Elizabeth." She drops her hand, but her smile remains. "We have gotten several compliments on the mural. Thank you for coming out to touch it up and give the inside a little face-lift."

I tuck my hands in my pockets and rock back on my heels. "My pleasure. I'll add a better sealant to the exterior this time. Should preserve the color for years to come."

"Elizabeth," a voice calls from farther back. My blood fizzles in my veins. A whirl forms beneath my sternum. *It's her. My otherworldly muse.* "Is the delivery truck here?" Her words fade as she enters the main floor and spots me with Elizabeth.

Her feet jerk to a stop as she goes rigid next to Elizabeth. Her twinkling eyes capture mine and I get the first *real* glimpse. Twilight-blue irises hold me prisoner for three breaths. During each inhale, I notice something new.

One... her eyes literally twinkle.

Two... the gold flecks resemble constellations.

Three... she is *my* constellation. *My Andromeda.*

She shakes her head and addresses me with a smile she no doubt grants everyone. But this is not the smile I want. Or the smile I need.

"Didn't mean to interrupt."

She goes to step away, but only takes two steps before Elizabeth speaks up. "Shelly, this is Devlyn, the artist who painted the mural."

The glimmer in her eyes arrests me. As if she wished on a star to learn my name. And today, her wish came true. Guess you could say mine did as well.

Shelly.

I scan through the random wealth of knowledge I stowed over the years and remember, in some beliefs, Shelly means "meadow." How fitting. In a blink, the meadow I plan to paint inside the shop has new meaning. A new purpose. A life all its own. I won't paint the meadow solely for the shop, but more so for her. A place of beauty, but not more beautiful than her. Scenery to let her imagination wander. To let her escape.

Blush tints her cheeks and she swallows.

Another random fact about the name Shelly… it means one of purity in Hebrew. Although Shelly has youthful features, the way she carries herself indicates maturity. Most women with her level of maturity don't blush. The fact she does is intriguing.

"My apologies." She offers her hand. "It's nice to meet you formally, Devlyn."

I slip my hand from my pocket and place it in hers. Soft skin with the occasional nick from a thorn and callous from the floral shears. But otherwise, smooth and warm and perfect against my own.

"Nice to meet you as well."

I don't want to free her hand, but know holding it

captive makes for an unpleasant first encounter. So, like a gentleman, I slip my hand from hers and stuff it back in my pocket. I do my best to ignore the tingle still on my palm. The lingering warmth where our fingers touched and hands clasped.

It's just a job. Just stop. Getting romantically involved is a bad idea. Always.

"At the end of next year," Elizabeth starts, snapping my attention back to her, "Shelly will take over Petal and Vine." A smile lifts the corners of Elizabeth's lips and eyes. Thin lines accent her cheeks and temples; years of wisdom and joy evident in those creases. Pride and delight and maternal love echo from her aura as she beams at Shelly. Within minutes, I learn Shelly is more than just an employee or coworker. She isn't just someone buying out a business. Shelly is family, even if not by blood.

"Congratulations," I say. And I mean the sentiment. Owning a business is no simple feat. "Elizabeth picked a wonderful woman to carry on her legacy."

Whack.

I need more than a mental slap.

What the hell am I saying?

First, I don't know Shelly. Not really. Sure, I caught a glimpse or two of her last year while painting the outside mural. Caught her from the corner of my eye, checking me out through the shop windows. Seeing her two weeks ago at the bar doesn't count.

Second, I barely know Elizabeth. I stumbled upon the job last year after my mother stopped by the shop to have an arrangement delivered to a grieving friend. She'd instantly fallen in love with the *cute flower shop*. Bragged about it for weeks, months. She also bragged to Elizabeth about her son who made everything more beautiful with a paintbrush. Not long after, I received a call and was asked to spruce up the outside of Petal and Vine.

I love my mother. Assume her intentions are honest and come from a place of deep affection for her only son. That is what I have told myself over the years. I have yet to convince myself it's true. Much as I appreciate her effort, she needs to stop meddling. Give me the opportunity to spread my wings. Find my way on my own. Let me be my own person. Without her.

As a child, her words and actions seemed harmless. I always thought of her as a role model, a strong woman with sheer determination. She didn't get to where she is today by standing quietly on the sidelines.

But as an adult, my lens of perception has changed. With age comes wisdom. With wisdom comes enlightenment. And with my developed awareness comes perspective and uncertainty.

I love my mother, but as more time passes, I learn with each word she speaks and act she commits, it is only to benefit her. To put her in the limelight. To make people fawn over her. To elevate her onto the shiny, stage-lit pedestal. She brags about her son because, in return, she gets praise for raising such a wonderful and talented young man. She glows under that praise and slowly transitions those conversations to focus solely on her.

In this one instance—tossing my name out to a prospective client—I make an exception.

Because, Shelly.

But god, I pray her meddling stops, and soon.

Another dose of crimson paints Shelly's cheeks and heats my blood. I memorize the color. Stash it away for the next time I have a brush in my hand and canvas beneath the bristles.

"Thank you. That's very kind of you." Her eyes pull me into her orbit and hold me steady. Her chest rises and falls in my periphery, over and over. Then she blinks and breaks the spell she cast. "I'll be in the back." She shifts her gaze to Elizabeth. "Let me know when the truck arrives."

"Will do."

Before another word is said, Shelly spins around and vanishes behind a wall of flowers. The second she disappears, I miss her presence, her energy, her aura. All things eidetic memory cannot replicate. At least the image of her is carved into my memory.

I blink a few times, shake myself back into reality, and look over at a smiling Elizabeth. Her smile speaks volumes, whereas her voice remains silent. The eye of an artist picks up on these small idiosyncrasies and uses them to convey deeper meaning in their work. As for now, I ignore the hidden message in her smile.

"Show me where you were thinking of placing the indoor mural," I say to steer the moment back to business.

In a blink, Elizabeth transitions into proud businesswoman and owner. She guides me to a wall opposite the entrance. Several tin pails, large and small, occupy the floor space. Eucalyptus stems, wheat sprigs, grassy bundles, lush greenery, cattails, and more fill the taller baskets on the floor. On a short shelf behind them, shorter pails are filled with lavender, sprigged red berries, oblong fiery flowers, blue thistle, baby's breath, fern stems, and wispy twigs with pink flowers that remind me of weeping willows and cherry blossoms. Off to the left, white and blush roses grow on a wooden ladder.

Visions of the meadow pop into my head. Various greens, hints of gold and brown, small splashes of violet and honey and berry, and subtle touches of white and indigo. With a slight shift of the pails, the illusion of a natural slate path in the mural will give patrons a feel of stepping into the meadow while shopping.

"It isn't much to work with…"

I hold up a hand and shake my head. "No, it's perfect." Beside me, Elizabeth beams. "Do you mind if I shift things around? Obviously while I paint, but also for when the mural is finished."

"Not at all. I trust your vision."

Hearing those words never gets old. When a client trusts you to bring the art to life, it is the ultimate gift.

"Thank you." I give her a sincere smile. "Also, a suggestion." Her brows lift as she holds my gaze. "When I finish the touchups outside, you may want to invest in a small awning. Nothing extravagant. But something that will shade the mural from the midday sun. It'll add years to the painting after I add the extra seal."

"I will look into them immediately. Thank you for the tip."

Elizabeth guides me back to the shop's office. I don't miss the opportunity to smile at Shelly as I pass. Her cheeks pinken again, then plump as she returns the smile. I don't know what it is specifically about this woman, but she steals my attention when we exist in the same space. Her aura controls the room and says *look at me*, and I cannot help but oblige.

But I shouldn't be caught looking at her like some creeper. So I shift my gaze and focus on the task at hand.

Elizabeth and I look over our schedules and coordinate—not as if my schedule is packed, but no one needs to be privy to such information. Minutes later, we both mark our calendars for the project to start in a few days. I give her a guesstimate of how long the entire project will take, mentally stretching the time frame longer than necessary.

Because, Shelly.

We walk out of the office and Elizabeth pats my shoulder. "Thank you again for doing this. Your art will add an elegant touch to the shop and make everyone's visit more pleasant."

I stop us near the table where Shelly studiously works on an arrangement, desperately trying not to make eye contact. But I need one last walk under the stars before I leave.

"If you don't mind, I'd like to bring you ladies drinks on the mornings I work. A token of my gratitude for the additional work."

Elizabeth waves off the idea. "Not necessary." Shelly

peeks through the sunset-colored petals with a small smile on her face. I let her hypnotize me for three wobbly heartbeats.

"True, but I'd like to anyway. So, what is your beverage of choice?"

"Relentless," Elizabeth mumbles, and I laugh. "If you insist, coffee. No cream or sugar." She pats my shoulder again. "You're too sweet, Devlyn."

Shelly steps aside and out of the arrangement's protection. And for two breaths, we don't speak. I don't know what it is, but this woman crosses my wires. Makes me forget how to function on a day-to-day level. For whatever reason, it doesn't bother me in the way it would with anyone else.

"What about you?" I ask, desperate for more than just her eyes.

She swallows, then wipes her hands on her apron. "I'm more of a tea drinker." She clears her throat. "Not sure where you'll be going, but I'll take any type of tea drink. With oat milk, if it comes with milk. If it doesn't, no milk is okay too." She purses her lips and attempts to hide a huff. Obviously upset with her slight rambling after being silent so long.

But I like her rambling. I like everything about Shelly. Even how different she is near me than she was when I saw her with friends not long ago. I like her shy side, but hope I get to know her outgoing side as well.

"Tea it is." I tip up one corner of my mouth, lightly tap the table between us, and take a step back. "I will see you ladies on Thursday."

Elizabeth gives an enthusiastic goodbye. But it is the quiet farewell from Shelly I hear the loudest.

I have zero intention of involving myself in any type of romantic relationship. With Shelly or anyone else. But non-romantic relationships aren't off the table. And I would very much like some type of relationship with Shelly. The fair-haired beauty with stars in her eyes.

FIVE

SHELLY

Lavender London Fog. That is the name of the tea Devlyn brought me today. The last four days at the shop, he has brought me something different. Hot teas. Cold teas. Tea lattes. Some florally, others earthy.

And I love each one of them.

Elizabeth smiles like a schoolgirl when Devlyn hands over her coffee and deposits a brown bag with fresh baked goods each morning. The bakery items are unique and different each day. Today, he brought two lemon-frosted lavender scones with a side of honey butter. Yesterday, it was brown butter pear galettes.

With his arrival each morning, my cheeks sting and neck heats. No doubt he sees the flustery embarrassment on my skin. But he doesn't say a word. Just smiles and says good morning.

I have never been so enamored with someone. Enough to blush like an adolescent.

And it is so freaking odd.

Shy is not my typical style. Sure, I quiet down on the first two or three dates with a guy, but I am not *quiet*. Not like this. Not as if I fear fumbling over my words or saying the wrong thing.

And let's get one thing straight, I am most definitely not dating Devlyn. Not that I wouldn't want to.

Devlyn is attractive with his sun-streaked, floppy brown hair, sharp, square jawline, and reserved nature that has me wanting to know more. To ask countless frivolous and meaningful questions. Without effort, Devlyn easily garners my attention. Lures me in. Holds me captive with unrestrained interest.

If Devlyn asked me out, my brain would conjure a hundred ways to word vomit yes in a heartbeat.

Someone stop my internal rambling. Jesus.

Devlyn is a nice guy. Quiet in ways different from my sudden shyness. His muted words and subtle smiles seem more his true nature. His way of processing the world around him without breaking it apart with meaningless words. In less than a week, I feel a sense of comfort from his taciturn nature. Like a warm hug you never want to end. This bewilders me in inexplicable ways. Drives my curiosity further. Makes me want to share more hushed moments in his presence.

When Devlyn exists in the same space as me, I see and think and process the world differently. Give myself a moment to *really* take in my surroundings. The bow of flower petals. The jagged edges of leaves. The soft brush of dried bunny tails. The potent scent of clove and cinnamon for the upcoming holidays. Each strikes me with new perspective. They aren't just plants in a shop to sell, but also a part of something more. Something bigger.

I sip the tea and sigh. "This is wonderful. Thank you."

Devlyn gives me his boyish smile, one that makes me, without hesitation, smile in return.

"My pleasure. Glad you're enjoying it."

Then he walks through the front room and out the door.

My brow furrows as confusion runs rampant. Not from what he said, but how I feel. The way I miss his presence the second he disappears. Such an off sensation. Is it weird that I enjoy the jittery calm only he delivers? Probably.

I sigh and sip my tea.

The touch-ups Devlyn has done to the outside mural have been minimal thus far. During my occasional work near the window, I have seen him add touches of fresh paint where the colors have dulled the past year. Blues and reds, but nothing extensive.

For the last four days, I fabricated reasons to be near the windows. Like I am right now. Stealing every opportunity to sneak a glance at the wall he paints. To daydream as I watch his arms flex and his head tilt as he works the brush over the concrete.

Watching Devlyn work is art in and of itself. The way his hair flops over his temple with each tilt of his head. The way he studies the wall with the end of a paintbrush pressed to his chin. How he zones out and becomes one with the art. How he only adds paint where he deems necessary.

Devlyn fascinates me in ways I never thought possible. Not solely how he views art, but also his physical presence.

I gawk at him way longer than appropriate. But no one stops me because no one is around to witness my lewd behavior. Hell, Elizabeth would probably encourage me. Tell me to spark a conversation with him. Push me to do more than spy on him through the window.

But she is in the office with a stack of bills and invoices.

So, I sip my tea, swirl the lightly sweet, floral flavors on my tongue, admire the man outside, and pretend to tend to the flowers at the front of the store. Flowers that need no organization whatsoever.

When lunchtime approaches, Devlyn steps inside. Perspiration glistens his brow, his temples, the line of his jaw, his philtrum, and I forget how to use words in the correct order. At least I stop myself from speaking early enough. No need to embarrass myself further. My hot cheeks have already done more than enough.

"I'm ordering lunch," he says before dabbing his mouth on the sleeve of his shirt. "Would you like anything?"

The leftover spaghetti I stowed in the fridge calls out. Tells me I should save my money and not waste food. Whispers that I should gracefully decline his offer. Especially since I need to save every penny with the shop purchase next year.

"I… uh…" I fumble for the answer. *No, thank you* sits on the tip of my tongue, yet the muscle won't curl properly to say the words. *Dammit.*

"It's my treat," he adds, a half smile pushing up the corner of his perfect lips and tempting me further.

My cheeks heat and I tuck my lips between my teeth. The action does nothing except make my embarrassment more evident.

Way to go, Shelly. He probably thinks you're batshit.

Get it together. Jesus. Take a deep breath, thank him and carry on.

"You don't have to buy lunch. I brought leftovers." I point toward the back, where our office-slash-break room resides.

Many moons ago, the shop was a house. But when the streets widened and the neighborhood became more commercial than residential, some of the houses turned into small businesses. At first, it was odd seeing houses turn into real estate agencies and restaurants and veterinary offices, but it didn't take long to become normal.

When Elizabeth purchased the building, it still had many of the interior walls. The previous owner ran a beauty salon. Hair, nails, facials. They may have had a massage room too. Completely understandable why the previous owner wanted the separate rooms.

Elizabeth had a vision when this place became hers. To have it as open and airy as a field. To make the atmosphere inviting. For the business to not look like an old home, but a unique storefront. Slowly but surely, she brought her vision to life. Watching the changes, small as they were, happen over the years has been wonderful. And I am so fortunate to have such an amazing business to step into when it changes hands.

The only original walls Elizabeth left intact were ones for a bedroom, bathroom, and the short hall leading to the garage. Now, the bedroom is the office-slash-break room —the bathroom en suite—and the garage is set up for storage and cooler space. All other walls were removed. Beams were erected to stabilize the ceiling wherever necessary. But now, over two thousand square feet are an open, usable storefront.

"Will they last another day?" I scrunch my brow, confused. *What were we talking about?* "Your leftovers," he clarifies, deepening that small half smile.

Right. *Dumbass.* "Oh, yeah. Probably. It's just spaghetti."

"Then eat it tomorrow. Let me get you lunch today."

Three. Freaking. Letters. Say yes. You know you want to eat lunch with him. Not just to sneak closer looks, but maybe to strike up a conversation. One where you use your words. In order. And not too quickly.

Say it!

"Uh, yeah. Yes. Lunch would be nice. Thank you."

He retrieves his phone from his back pocket, unlocks it, and scrolls. All the while, I simply stare at him. Watch as he hunches over the phone, the thumb of one hand scrolling while a finger of the other hand presses his lips.

Oh, to be that finger. His head pops up and heat hits my cheeks at being caught.

He simply smiles.

"Sandwiches or sushi?" I laugh a little too hard and he leans closer. His scent hits my nose and I stop laughing. Remind myself to breathe, slow and steady breaths. *God, he smells good.* "Maybe over lunch, you can tell me why that's so funny."

Suddenly, lunch feels like a date. But I don't know Devlyn. Not really. Not that I knew the guys I dated either. So I brush off the notion and think of it as two friends eating a meal together. Like I would with Gavin or Jonas or one of the guys from the tattoo shop.

"Sandwiches. And yes, I'll let you in on the joke."

Devlyn picks a delicatessen two miles up the street and we both choose sandwiches. He asks what Elizabeth likes and I give him her typical order.

See, Shelly. Just friends. He's buying Elizabeth food too.

He places the order for delivery, then says the food will arrive in a half hour.

The next thirty minutes take hours to pass.

Devlyn goes outside to clear some of his supplies from foot traffic. Me... I wander the store and pretend to straighten the already clean and organized shelves and flower buckets... while watching Devlyn... through the windows.

Am I a lost cause or what?

I force myself away from the windows and head for the office. While we wait for lunch to arrive, I clean the small card table we eat at in the break room. Spray it down with all-purpose cleaner and wipe with a little too much gusto. After I straighten the napkins in the holder and resituate the salt and pepper shakers, I exit the room.

Elizabeth busies herself with bouquets and table settings for an upcoming Halloween wedding. Seeing the bride's vision come to life has been impressive. Dark red and vibrant orange roses mixed with black calla lilies and black wispy spirals. As usual, Elizabeth places each stem in the perfect place. Her arrangements are always immaculate. Perfection.

My goal is to one day create bouquets and arrangements as coveted as hers.

I step up to the tall banquet-length table we use to arrange. Classical music plays in the background, loud enough to hear, but not so loud it hinders conversation. Elizabeth is in the zone as she shifts and adds stems. I don't want to mess with her chi, but I don't want her to miss lunch either. We generally don't eat at the same time, but I always give her the option to go first.

"Hey," I say softly. She peers up from the flowers, gives a small smile, then returns to the piece in front of her. "Devlyn insisted on buying us lunch. Got you cheddar and turkey on rye. Should be here any minute."

"He's so sweet. You eat first." She snips the end of a rose and feeds it into the vase. "I still have a bit to go until this one is finished and I don't want to leave it half done."

"Are you sure?"

She leans back from the flowers, twists the vase left then right, scrutinizes the arrangement from every angle, then returns to her original position. Although I have learned a wealth of knowledge from Elizabeth over the years, seeing flowers the way she does isn't a skill you learn. It simply exists. Elizabeth has an uncanny eye for arranging. A true gift.

"Yes." She lifts her gaze. "By the time you finish up, I should be done with this one."

I nod and watch her work.

In the beginning, I followed her every move for hours. Observed the way she selected flowers. The precision in which she clipped the stem. How she started an arrangement or bouquet, then brought it to life as she added one flowering stem after another.

In some regards, watching Elizabeth with flowers was similar to watching Devlyn with paint and a brush. Both mesmerized me with how they viewed the piece and how their fingers seemed to move without instruction. It isn't a job to them. Put simply, it is an extension of them. Their creativity brought to life.

Devlyn steps up to the table with a large brown sack in his hand. "Lunch arrived."

"You two enjoy. Just set mine in the fridge and I'll get it soon." She slides a black calla lily into place then looks at Devlyn. "Thank you for lunch. Was kind of you."

"You're welcome."

Without a word, I lead the way to the break room. Take a seat near the wall and am surprised when Devlyn slides the chair out to my left instead of across the table.

Is it normal for friends to sit so close?

Don't put the cart before the horse. Is Devlyn my friend?

He digs through the bag, oblivious to my internal

inquisition, and pulls out three sandwiches, individual bags of potato chips, small paper cups of fresh fruit, and bottled waters. He picks up Elizabeth's sandwich and sets it in the fridge, along with her fruit and water.

Brown butcher paper crinkles in the otherwise silent room as we unwrap our lunch. I use the paper as a placemat and dump out my chips. Then pop the lid off the fruit cup and water, ready to dive in.

The first few minutes of lunch pass in silence as we satiate our stomachs. Covertly, I side-eye Devlyn as he eats. Watch the muscles of his jaw work as he chews. Lick my lips when he swallows.

Do you believe what you eat says something about your personality? If so, what does the Cuban without mustard or pickles say about Devlyn? While on the topic, what does the roasted veggie with brie and orange marmalade say about me?

Most of my guy friends eat anything you put in front of them. Does that mean they are more open? Can't be sure. I mean, I am kind of picky with food—eating familiar dishes to avoid change. Is that a personality trait that extends into the rest of my life? Is that why I am picky with men? Not that men are the same as sandwiches, or food of any kind.

"How long have you worked here?" Devlyn asks, startling me back to reality.

I swallow my bite then sip my water, praying I don't have a piece of spinach stuck between my teeth. "Sixteen years next month. It's the only job I've had, but I love it. Wouldn't change it for anything."

"Wow." He pauses and stares at the pressed meat and cheese in his hand. "You don't look old enough to have worked here so long." He bites his bottom lip and I don't hide my blatant stare. His bottom lip looks tastier than my sandwich. "If you don't want to answer, I'll understand..." He swallows and my eyes refuse to look up from his throat. "How old are you?"

Some women lose all sense of reason when someone asks their age. Me? I don't care. Age is just a number. Age happens to us all. No sense in dwelling on something that happens regardless of how you feel about it. I say, never be ashamed of all you endured in your lifetime. Scars from years past can be painful, but they also remind us how far we have come. What we endured to get here. Own your-self—age and body, scars and wrinkles.

My gaze drifts up his throat and finally lands on his eyes. "Thirty-two. You?"

He tilts his head to the side and studies the contours of my face. On cue, my cheeks heat. His stare doesn't unnerve me. It is more like he *sees* me. Sees the parts no one else does. It intrigues me more than unsettles.

"Twenty-two."

A myriad of emotions swirl through my chest at hearing his age. Devlyn is *young*. Much younger than I suspected. A voice in the far corner of my mind says he is *too* young. Ten years is a big difference. Maybe not when the younger person is in their thirties, or older, but that isn't the case.

Should I be uneasy with my attraction to Devlyn? Hell, when I graduated high school, when I stepped into the adult world, he was finishing third grade. It feels… strange, wrong, to find him physically appealing. To watch him through the window as he works because of some newfound mental addiction. To think desirous thoughts about him and what his lips would feel like pressed to mine.

It feels wrong. Yet, it doesn't.

We are both adults. Yes, I have a decade on him. Yes, people might stare longer than usual or say off-putting statements. But societal standards are absurd. Invisible lines drawn to make others feel guilt or shame for loving someone or something that others deem controversial. In general, I am not the type to buck the system. But when it comes to pivotal topics, I am front and center.

Is age difference one of those topics? Potentially.

No one I know has been in this particular situation. The opinions of others have never bothered me in the past, but this feels different.

"Does that bother you?" he asks, jolting me from introspection.

I meet his gaze. Stare at his translucent green irises, so similar to stained glass. For the first time, I study their depths close up. See beyond the man. Deeper. Through the window, getting a glimpse of his soul. Without a doubt, his soul has lived more than one lifetime.

"No," I answer just above a whisper. I sip my water then speak with more confidence. "No, it doesn't bother me. You?"

He shakes his head. "Nah. Age is a number, tossed out

every year by someone who wanted to mark time. I don't let it rule how I live."

Such a profound statement from someone barely in adulthood. Quite philosophical.

The room quiets and we go back to our lunch. I do my best to not blatantly stare at Devlyn. Every few breaths, though, I glance to my left. The more I get to know Devlyn, the more fascinated I become.

"So," I start, wanting more conversation in our limited lunchtime. "When are you starting the interior piece?" I stab a tangerine segment and study the piece of fruit longer than necessary.

"Tomorrow."

I perk up at the news. Granted, he was only touching up the exterior, but I assumed the exterior would take another week.

"Oh," I squeak out. Heat blooms over my cheeks at my juvenile response. "Thought you'd be outside longer."

Eyes on his water bottle, a hint of a smile glints his face then disappears just as quickly. "No. After lunch, I'm applying the sealant. Then it's finished." He pops a potato chip in his mouth then meets my wide eyes. A confident yet laid-back vibe rolls off him.

I like the feeling more than I should.

Then a sudden burst of panic infiltrates my bloodstream. With Devlyn inside the shop eight-plus hours a day, for the next week or longer, will I be the creepy voyeur lady? Yep, that sounds like me. The woman who stays in his periphery at all times, gawking. The woman trying to put the Devlyn puzzle together. The woman asking endless questions to learn everything about him.

Ugh! Please don't let him find me as disturbing as I do.

"That's great. Guess I expected the touch-ups to take longer."

I finish my fruit cup and stare down at the brown butcher paper, wondering if my embarrassment will swallow me into the pits of hell.

Devlyn strikes me as the intuitive type. Aren't most artists? That said, there is no possible way he doesn't pick up on my attraction toward him. Or my occasional self-consciousness, which is most peculiar. Ask any of my friends if I am shy, laughter would fill the room. Every one of them would say I don't have a timid bone in my body.

Until Devlyn, that statement held truth.

"Some colors fade easier in the elements. I touched them up. The sealant will help, and Elizabeth is adding an awning."

Why does it sadden me there won't be a reason for Devlyn to return in a year or two? Unless I figure out some other project for him.

"That's great." Is that the only response I am capable of speaking? My words lack enthusiasm, which makes him smile. I really like his smile. It isn't artificial or something he hands out to everyone.

He crumples up his sandwich paper and deposits it in the bin with his other lunch trash. All too soon, conversation time ends. Rather than feel down, I inwardly smile at seeing him inside for the next week. Fingers and toes crossed it will be longer.

Devlyn keeps to himself for the most part, and I don't mind. The trait adds to his allure. Gives me ambition to learn more about him through conversation. Devlyn may be quiet on the outside, but something tells me the inside is the polar opposite. Eclectic and mysterious and affectionate. Perhaps a little loud and overzealous.

Maybe, just maybe, I will find out.

SIX

DEVLYN

The past ten days at Petal and Vine, constantly inhabiting the same space as Shelly, reminds me of *The Mulberry Tree* painting by Van Gogh. Subtle hints of color illuminating vitality and brilliance. A hidden fire, out in the open, waiting for the right kindling to set it ablaze.

Oh, how I want to be her kindling.

But after years of solitude and single-minded focus, I feel so out of my element in personal conversation. Sharing pieces of myself with someone, especially an attractive woman.

It isn't the actual conversation I find challenging; I speak with strangers often.

Conversations related to business flow with ease. Someone purchases or praises my art online or in the community, my introversion takes a back seat. The typical interaction at exhibitions, some might say I don't shut up. Shoptalk doesn't make me uneasy.

But talking about something other than art—my pieces or someone else's—isn't something I do often.

While Chet was in town, even our conversations were clipped. Not that we didn't have anything noteworthy to share, we just understand each other. Understand the inner workings of the creative brain. That we don't necessarily voice everything we think or feel or perceive. Instead, we digest it in our head and translate it via art. Some on a sketchpad, others on canvas, and many with another medium.

Oddly enough, I enjoy conversations with Shelly. Conversations about something other than work or art. With each passing day, she opens up more. As do I. Like the petals of a morning glory. Slow and steady, then all at once.

Since walking through the doors of Petal and Vine, I have learned a lot about Shelly.

Her preference for pink is unrivaled. Pink isn't the only color she wears, but it is somewhere on her person each day. Whether it be accents in the attire or the elastic securing her ponytail.

She prefers tea lattes over tea with a splash of milk, but won't disclose this. There was no disguising the twinkle in her twilight eyes when I handed over the extra spicy chai tea latte. Never had I seen someone so excited for a drink.

Which is why I bought her the same drink today.

"Enjoy the rest of your day," Shelly says to an older man leaving with a bundle of flowers in paper and twine. The bell over the door jingles, the man waving goodbye as he exits. My eyes are glued to the door when I feel Shelly sidle up to my right. "Looks dreamy." Her voice soft and fantastical.

I twist and take in her profile, her gaze lost in the meadow on the wall. *Her meadow.* The one I painted with her in mind.

Whimsical weeping willow branches in the foreground. Tall grasses a pale green and golden brown. Wild purple flowers and sunset-colored echinacea buds. Common daisies and bold-blue cornflowers. And a small cobblestone path that starts at the floor and trails a few feet into the meadow before disappearing.

"Good. Was the impression I wanted to give."

She stares at the meadow. Studies the intricate lines and detailed strokes. Meanwhile, I revel in the contours of her profile. The minor slope of her forehead and prominent arch of her brow. The subtle angle of her nose, slight flare of her nostrils, and dip of her philtrum. The plumpness of her lips, the bottom fuller than the top. And the strong yet soft line of her jaw and chin.

Shelly is real-life art. An artist's model. A muse. A goddess.

I shake my head. Shake away the fantasy of something more.

It's just a job. Nothing more. Never anything more.

Shelly snaps her gaze away from the meadow and meets my stare. The usual sparkle in her twilight eyes is muted, duller, less dazzling. I want to ask her the cause of her sudden mood shift. What brought on her melancholy?

But I don't, fearing I already know the answer.

After I leave Petal and Vine tonight, I won't return. Not for work, anyway. And this fact displeases her.

A twinge expands in my solar plexus. Reminds me not seeing Shelly every day will be difficult for me as well. Something I am not used to... missing another person.

What alternative is there?

I don't want this to be it. The end. The last day I see her. But I don't want to give her the wrong impression. Don't want to lead her on and spread false hope. It wouldn't do either of us any good. Still... this can't be it.

"Would you want to hang out sometime?" The words leave my lips in a rush. Then I mentally smack myself as they replay. *What the hell are you doing?* But it is too late. The offer has already been extended. Perhaps I should amend it. "As friends," I clarify.

Her eyes dart between mine, searching for unspoken clues.

Good question. If you find answers, let me know.

"Uh..." Her teeth nibble at her bottom lip. In the periphery, her fingers tug at her waist apron. "Sure, I guess. Sounds nice."

God, how does she make apprehension look adorable? Her hesitation makes my heart beat faster and breath come in bursts. Spreads warmth in my veins and stirs me to life. Gives me an inkling of hope for something more. Something I swore off years ago.

But it shouldn't give me hope. It can't.

Shelly is a friend. Only a friend. Plenty of men and women have strictly platonic friendships, and so can we.

Keep telling yourself that. Maybe if you repeat it enough, you'll believe it.

"Before I leave, we should exchange numbers," I say, then add with too much enthusiasm, "To coordinate." *Take a fucking pill already. Jeez.* "What do you think about lunch and a museum?"

Seriously, this feels like more than friendship. Asking her to lunch and the museum sounds more like a *date.* But what do I know? I haven't had many female friends since high school. That is what happens when you keep to yourself. So what do adult, opposite-sex friends do?

The museum sounds like a safe atmosphere to visit with a friend. Lots of people. Plenty of distractions.

At least it isn't my house, on my couch, with the bedroom in close proximity. Or worse, my studio. Although my desire to be intimate with a woman is minuscule, I fear the temptation of having Shelly in my space. Near my bed. Near my creations. Her scent in the air and on fabrics. The image of her permanently etched in each room she enters. God, it would make my home my own personal torture chamber.

"I haven't been to a museum since I was a kid. I'd love that."

Her smile is worth every questionable thought. Worth the agony of where we go—as friends—from here. If a day at the museum excites her, I wonder what other places will?

"Great." I almost slip and add *it's a date.*

For a moment, we stand there, unsure what to do next. The corner of her mouth twitches, and I drop my gaze.

Before temptation gets the better of me, I face forward and start cleaning up my mess. This snaps Shelly into action and she goes back to her workspace and cleans up the table. As I gather the last of my brushes, she fills the low-stocked flower pails with more blooms and tidies up the shop.

When she locks the front door and flips the welcome sign to closed, I wilt like a thirsty flower. She does a few last-minute tasks and then we exit through the back door.

After I stow my supplies in the back of my SUV, we stand unmoving, unspeaking, between our cars. I barely know Shelly, but today feels like goodbye. Like letting go of someone important. And I don't like the pang beneath my diaphragm. The ever-increasing twinge between my ribs.

"Talk to you later," I say as I reach for the door handle. "Drive safe."

"You too. Talk to you later."

We get in our cars and I wait for her to leave first. When her car is out of sight, I drop my head on the steering wheel and close my eyes. Take a deep breath. Then another as I wrap my fists around the wheel.

"What *are* you doing?"

Of course, I don't answer myself. What the hell would I say? I have no legitimate answer. Wish I had an idea of what happens next. Wish someone would give me advice on where I go from here. I don't need step-by-step instructions, but a look in the crystal ball wouldn't hurt.

If I keep the boundaries clear, keep us both on the same page, everything should be fine.

Shelly and I are friends.
Only friends.

I STARE AT MY PHONE SCREEN, WAITING FOR A RESPONSE like a needy teenager. Like a boy desperate for attention or affection or both. No matter how hard I stare, no matter how long I keep the screen awake, a response doesn't come.

And I hate how much this bothers me. I hate how I can't look away or put the phone down.

Three hours have passed since we left Petal and Vine. Three hours is both too long and not long enough.

I wanted to wait longer to text her to set up our "friend date." I hate the word *date*. But what else do I call it? Casual meetup? Get together? An engagement or rendezvous? None sound right. Especially the word *date*.

I hate myself.

Hate the inner workings of my mind and how I over-analyze every little detail. Hate that she hasn't answered me, and it has only been ten minutes since I sent the message. Hate how I have worked myself up over something I deem friendship.

Have I ever been so frantic to hear from a *friend*? No. No, I have not.

Rising from the couch, I lock my phone, stow it in my pocket, and head up the stairs to my studio. If anything distracts me, it is a pencil or charcoal or brush in my hand.

As I reach the landing, I laugh at myself. A little too hard. Why? Because I plan to use my art as a means to escape the thought of Shelly. But as soon as I fill in the blank canvas or heavy stock paper, it will be her I see. Best if I own and accept facts… there is no escape. Not when it comes to Shelly.

I am sick. Sick in the head and a glutton for punishment. My own worst adversary.

Sitting on the stool at my drafting table, I flip to a new piece of stock. Grab my charcoals and blending tools. Turn on the repeat playlist I listen to in the studio. Then, I hunch over the paper and let my fingers and mind roam freely.

I smudge a lock of hair near the corner of her eye and angle of her jaw when my phone chimes. Jolting at the sound, I sit up and set down the blending stump. Staring down at the table, I know the profile of the woman on paper is the person who just texted.

It is no secret I keep to myself. Not that I don't have friends or socialize with people. I simply prefer solitude. Family and friends know this about me, and only reach out when something noteworthy happens. Texts and calls are never just a *hey man, how's it going?*

So, when I pick up the phone, I know exactly who texted. The woman I messaged over an hour ago with a date, time and place for us to meet for our non-date.

Shelly: Sunday works. I haven't been to the Black Cat Tavern yet.

Devlyn: Perfect. Meet you there at 12:30.

Meeting Shelly at the restaurant versus picking her up

and riding together sends a clear message. *This is not a date. We are just friends.* Opposite-sex friends who enjoy each other's company. That is all. Period.

In college, I had female friends. We shared meals and philosophical conversations all the time. So I know friendship with Shelly is possible. I can do this.

If I tell myself this enough times, perhaps I will believe it into existence.

Shelly: I'll be the cute one in pink. See you then.

Her comment is meant to be funny or endearing. But of course, my mind veers down every other path. Searches for every hidden meaning in her words. Focuses on the way she refers to herself as cute. Pictures of different pink tops or attire she has worn in the short time I have known her.

And I hate that my mind does this. Sends me down a road I should not travel.

Why? Why do I torture myself? Overthink and scrutinize every word someone says. Look for a double meaning that, more than likely, isn't there. Look for reasons to reschedule or cancel. Or worst of all, look for clues that say this is a *good* thing. That a friendship with Shelly is exactly what I need. To feel alive again and get past the shadow masking my heart.

Since the day Kelsey put my heart through the shredder, I refuse to believe romantic happiness is an option. The heartache she inflicted still haunts me. It sets the tone for every interaction I have with a woman. Causes me to doubt the intention of every woman. Causes me to question my own feelings. Destructive as it is, what Kelsey did changed the way I perceive romantic relationships. The harsh way she ended our relationship, the way she threw our love in the trash, it made me turn my back on love and trust.

It irritates me she still has this power. Over me and the way I live life. Over my happiness and future. Over my heart and the love I could give another.

My mother and her frigid, heartless temperament toward me didn't help matters.

Maybe Shelly is the key. The one person to unlock this darkness that has consumed me for far too long. The sunshine after the storm. The light at the end of a very long, dark tunnel. Hope. *My hope.*

My relationship with Shelly doesn't have to be romantic to be fulfilling. Romantic ideals cloud what matters most. Connection. Trust. Loyalty. All components of a solid friendship.

Repeat the word friendship enough times and you might spur it into existence. Eat, sleep, rinse, repeat.

"Play it by ear," I mumble as I stare down at her charcoal profile. "Maybe Shelly is exactly what you need."

More than I realize.

SEVEN

SHELLY

I scream and all but evacuate my skin as Gavin laughs inches from my trembling frame. "Jerk!" I slap his cloaked form and he laughs harder.

"Your expression was priceless."

"What? My *I almost pissed myself* face? How sweet of you."

He lifts the terrifying mask from his face and juts out his lower lip. Not fair. Just because he is my brother's best friend and my best friend's husband, it doesn't mean he gets a free pass. He needs to learn his lesson. And grovel a bit.

"I'm sorry, Shell." His pout becomes more prominent, but I really want him to work for it. So I purse my lips and narrow my eyes, then firmly plant my hands on my hips. "Really, I'm sorry." The corners of his eyes down-turn, a telltale sign his apology is genuine.

Relaxing my stance, I nod. "Apology accepted." I jab a finger in his chest. "But don't do it again."

Cora waddles toward us, one hand on her rotund belly and the other carrying a bottle of water. She surveys the situation, then gives Gavin a stern yet affectionate look. "What did you do?"

He holds his hands up in surrender. "Nothing. Just some Halloween fun. I swear."

"Mm-hmm," she mumbles. "And your version of fun versus mine and Shelly's is totally different. Please, don't give my friend a heart attack. Or I might have to hurt you." Gavin gives Cora a look that says *oh, really*. She arches a brow. "Don't press your luck, mister. I may be ready to pop any day, but I'll still go to bat."

For a second time, and for Cora's benefit, Gavin apologizes. "Sorry, Shell. Just trying to liven up this party. If Micah didn't have to work, I'd have someone else to joke with."

My dear, sweet, sometimes pain-in-the-ass brother. Over the last year and a half, he has become a new man. A better man. Mature and caring and respectful. But put him in the same room with Gavin—best buds more than half their lives—and all levelheadedness disappears. I love my brother. Love Gavin like a second brother. And like any sibling does, they both get under my skin from time to time. I always forgive them, but it's fun to watch them squirm first.

"Yeah, yeah." I narrow my eyes and give him my best death glare. "Next time, I may not be so forgiving." Lies.

Panic fills Gavin's eyes. Beside him and a step back, Cora clamps her lips impossibly tight to not laugh. Cora knows me better than anyone. Which is how she knows I am messing with him. Knows I am giving him shit, just like he did to me moments ago. She loves it as much as I do, if not more. My cheeks sting as I fight the urge to laugh. My faux seriousness on the verge of crumbling any second.

Thankfully, it doesn't have to.

"Promise, Shell." Surprising me, he hauls me in for a hug. Forces the air from my lungs. "Won't do it again." He releases me and holds me at arm's length. I pat his shoulder in acceptance. "Let's eat."

"I vote yes to food," Cora answers and I agree.

Gavin wraps his arm around Cora and kisses her temple as we wander toward the spooky-themed buffet.

Tonight is similar to our Sunday night get-togethers. Tons of food. Music in the background. Good conversation between friends. Not everyone is here, but most of the group has gathered. Tonight's festivities will end with cobweb cleanup and candy inventory instead of leftover burgers and talks of seeing each other in a week. With Sunday around the corner, we will gather again in no time.

Halloween is different this year. Still fun, but more adult than previous years.

With Cora pregnant—very pregnant—her costume of choice is more about comfort than fun this year. Black maternity leggings and a top that says *The goblin stole my candy* with a cute, animated goblin baby on her belly.

Autumn is also pregnant. Although her belly is less round, her outfit is practical as well. She and Jonas will welcome their new bundle of joy a little more than two months after Cora and Gavin. They decided not to learn the gender ahead of time and, every once in a while, I hear their whispered exchanges of baby names. Some male, some female, and a handful of gender neutral. Watching both couples share openly affectionate moments and fawn over their upcoming additions warms and jump-starts my heart. Has me wistful as I think back to missed opportunities. Has me questioning when my life steered down this path. The lonely path.

I sound envious. To say I am not, would be a half-truth.

So much has changed in such a short period of time. For everyone. Everyone but me.

My friends and family seem to have their lives figured out. On track. Moving forward. Marriage, cohabitating, starting a family, buying a home. They have it all figured out.

Me... I feel stuck. Stuck in singledom. Stuck in place. The next phase of my life in my sights, but just out of reach. And I hate how immovable life feels. In a continuous loop with no forward motion.

As with our Sunday get-togethers, tonight's shindig is at Jonas and Autumn's place. Their new house. Their gorgeous, *we are definitely adulting*, new house.

The house isn't grandiose, but it is a big step up from the small two-bedroom they lived in previously. Now, they have two stories and double the bedrooms, which they will need once their new addition arrives. Clementine, Autumn's firstborn, has been the sweetest helper since learning she will be a big sister. Doing extra chores, talking to Autumn's belly, getting drinks or snacks or blankets for her mom.

Her sass makes an occasional appearance, but she makes up for it with pampering later.

Tonight, Clementine plays hostess. Tidying up the buffet table, greeting everyone, offering drinks. Jonas and Autumn rave over Clementine helping with the decorations too. Hanging fake cobwebs with plastic spiders. Carving ghoulish faces into pumpkins and toasting the seeds. Stabbing fake tombstones in the front yard and stringing tattered sheets to large oak tree limbs. And instead of the usual rock music we listen to, haunted house music plays from the front porch.

"Aren't you trick-or-treating?" I ask Clementine as we fill our plates with finger foods. Some actually look like fingers.

"Yes." She munches on a deviled egg that looks oddly like an eyeball. "Mr. Jonas is taking me out soon. I'm super excited, Miss Shelly." She bounces on her toes. "One of the kids from my new school said our neighborhood gives out *whole* candy bars. Like the big ones you get at the store." Her eyes widen and jaw drops.

Oh, to be young again. To have simple things—like regular-sized candy bars given on Halloween—bring you joy.

"That's amazing!"

"I know, right?"

"When I was your age, we would trick-or-treat around our neighborhood, then go to my friends' neighborhood. If it was a weekend, we went to as many houses as possible. Some years, we had candy for months."

"Wow." Clementine peers up, awe in her expression. "Maybe Mr. Jonas will do that for me next year, after my baby brother or sister is born."

"Maybe. Just make sure you ask days before. You have to make a plan."

Clementine salutes me. "Yes, ma'am." Spartan appears out of nowhere and sniffs along the edge of the table. "No, Sparty. Mama said you can't eat the people's food. It upsets your tummy. Come on." She steps away from the table and Spartan follows without another word. "Later, Miss Shelly."

"Later, cutie Clementine."

I load more food onto my plate and head for the living room. Plopping down on the couch between Cora and Autumn, I scoop up spinach artichoke dip that came from a carved pumpkin mouth. Listen to my friends discuss pregnancy and pending motherhood. Sit in silence and wonder if I will experience more than solitude one day. If I will experience the pangs and joys of pregnancy and motherhood.

Part of me still envies their lives. The natural progression. Attaining happiness and love.

My inner romantic reminds me I will walk the path too, when the time is right. To just be patient. Quit looking at every guy I meet as a potential love interest. Let nature run its course. Things will pan out on their own. Bloom when the time is right. That I just need to stay confident and calm.

My time will come. I want to believe this. Need to believe this. But some days, convincing myself is more of a challenge than not.

Jonas hooks Spartan on his leash before he and Clementine kiss Autumn goodbye.

"Don't pick up anything heavy while we're gone, Mama," Clementine says with a stern expression. I swear that girl will make others bow to her one day. Once Autumn agrees, Clementine skips out the door, telling Spartan they are going to get the best candy stash ever.

"Is it wrong to be happy I don't have to do the trick-or-treating this year?" Autumn laughs and Cora and I join her.

"I'm just waiting for all the Halloween candy to go on sale tomorrow, so I can buy my own stash," I admit. "That's the only trick-or-treating I'll do." We laugh again.

"Get me some," Micah says, entering the room with Peyton at his side and surprising us.

"Thought you were working, big brother."

He kisses me on the forehead. "I was. We got out early. The owners decided to give management an early night." He waves a hand around the room. "So, here I am. Ready to indulge in mountains of sugary, ghoulish treats and torture people I love." I narrow my eyes at him and he sticks out his tongue.

"Help yourself. There's food and drinks in the kitchen and dining room," Autumn says.

Peyton gives us hugs, then she and Micah wander toward the buffet hand in hand.

I stare after my brother and his wife of less than a

month, and smile. More than anyone else in our circle, they give me the most hope. If they were able to forgive and let go of the horrid history they share, overcome crazy obstacles thrown at them, find love and a happily ever after together, how can I not believe in a happy ending for myself?

Autumn rises from her seat next to me and dashes for the hall, grumbling about the constant need to pee as she walks off. Not a second later, Micah plops down and knocks my arm with his.

"What's up?" I ask.

"You look better."

I cock a brow at him. "Thanks, big brother. You really know the way to a woman's heart."

He rolls his eyes. "Ugh, you know what I mean. You're smiling more since I last saw you." He sets his plate on the coffee table then wraps his arm around my shoulders. "No offense, but you look happy. What changed?"

Everything. Nothing.

My life is pretty much the same. Work eight to ten hours a day, five to six days a week—depends on time of year, orders, events, and staff. Each day, I go home to my empty apartment, eat something simple or order delivery, and watch an episode or two of my current television drama. On occasion, I sneak in a romance movie on Hallmark or Passionflix.

Oh yeah... I also have a new friend. A new male friend.

Is that what Devlyn is? My *friend*? That is not a question even *I* can answer. Devlyn feels like more than a friend, yet not a romantic interest. At least, that is what I tell myself. Over the past two weeks, I have gotten to know a fraction of what makes the man. But Devlyn is still a mystery, and I feel a bit like Nancy Drew trying to figure him out.

"Work's been good. Tonight's been fun with everyone." I bite the end of a dough-wrapped mummy dog. "Just so happy for Cora and Autumn."

Micah narrows his gaze; his twin eyes study mine in search of falsehoods. But nothing I said was a lie, so…

He lays a hand on my shoulder, his thumb stroking back and forth as his eyes resume their normal shape. "You know you can talk to me about anything, right?" I nod but don't say a word. "Just need to know everything is okay. That *you're* okay. I need you, Shell."

I don't miss the undertone in his words. Fear. Worry. Love. The backs of my eyes sting. An expanding ball of emotion forms in my throat. A tsunami of love builds in my chest. Micah isn't emotionally detached, but he also doesn't freely share how he feels. For him to openly express such things, it hits harder than expected.

I never lie to my brother. Not about the important stuff, anyway.

As of now, there isn't much to share with him about Devlyn. When something notable happens, he will be one of the first to know. After Cora.

Now, though, Devlyn and I are friends. Nothing more.

"I need you too, big brother." Twisting in my seat, I snake my arms around his torso and hug him hard. "Love you."

"Love you, too." He feigns a cough and I shake my head. "Sorry. Trouble breathing." He smacks his chest over his lungs.

In the affection department, Micah and I have been opposites for years. Since he and Payton became serious, he leans more toward the mushy category and I don't think he knows how to handle it. So I give him a free pass. Let him fake his cough rather than own his emotion. But I love how Peyton has made him a better person. Caring and soft and more sensitive.

The night carries on like our Sunday get-togethers, with added special treats and a mountain of candy. With each new conversation, bout of laughter, and hug given, I am thankful to have this tremendous group of people in my life. People I love and who love me in return.

Perhaps one day, I will have someone special at my side. Someone new to our inner circle.

One day.

FIFTEEN MINUTES EARLY. BETTER THAN BEING LATE, I suppose.

I park in the lot for the Black Cat Tavern, but don't shut off the car. It may be the beginning of November, but the cool weather won't hit this part of Florida for at least another four to six weeks. So, I scroll through social media and clear notifications while the air conditioner blows my hair and dries out my skin. I click the heart reaction on a few Halloween photos friends posted. Comment on those same posts with praise for costumes or treats or candy hauls.

Then I look out the windshield and spot Devlyn's black SUV. A BMW as mysterious as the artist himself. *How does he afford such an expensive car?* Maybe artist incomes are better than I realized. Murals on flower shop walls don't pay for cars like his. With his talent, he probably commissions work often, sells pieces online, and isn't hurting for paychecks. Or women.

I shake my head at the errant thought.

Devlyn is a good-looking guy, no sense in denying it. Beautiful in an unconventional way. Some may disagree due to his lack of thick muscles, but I see beyond the outer layer. Sure, I can lie to myself until blue in the face, but doing so is pointless.

I enjoy looking at him. Being in the same space as him. Talking with him.

Our conversations, even the most mundane, are my favorite. Less than twenty words might be shared between us and the conversation feels profound. Those brief, meaningful conversations are one of his most attractive features. One of many.

I cut the engine, stow my phone in my purse, and step out. Before I close the car door, he spots me across the lot. He stops walking and locks on to me with his sunglasses-covered eyes. As if my mere presence is a beacon. And that notion does strange things to my head and heart. Makes me dizzy. Has my stomach in knots and my pulse jumping hurdles. Makes my knees weak.

My reaction to him gives me pause. Has me unsure how to proceed after such an emotional response. On unsteady feet, for sure.

Devlyn has given me no indication he likes me more than a friend. All the kind gestures—drinks, lunch, conversations—weren't only bestowed upon me. Elizabeth was included in those treats, although she may argue that he included her to disguise his true intentions. That said, he also hasn't given any signs to state the opposite either. When he suggested we hang out, spend time together, just the two of us, he emphasized the word friend. A little too much. Like he needed to stress the word before I agreed. Still not sure if the emphasis is for my benefit or his.

I try not to give it much landscape in my head.

His stride resumes, picks ups steam, and he reaches me five breaths later. "Hey," he says. "Sorry you had to wait."

I shake my head, then swallow past the dryness in my throat. "No need to apologize. I haven't been here long. Didn't want to be late. So I occupied myself with the black hole that is social media." Cue rambling Shelly. God, he must think me an idiot. I sure as hell would. The babbling woman who blushes more than any person her age.

I bite the inside of my cheek to stop myself from blurting more nonsense, and I swear he notices. A half smile flashes on his lips and has me biting a little harder.

"Hungry?" I nod, not trusting myself to speak without blathering, and he gestures toward the restaurant. "Let's eat."

We step into the restaurant and I silently thank whoever manages the air conditioning in here. You would think it was the peak of summer at the rate I am sweating. The host seats us, hands over menus and indicates the server will be with us in a moment, then walks off.

Devlyn and I lift the menus like shields and I almost laugh at our identical behavior.

Is he as nervous as I am?

Devlyn is always cool and collected. A perfect example of chill. Him on edge is unimaginable. Impossible. Preposterous.

We place our order, and now the only thing we have to shield or distract us is two glasses of water. And I should try to pace my drinking. Take small sips and not too many. Repeated trips to the bathroom will do nothing but kick my anxiety into overdrive and embarrass me to no end.

"How was your Halloween?" he asks as I study the ice cubes in my water.

I peer up and spot genuine interest on his face. His gentle smile and pale-green eyes calm me a fraction. "Good. Hung out with friends, had spooky-looking food, handed out candy. You?"

He plays with his straw, but his eyes don't deviate from mine. His stare isn't intense or uncomfortable. If anything, eye contact with Devlyn feels automatic. Natural. Effortless. As does his company. And this poses question after unanswered question. Because I get the sense he doesn't want anything more than this. Lunches and trips to museums and whatever else it is non-romantic, platonic friends do. Together… but not.

I think back to all the times I'd hung out with Jonas before he and Autumn were together. Our friendship came naturally. Our connection more like siblings or cousins. Things have always been straightforward and comfortable with Jonas. The definition of our relationship always clear and never tricky or confounding.

Not like with Devlyn.

Don't think I will ever regard Devlyn with that same brotherly mindset. The idea is ludicrous.

"Quiet. Not a lot of kids live in my neighborhood. So I get a small bag of candy and make sure it's something I'll eat eventually." He laughs and I follow suit.

"I hand out candy if I'm home, but it's minimal too. But don't be fooled, the day after, I'm the lady raiding the shelves. For myself and the shop."

"Hmm. Too bad I didn't start the mural later. Bet you have good taste." My eyes widen a fraction. "In candy choice," he adds.

I love how he feels the need to clarify. As if I didn't know he meant the candy.

Lunch arrives and silence settles over the table. I dig into spring greens piled high with turkey-craisin salad, feta, veggies, and sweet dressing.

Every now and then, I peek up from my food to find Devlyn staring. Not the creepy type of staring that makes my skin crawl. But the type that makes my chest and neck and cheeks hot. The type that makes my throat dry and causes me to swallow over and over.

The server returns as we finish our lunch. Her eyes

dart in my direction, a big smile on her face. "One check?" she asks.

My brows pinch together as to why she asks *me* this. Not that I am the type to assume the guy always pays or that Devlyn will pay for my lunch. But something in the way she looks at me while she asks has me thinking there is an underlying assumption. One I am not privy to.

"I'll take the bill," Devlyn speaks up.

The server shifts her focus to Devlyn as her cheeks pinken and eyes widen. "Oh. God." She closes her eyes a beat and shakes her head. "I am so sorry. I just assumed he was…" Her eyes come back to me, her blush darkening. *What am I missing here?* "Your son or little brother."

What. The. Fuck?

I stop breathing. Stop every motor function I control.

She thought he was my son? She thought Devlyn was my son?

Jesus. How old do I look?

Yes, Devlyn looks young. Maybe a year or two younger than his actual age. But there is no possible way we look that far apart in age. That I look sixteen-plus years older than him. Do I?

How many people over the years have told me I look young for my age? How many have asked what skin regimen I use because of my youthful appearance? Far too many to count. So, how is it this woman thinks I am Devlyn's *mother*?

Soon as Devlyn hands her a card with the check, she bolts from the table. No doubt she is as mortified as I am. Just for different reasons. Bet this curbs any future assumptions she'd voice aloud.

"Hey," Devlyn says from his seat across the table.

I want to look up. Want to stop staring at the same drop of condensation on the water glass. Want to unhear that my lunch partner, the guy I have an undeniable crush on, looks young enough to be my *son*. Or that I look old enough to be his *mother*.

My stomach flips and I close my eyes. Take a few deep breaths and beg the contents to stay down.

Calmer, I open my eyes and look up. Meet his gaze and try to read the unspoken thoughts in his expression. But the server returns, hands Devlyn the check presenter, apologizes again, and wishes us a good day before she dashes away.

Exiting the restaurant is a blur. I barely hear or register Devlyn telling us we can walk to the museum. I just follow alongside him, trusting he won't let me stray or bump into anyone.

Most opinions don't hit me like this. Don't render me speechless. Don't muddle my thoughts so thoroughly.

But her assumption is a slap in the face. A punch to the gut. It makes me question myself. Makes me question if hanging out with Devlyn, as friends or something more, is a good idea.

I want this—us—to be a good idea. I want it to be more.

Ten years may divide us, but I have never felt closer to another person. Does that make this—us—wrong? If only I had the answer.

EIGHT

DEVLYN

I HATE THIS. HATE THAT SOMETHING SO TRIVIAL bothers her this deeply.

Yes, there is a ten-year age difference between us. Yes, I look younger than my actual age. But damn, I sure as hell don't look young enough to be Shelly's child. And Shelly sure as shit doesn't look old enough to parent a grown-ass adult.

What bothers me most is how deeply the woman's preconceived idea sticks. How Shelly has let it sink its claws in, make roots, and sour her mood. And the mood for the day.

More than anything, I hate how much I care. How my mind won't let the matter go. And how much I want to storm back into the restaurant and complain. Question the server's ability to see clearly or think before opening her mouth. My heart isn't cold. Cruelty isn't how I approach situations. And dammit, I shouldn't care this much.

I *can't* care this much.

Things between me and Shelly should stay casual. For her sake and mine. Shelly is my friend. *Just a friend.*

Friend or not, I damn sure won't let anyone drag her down or make her feel less than. Intentional or accidental.

Distress turns her aura stormy gray, and I don't like the shift in her energy. I much prefer the raspberry red I often see around her. The passion and strength and love. Qualities that magnetize me to her.

I bump her arm with mine as we walk past storefronts. "Hey." She doesn't lift her gaze. Doesn't answer. Just keeps her eyes ahead and semi-downcast, still in a daze. So, I bump her again. "Hey," I repeat, a touch louder.

She snaps out of her momentary fog and grants me her full attention. A nameless emotion burns white hot inside me as I stare back at the dulled color in her irises. Eyes that would no doubt shimmer in the sun. Radiate and add a new layer of appeal. An appeal I work hard to shut down.

Just a friend.

"Sorry," she says just above a whisper. "That was just…" Shelly leaves the rest unsaid. Leaves me mentally bereft.

Nope. Not having it.

I reach for her elbow, steer her away from other people on the sidewalk, and stop us under a store awning. "Was just what?"

I shouldn't care this much. Shouldn't worry about a statement from someone neither of us will see again. But it isn't so much what the woman said that bothers me. It is the fact Shelly is so thrown off by the misunderstanding.

"Does it not upset or frustrate you? What she said." She points down the street toward the restaurant.

Please don't let her think I am dismissing her feelings. "Actually, no." Her forehead scrunches in confusion, disbelief, hurt. I hurry to explain my reasoning. "Shelly, if I let other people's opinions rule my life, I would be disappointed or depressed or irritated more often than not. I'd rather spend my energy on what makes me happy." I glance down the sidewalk, let my eyes lose focus. "The last time I let someone's words consume me, it almost cost me my life." Blinking, I turn back to her. "And I won't do that again."

Her dazzling twilight irises glass over. Breathtaking and tragic at the same time. The idea of Shelly in pain—whether physical, mental, or emotional—bothers me on an unhealthy level. But seeing her exposed and vulnerable, seeing her look at me with hundreds of questions in her eyes, has my soul begging for more. More of her heart. And me giving her more of mine.

I should not want either.

I cannot want either.

She lifts a hand and sets it on my forearm, giving a light squeeze. "I'll do my best to let it go."

A strand of her hair catches the wind and grazes her cheek. And god, do I want to tuck it back into place. Brush my knuckles over the apple of her cheek and reassure her. Tell her everything will be alright.

But I leave my hand at my side. Refrain from speaking such reassurances. Don't move an inch. Because friends don't touch each other that way. Not the way I want to touch her.

"Good," I choke out, then clear my throat. "Shall we?" I offer her my elbow and smooth out my expression. Act as if we didn't just share emotional intimacy.

She loops her arm with mine and straightens her spine. "We shall."

We walk two more blocks, our steps leisurely as we take in the city. Most of Downtown St. Petersburg is plastered in art. Paintings by local artists on the sides of buildings. Sculptures in front of local businesses. Even some of the older structures are art without effort.

Soon, I steer us toward the Morean Arts Center, where the local Chihuly Collection is on display. Although sculpture and glasswork are not my specialty, I appreciate the love and labor and artists who construct such astounding masterpieces.

"Oh, wow." An air of awe occupies Shelly's expression. "I haven't been here, but I've heard wonderful reviews about the exhibit."

"Well, then I'm glad we came."

Gone is her morose mood from the restaurant. Now delight and anticipation set her aura on fire. Excitement and a hint of passion. The shift soothes something deep inside. Something I won't question or spend time trying to figure out. Not now.

After we go through check-in, a curator in the museum explains the rules while inside. As with most museums, there is no touching. Unlike most museums, you have permission to take photos.

Without hurry, we go through each room. Read the placards and learn about Dale Chihuly and his glasswork. Stare at the blown glass that defies logic or gravity. His pieces are pure imagination brought into existence. His gift to the human eye. Globes in various sizes. Bowls resembling ocean waves. Spirals and pillars and tentacles.

With each room we enter, each new piece we see, I study not only the displays but also Shelly. Really study her. How she reads about each display thoroughly. How she steps back and looks at the display from afar. Then steps closer and takes in the intricate details. The fine lines and layers of color woven into each piece. The unprecedented design and craftsmanship.

She sees each piece as more than just *pretty* or *neat*. She finds inspiration in the work. Looks at it from one angle then another. I would swear she *feels* the art. Immerses herself in the mind of the man who created each piece and display.

When we walk beneath the *Persian Ceiling,* I swallow past the dryness in my throat. Breathe deep and work to calm the ever-expanding organ beneath my sternum. The one that should *not* be beating so profusely. Yet, I can't stop what happens naturally.

Not when it comes to Shelly.

Under the lights and strategically placed glass pieces in the *Persian Ceiling* is a rainbow of color. The space is a sea of stained glass and wonder. The sight of Shelly beneath the art, reds and blues and yellows splashing her cheekbones and neck and jaw, stuns me. Renders me speechless. Bonds me to the floor where I stand. Robs me of breath and reason and practicality.

And I do nothing to stop or fast forward the moment. I can't. Not when I see her like this. Not when it makes me eager to dip a brush in pigment and paint her in this new light. A spectrum in a world of gray. A myth brought into existence.

"I found one," she whisper-shouts.

I snap out of my Shelly-induced stupor and step closer to her. "Found what?" With my fantasizing, I have no idea what it is we are looking for.

"A cherub."

Ah, yes. Chihuly and his affinity for the childlike angel. "That you did."

While Shelly scans the ceiling to locate more, I remain a step back and watch her. Watch her fascination, her excitement, her eagerness to find the next special piece in the art. I don't need to search for cherubs. My eyes on her is all I need in this magical place.

Once we leave the *Persian Ceiling*, the rest of the museum tour speeds by. Wraps up far quicker than I would like. In the gift shop, we each buy a small token to remember the museum and our visit. Not that I need a token to remind me of today, or any day with Shelly.

We step out into the warm November air and pause. After getting swept up in the whimsical world of Chihuly, we both need a minute to reset ourselves. Find our footing back in the real world.

A voice in my head tells me to ask Shelly to dinner later. Well, only a couple hours from now. The words are on the tip of my tongue. Ready to spill out and be heard by someone other than myself.

As I open my mouth to ask, another voice speaks up. Reminds me of the last time I gave too much of myself to another. Reminds me of the heartache and pain and dark, dark days that followed when she ripped me apart. When she left me to waste away. When she abandoned me without care.

And the fear from that singular moment is why I bite my tongue. Why I seal my lips and close off my heart. Because if I ever let anyone that close again, if I allow myself to be truly vulnerable, it sets me up for loss. For anguish. For the darkness.

I can't go back to the darkness. Not again. Never again. Who would pull me out?

"Ready to head back?" I mutter. This time, I don't offer my arm. Don't add pep to my voice. Don't glance in her direction.

And she picks up on the sudden mood shift.

Shelly wraps her arms around her middle and looks in the direction of where our cars are parked. "Sure."

No doubt, she probably wishes we didn't have to walk back together. Not after my abrupt coldness.

But shutting her out like this is the only way. The best way. All I know. She may not be grateful now, but she will eventually thank me. When she moves on and finds someone worthy of her smile and warmth and heart. Someone who won't love only the idea of her.

All too soon, we arrive back in the lot. The lukewarm goodbye we exchange is pathetic. Friends give better farewells than this. Usually a *see you soon* gets said at some point. But not with us. Not today. And I hate that I did this. Put a damper on our *friendship*. Ruined a perfect day.

But it has to be this way.

Not a complete asshole, I wait until her car starts before walking to my own. Behind the protection of tinted windows, I stare, stare, stare at Shelly's red Beetle. Watch for any sign of dismay; a look of disgust toward my car. But nothing comes. So I wait impatiently for her to drive away. And maybe flip me off. But she sits idle a moment, and I wonder if something is wrong with her car.

I narrow my eyes and look through her windshield. With the blinding sun, it is difficult to see her. See what she is doing. If she needs help.

Maybe she is waiting for me to leave. Wants me gone before she drives away. Just as I give the thought merit, her car rolls forward and exits the lot. No slow down to smile or wave. She just… leaves.

My knuckles pale as I grip the steering wheel tighter. I close my eyes, bang my forehead on the leather, and berate myself. Mentally slap myself upside the head.

"Did you really need to do that? Did you really need to fuck up something good?" I ask myself aloud.

Yes, I did. Because although I keep telling myself Shelly is just a friend, my thoughts continue to step over the invisible boundary. The boundary dividing friends and lovers. A boundary I dare not cross. A path I refuse to travel down. Not again.

If Shelly and I don't cross the boundary, if we remain strictly friends, neither of us will get hurt. Defining the line today was for the best. For me and her and our friendship.

Did I need to be so cold when defining said line? No. But I don't know how else to set the tone for our relationship. Our friendship. And the definition of us definitely needs to be precise. Black and white. No gray. No color.

Lifting my head from the wheel, I take a deep breath and attempt to clear my cluttered thoughts. I put the car in gear, exit the lot, and drive home in a fog. I speed down the road faster than responsible. Faster than safe. And in no time, with no memory of the trip, I park in the driveway. Amble out of the car. Unlock the front door. Kick off my shoes. Wander through the house and take the stairs two at a time. Step into my studio.

And breathe.

I close my eyes and inhale. Find comfort in my safe space. In my solitude. In my art.

Then I pick up a blank canvas, park it on the easel, sit on my stool, and paint. A woman in full spectrum with wonder and delight and amazement in her twilight eyes. A woman, no matter how hard I try, I can't erase from my mind. A woman I will apologize to sooner rather than later.

Because there is not a chance in hell I won't be seeing her again.

Even if it hurts.

Even if it breaks me.

Even if I should walk away.

"Ouch!" I bring my thumb to my lips and suck on it.

When was the last time a thorn stabbed me? Years ago. Probably not since the first or second year I worked at Petal and Vine.

Yet, here I am. Getting stabbed by flowers with a vendetta. Really, they have no discord with me. But picturing a flower with revenge in its veins gives me a reason to laugh. Imagining every thorn prick brings the flower joy is the only humorous way to deal with the sting.

Why do some of the smallest wounds hurt the most? Thorn pricks, paper cuts, the slip of a needle tip while you sew.

I step back from the arrangement table and study the full vase of blooms. Contemplate adding more filler or flowers. Maybe a little of both. Anything to keep my hands and mind busy. To distract me from what I have been waiting to hear. What we all are waiting to hear.

Baby Clara is on her way.

Any second, Cora will go into labor. Baby Clara will make her debut. Everyone in our circle is on edge, eager and ready.

Elizabeth and I decided not to take on any major orders in the two-week window of her due date. Which happens to be tomorrow.

Our part-time employee, Francine, is on standby. She typically works two days a week, less than sixteen hours, to help out when either Elizabeth or I am alone, or we have major events to work on. She will work more hours if either of us is under the weather, but prefers the lesser hours. Plus, she told Elizabeth early on, her minimal time here each week gives her a sense of purpose.

Our delivery drivers, Joe and Melanie, won't be affected much. They come and go with orders, but keep an eye open for delivery and store updates.

With the impending arrival of her first grandchild, Elizabeth has busied herself more than usual. And driven me a bit crazy, to be honest. For the last twenty minutes, she has swept the same section of the shop repeatedly; not a speck of dirt to be seen.

But I don't blame her.

If I were in her shoes, I would be jittery too. On edge. And I am, but my anxiety is nothing compared to that of a parent waiting to become a grandparent.

Any minute now, my niece will enter the world. We may not be genetically related, but Cora is one hundred percent my sister. Always.

The arrival of baby Clara will change all our lives. In a

good way. I never thought it possible, but her birth will bring us all closer together. Bond us in a way we never imagined. Start a new phase of our lives and expand our friendships.

"You okay?" Elizabeth points to my hand.

"Yeah. Just zoned out and the thorn attacked." I narrow my eyes at the thorny flower in question.

Elizabeth laughs. "They get you when you least expect it."

I go back to the arrangement, one of several premade bouquets we have available. Elizabeth and I wanted an abundance of grab-and-go flowers in the case so Francine won't be overwhelmed in our absence.

Elizabeth switches from sweeping to dusting, mumbling to the flowers as she moves through the shop.

I insert the next stem into the vase, then twist the arrangement left and right to see where I need to put the final flowers. My gaze drifts toward the front of the store. Toward the beautiful meadow painted on the wall. The wispy grass and abundant wildflowers. And I zone out again. Imagine myself in a magical place like the one Devlyn created.

A little more than a week ago, Devlyn and I shared the best and worst day. Between the age mentioned by the server and his aloof behavior after the museum, I considered throwing in the towel on our friendship. Everything about us is new. So breaking ties with Devlyn wouldn't be the same as losing a friend I'd had most of my life.

At least, this is what I've told myself every day I'd considered texting him.

Then Devlyn took me by surprise. The next day, he reached out.

When the notification popped up on my phone, I expected to see a text with *it's been fun* somewhere in the bubble. Those words were nowhere to be found. What I saw instead was an apology. A real apology. More than the basic *I'm sorry*. His message read… *I didn't mean to be such an ass. It's a long story. But I'd love another chance at friends. Please.*

I have never been the type to hold on to anger toward another person. Not unless they did something major. Something unforgivable. Ninety-nine percent of the time, I forgive easily and let the past roll off my shoulders.

With Devlyn, though… the man needs to figure out what he wants.

He dishes out the word *friends* more than an all-you-can-eat buffet. Not sure if the constant reminder is for me or him. Either way, it leads me to believe two things without hard evidence.

One—he fears anything beyond friendship with a woman. The thought hurts my heart on so many levels and stirs up a list of questions as to why. Two—part of him wants more than that with me. More than friendship.

More than once, I've wanted to ask who broke his heart. Who made him so anti-love. To love someone is human nature. His vehemence to avoid love has to stem from past hurt, past pain. Putting him on the spot, coming out and asking him who did this to him, won't yield answers. And with our friendship so new, so on the edge of tipping one way or the other, asking would only push him away.

In his own time, and however he processes things, Devlyn needs to work through his emotions. I simply ask him not to rake me over the coals in the process.

Since his apology, we text or talk daily. No philosophical or life-altering chats. Just normal day-to-day stuff. Conversations similar to those I have with any other friend. Chats about work, strange clients, weird conversations we overheard at the grocery store, great jokes someone shared. And like all new friendships, we learn each other's quirks and boundaries.

Another change since the apology… we hang out a lot. Like every other day. For my own sanity, I compare time with Devlyn to hanging with Jonas or Gavin. We meet up at restaurants, eat pizza or Chinese or sandwiches. Talk, laugh, and ask questions. Nothing too deep, though.

My cheeks have stung more over the past few days than any previous time. Devlyn makes me smile. Often. More often than a friend.

Our late-night phone calls—Devlyn is anti-text whenever possible—aren't like the calls Cora and I shared as kids. The kind where you stay on the phone all night, trying to find something, anything, to talk about. Conversations between Devlyn and I hold more definition, more purpose.

Last night, we talked about college. How my experience compared to his. The way he spoke about art school and the people—professors and student body— enthralled me. His experience sounded otherworldly. In a sense, I suppose living and breathing art is a different way of life.

I shared my time at college, which was boring in comparison. How I originally studied interior design, then switched gears to get my bachelor's in finance and business. Working at Petal and Vine fulfilled my creative heart. Learning how to successfully own a business was more important for my future.

Time and conversations with Devlyn are a nice change of pace. A change I didn't see coming, but enjoy more than expected.

I take the finished vase of flowers to the open-air cooler, then return to the table and clean up. As I brush stem bits off the table into the bin, Elizabeth appears out of nowhere.

"It's time!"

My eyes widen. "*Time*, time?" She nods and I drop the can to the floor. "Okay. Shit." I fumble with my apron strands. "Grab our purses. I'll flip the sign and lock the door."

A minute later, we dash across the lot. I tell Elizabeth I will call Francine on the way. We hop into our cars and speed toward the hospital. Most of the drive is a blur of bumper-to-bumper cars, red lights, and finger taps on the steering wheel.

Cora consumes my every thought until we reach the hospital.

Is she in pain? When did her labor start? Is she all deep, practiced breaths and cool as a cucumber? Or is she detaching Gavin's hand from his limb and screaming at the hospital staff? Will she be in labor ten more hours or two?

I park a few spaces down from Elizabeth, jump out and press the lock button on the fob, then jog to catch up. She presses the button for the elevator car more times than an impatient child. I don't say anything to stave off her anxiety. Instead, I lay a hand on her upper back and draw small circles. Soothe her as best I can while she worries over missing this monumental moment.

The doors whoosh open and we dart inside the elevator. Elizabeth smashes the button once, twice, then takes a step back as the doors close. Seconds later, the elevator doors open to the labor and delivery floor. Elizabeth runs to the nurses' station while I go to the waiting area, where I spot Jonas, Autumn, and Erin.

"Any news?" I ask when I reach everyone.

"Gavin came out to update us a few minutes ago. She's eight centimeters dilated. Shouldn't be much longer," Jonas shares.

Admittedly, I know nothing about pregnancy or having babies or motherhood, except for the basics and what I have heard recently. This whole centimeters-dilated thing is jibber-jabber. A foreign language only parents and parents-to-be know. I want to ask how many centimeters she has to be dilated before she has the baby. Babies are big, so it has to be a lot. Right?

Autumn chuckles at my deer-in-headlights look. "Shelly, ask me anything."

Autumn must have a sixth sense. Probably hears my inner monologue and confusion. In another couple of months, our friends will gather here again. For Autumn and Jonas and their new arrival. Probably best to ask now.

"The centimeters thing…" I pause and Autumn nods for me to continue. "What's the magic number? Like twenty?" Sounds legit.

Autumn laughs, then grabs her belly and stops. "Don't make me laugh. I'll pee." My eyes widen. Do I ever want to be pregnant? The big belly, the whole squeezing a watermelon from your body thing, the fear of peeing your pants. The more I think about it, the more I don't think I want to be. "Ten. Ten is the magic number. She's almost there. Which means it won't be long. Within the hour, most likely."

Oh. Well, that is good news. But how the hell does such a big baby come out… No. I don't want or need to know. I zoned out during that part in health class for a reason. The entire concept is just too painful.

"I'll get us drinks," I offer. "Any takers?"

With everyone's drink order, I head downstairs in search of the hospital cafeteria. It isn't long before I pop two coffees, two hot cocoas, and a pile of creamers, sweeteners, and stir sticks in a cup carrier. When I step off the elevator in labor and delivery, Jonas is pacing with a larger-than-life smile on his face.

I rush over to him and Autumn, noticing Elizabeth's absence, and set down the drinks. "Is she here? Did I miss the excitement?"

Jonas shakes his head. "No, but she's pushing now. Elizabeth went in the room while you were gone."

For the next thirty-seven minutes, Autumn, Erin, and I sit in uncomfortable chairs while Jonas continues to pace. Autumn and I sip hot cocoa while Erin drinks coffee and Jonas takes the occasional sip. I continue to watch my friend. Watch as he wears a new pattern into the shiny, bleach-scented linoleum. Watch as he picks at the edges of his nail bed with other nails. Listen to the scuff of his boots and occasional huff from his lungs.

No doubt, he is envisioning the day he and Autumn return to this floor. What it will be like when his girlfriend gives birth. How his family will be as they wait in this very room. What their smiles will look like when they meet their new grandbaby or niece/nephew.

I rise from my chair and step into his space. He pauses his trek and meets my eyes with his antsy ones. "You okay?"

He nods. "Yeah. Just trying to absorb it all. It'll be different when Autumn's on the hospital bed and I'm in the delivery room." He takes a deep breath. "I'm just trying to not freak out."

Hooking my arm with his, I steer him toward the chairs. "Sit." He obeys. "There is nothing to worry about. We've gotten happy and healthy news about their baby and yours." Autumn laces her fingers with his. No doubt, she has dealt with his anxiety more than either will admit. "And I can't wait to meet my next niece or nephew." The three of us laugh.

"Who would've guessed?" Jonas's question is rhetorical, but I answer anyway.

"What?"

"That we'd all be here. Less than three years ago, we hung out at the bar every week. Listened to horrible, but hilarious karaoke. None of us were where we are today. In relationships. Having children."

Erin glimpses my way and I spy the subtle, quick wince. I want to say, *"I feel you, girl."* But I keep my lips shut. Jonas rambles because his nerves are shot and his thoughts are scattered. Although Erin and I are definitely not the same women we were three years ago, neither of us is in a romantic relationship or expecting a child. His comment isn't meant to offend, so I don't take it as such.

"We're adulting," I tease. "You guys"—I point down the hall, then between Autumn and Jonas—"are just adulting hard core."

Erin laughs and we follow suit. Then Autumn stands up with an *oh-shit* look on her face.

"Where's the bathroom?"

Jonas is at her side immediately. "I'll walk you." I love how sweet my friend is. How attentive he is with Autumn. Jonas has always been such a good man. And it makes my heart happy he and Autumn found each other.

For years, I worried about him. Long before Gavin returned to Florida, I watched Jonas pine for Cora. And Cora almost gave in to the idea of a romantic relationship with him. Almost. But Jonas was the bigger person. He put aside his feelings for her and encouraged her to follow her heart.

Karma, in return, brought Jonas and Autumn together. And I honestly believe everything went according to plan.

Sometimes you have to deal with pain and heartache before you get your happily ever after. Which is what I keep telling myself. One day, I will get my happy ending too.

Elizabeth dashes into the waiting room with the biggest smile on her face. Peter—a.k.a. Mr. Davies—appears out of thin air. *Has he been here the entire time and I ignored him?* His smile is as big as Elizabeth's and I have my answer. Obviously, he arrived before us and was in the room.

"She's here!" Elizabeth says louder than ever before. "Seven pounds, eight ounces. And she is perfect." She steeples her fingers in front of her lips. Her smile locked in place. A smile that will never fade.

"When can we see them?" Erin asks.

"In about fifteen minutes. They're getting cleaned up and settled," Peter states.

By the time Jonas and Autumn return, we are allowed to see Cora, Gavin, and Clara. We wander down the hall and, one by one, enter the room.

The hospital room is unlike any I have seen. So spacious and welcoming. Cora lies in a hospital bed that looks more comfortable than most regular beds. A rocking chair and stool take up the corner by the draped window. A small sofa and table sit opposite the bed. And tucked in the corner near the door is a collapsible bed. The room has everything for the new family.

A small, clear bassinet sits parked next to Cora's bed, empty. I step farther into the room and locate my best friend. And she is positively glowing. Baby Clara rests peacefully in her arms, snug to her chest, fast asleep. Cora stares down at her in what can only be described as pure amazement. Gavin watches them both with similar awe in his eye.

And I want to cry. Shed a million tears for my friends and this newfound joy in their lives.

Cora peers up and sees me near the foot of the bed. "Hey," she whispers.

"Hi."

"Does Auntie Shelly want to hold her niece?"

I nod because I can't seem to find my words.

Elizabeth appears at my side then guides me to the rocking chair. Gavin scoops up Clara so gently, I mentally gasp at how different he is as a father. Such a beautiful sight. He sets Clara in my arms and reminds me to support the back of her head. And we just rock.

Clara doesn't wake. Her eyelids flutter now and again. Her lips twitch just as often. She makes the sweetest little sounds. And she smells amazing. All I do is stare at her and whisper how lucky she is to have such a wonderful mommy and daddy. That she is loved by so many. And when she gets older, I will do all the fun stuff with her.

"Do you want a picture?"

I peer up to see Jonas waving his phone in the air. "Please."

He snaps several pictures and then Clara goes to the next set of arms as I evacuate the chair. Jonas sends me the pictures and I ooh and awe over them. Then, I send a photo to Devlyn.

Shelly: My best friend just had her baby. Isn't she precious?

The small bubble pops up and dances a beat.

Devlyn: Two beauties in one masterpiece.

I stare down at the screen. Read his response. Then read it again. And again. Question if I misunderstand the message. But no matter how many times I read it, I decipher it the exact same way. Each time I read it, I hear Devlyn's voice telling me I am beautiful. That I am a masterpiece.

And it confuses me. *Devlyn confuses me.*

One minute, he says the sweetest things. Compliments me like a lover and not a friend. Leans in closer, hooks my arm with his, watches me from a distance. He inserts himself in my life in ways unlike any other friend.

Perhaps he doesn't know I notice his eyes on me more often than not. That I don't feel the weight of his stare on my profile. The slight shift in his posture or held breath. But I notice every glance. Feel the way his eyes scorch my skin. I see it all. Feel it all.

Then, abruptly, he gives me the cold shoulder. Skirts around a past he hasn't gotten over. A past that keeps him from moving forward. When it comes to love and trust and his heart on the line, anyway.

So… I remain his friend. Act as I do with Jonas or Gavin or any of the guys in the tattoo family, and maybe sometimes with my brother. Try not to say anything flirty or dreamy or lovey. Do my damnedest to remain neutral.

But when he says stuff like this, when he tells me I am beautiful, I don't know what to think or feel or say. Do opposite-sex friends compliment each other's appearances? Sure. But Devlyn isn't like any guy friend I've had. When Devlyn tells me I am beautiful, the sentiment is layered with complexity and hidden meaning. So hidden, I don't think he even knows what is underneath.

Gah! Devlyn is a frustrating man.

Since I sent the picture of me with baby Clara, since I provoked the conversation, talking baby-related stuff wouldn't be awkward. Would it?

Shelly: Thanks. I've never given thought to having kids. You?

Devlyn: Not so much. Even if I did, I'd want to be in a long-term relationship first. Don't see that happening anytime soon.

This man is like a damn seesaw. A mood swing waiting to happen. I press a loose fist to my stomach as nausea begs for relief. His text is another reminder. A reminder I don't need, but receive almost daily. A reminder that feels like a constant slap to the face.

Friends. Devlyn and I are only friends.

His random sweet words, charming smile, and desire to spend time together throw me off balance. Make me question my sanity and perspective. Make me ask myself if I am interpreting his words through a romanticized lens. Because I have no clue.

God, he makes me dizzy.

Shelly: Well, they're asking us to go. Talk to you later.

Devlyn: Later.

No one asked us to leave yet, but probably will soon.

Cora and Gavin must be exhausted. No doubt baby Clara is as well.

The conversation with Devlyn needed to end, though. We haven't known each other long, but part of me *knows* him. And every once in a while, I want to smack some sense into him. Tell him to wake up and see what is right in front of him. Ask him what I can do to help heal his heart.

But I don't. I won't.

As always, I keep my eyes forward, mouth shut, and just go with the flow. And I pray one day it will all work in my favor. That I will find the love I have been looking for. Without mixed signals and crossed wires.

If that person happens to be Devlyn, I would be surprised.

If that person happens to be Devlyn, I would show him what being loved is really like.

TEN

DEVLYN

Dɪᴅ I ғᴜᴄᴋ ᴜᴘ?

For days, Shelly has been in a funk. Absent is the timid yet passionate woman I met more than a month ago. In her place is a more lackluster woman. She gives no indication I am to blame, but the pang in my gut says otherwise.

I want to ask what happened. What has her more hesitant and quiet? What has her avoiding eye contact?

But I don't say a word. I won't.

Asking questions leads us down a path of uncertainty. A path where I ask the questions, but won't answer hers. A path that muddles the lines of friendship, once again. And as much as I'd love to wipe the friendship line from existence, my heart trembles at the idea.

I am not a cold person. Not empty or devoid of emotion. Not intentionally. I do *feel* things, emotions. Love and happiness. Hurt and sadness. Joy and pain. The good and the bad. I feel it all.

Years back, prescribed by my dear mother, I visited a therapist regularly. My mother had it in her head that I was empty inside. Soulless. The irony isn't lost on me, but maybe she assumed this because I didn't express myself in a way that made *her* happy.

With each therapy session, my mother sat in the room —something abnormal on all accounts, but she insisted upon it. With each session, I opened up more. Expressed what I dealt with in school and how it made me feel. Mother wasn't keen on my responses. Perhaps they didn't suit *her* needs. She told the therapist she'd done her own research and was convinced she knew what was *wrong* with me.

Thanks to my mother, in one session, the therapist teetered on the idea of me having anhedonia—the inability to feel pleasure.

What a crock of shit—the doctor and the prognosis.

For years, all I felt was the good, the wonderment, and the delight in the world. There had never been a dark cloud in my sky. Sometimes, I experienced the pleasure a little too much.

And perhaps, that is the problem.

I feel *too* much.

But isn't feeling too much part of being a creative? A fault in the genetic makeup of an artist, any artist. We feel *everything*. Which is why we create. Why we draw or paint, journal or write, sculpt or build, play instruments or sing. So we have a way to release the pent-up emotion, a way to express what consumes our mind and soul. So we don't lose our minds. Mostly.

Shelly and I walk along the park trail. I stay just a hair back so I have my favorite view of her profile. The one I stare after too much, yet not enough. Sunlight filters through the trees and dances over her prominent cheekbones, her toffee-blonde ponytail, the column of her throat. The play of light heats my skin more than hers. I lick my lips, swallow, then avert my eyes forward.

Don't go there, Templar.

"Hey." I bump her arm with mine. Her gaze shifts from the path, but only for a second. "Everything okay?" A shiver shakes her frame, but she tries to disguise the action by tucking a nonexistent stray hair from her cheek. A cold front swept through yesterday. The air a touch crisper today, but not cold. The sun warms us as we walk through the park. A hoodie on me, as well as her. "We can head back if you're cold."

She stops walking and I follow suit. In the front pocket of her hoodie, her hands squirm. Too fidgety to be from the temperature.

Is she nervous? Why would she be nervous?

Before I open my mouth to suggest we turn back, she speaks up.

"I'm not cold. And…"

She lifts her eyes to the trees. Her twilight irises twinkle in the sunlight as she thinks of what to say next. Moments such as this, I wish for telepathy. The ability to hear her thoughts. Hear them unfiltered straight from the source. To know what confounds her so deeply.

Then, I nix the idea. Because with the thoughts I want to hear comes the sentiments she keeps to herself. The ones I want to hear, want to reciprocate, but refuse to accept or return.

"Sorry," she says after a long pause.

"Why are you apologizing?"

She lowers her gaze and I come eye to eye with Andromeda. Immerse myself in her starry eyes. Swallow past the expanding lump in my throat. Berate myself for leaving my sunglasses in the car because, right now, I feel completely vulnerable. Exposed. Nude in a crowded room. I love and despise the feeling. I crave and evade the eddy beneath my diaphragm. Beg for more while wanting to bury myself deep in the earth.

"Sometimes, it's hard being your friend."

My brows tighten. What does she mean?

Yes, I have been wishy-washy. Been open and interested one minute, then cold and reserved the next. I know this. But the stony mask is my shield. How I protect myself. How I protect her.

"Not sure what you mean." I truly haven't the slightest idea. And guessing will only dig a deeper hole.

Her steps resume and lead along the path again. Without hesitation, I follow her. "You confuse me."

"How?"

"I've had guy friends all my life. When you have an older brother, it just happens." I nod and hum, although siblings are foreign territory. "And none of them have been like you."

Is this a compliment or an issue? Her tone gives nothing away.

"Thanks," I say on a wince.

She laughs and knocks my arm with hers. I take it as a good sign. "Don't be a weirdo."

Laughter bubbles in my throat. "It's who I am." I shrug as if my awkwardness is common knowledge.

"What I mean is, none of my guy friends really connect with me." I stop breathing for one, two, three strides. "We have stuff in common," she continues as if her declaration is no big deal. "But they never seemed to get me. Not like you do."

I do get her. With Shelly, everything clicks into place.

At one point, everything clicked with Kelsey too. Or so I thought. Then, she pummeled me with her proclamation and I lost sight of all perspective. Doubted every gut instinct I felt. Because how did I not see that coming? How did I not know my girlfriend of three years, who seemed happy and in love with me, wanted to break up?

Is this where things are headed with Shelly? Down the path of promises and hearts on display. Souls exposed and futures on the line. Not sure I can walk down that path again. Not after where it led me last time.

Shelly is not Kelsey. Shelly has years of wisdom and heart guiding her. But if I let her all the way in and lose her, the end would be pure devastation. For us both.

"Not sure what to say."

Part of me wants to nix our friendship. Call it quits before it becomes something more, deeper, unbreakable. Before either of us navigates this irreversible path.

I should walk away now, say goodbye as we go our separate ways. But abandoning Shelly is impossible. Just the idea of walking away steals my breath. Forms a fault line in my heart. Has me mentally bending at the waist and retching.

I hate the piece of me that needs her. Needs her aura and light. Craves her smile and warmth. Begs for her timid conversation and unrelenting attention.

I also love how much I need her.

She spins around, walks backward, and grants me the smile I see every time I close my eyes. "You don't need to say anything. I just wanted to tell you." She spins back and walks beside me again.

The next quarter mile of our walk around the lake is blanketed in silence. Our pace leisure. Her arms swing at her sides as she glances up at the trees. I shove my hands in my hoodie pockets to avoid reaching for hers. Wouldn't be surprised if my body did it involuntarily. Not with the level of gravity Shelly harbors.

Her behavior the last few days wiggles its way to the surface. The uncomfortable, tense silence. Her stiff posture and dejected body language. I work to force the memory away but fail miserably.

"Can I ask something?"

"Yes."

Deep breaths. It's just a question and I am probably overreacting. Still, my stomach twists and flips. "Did something happen?"

"Not sure I understand?" Her gaze falls from the trees and heats my cheek, my jaw, my neck.

"The other day, you texted about your friend having her baby. You seemed really happy. Since then, not so much. Did something happen?"

A chill blankets my skin the second she looks away. Shelly stays quiet for several paces, and I wonder if the question was too personal or somehow upset her.

We happen upon an empty bench by the lake. She ambles off the path and goes straight for the bench without a word. I stay a few feet back until we both sit. Out of the corner of my eye, I watch how intently she focuses on the lake. Watch as she searches for a way to tell me what occupied her mind. What had a gray cloud floating over her.

"This is going to sound stupid." Her eyes scan the bank of the lake as she works her jaw back and forth.

When she doesn't continue, I bump her shoulder with my arm. "Nothing you say is stupid."

She laughs without humor. "Just wait." I grant her the time she needs. Don't interrupt while she compiles the words in her mind. And then she spills her secrets. "I read too much into your response after I texted you that day."

"When your friend had her baby?"

"Mm-hmm."

What did I say? Think, think, think.

I go back a few days in my memory bank. Remember the picture she sent of her with the baby. Recall the way I stroked her cheek in the image before I replied. Then, I hang my head. Mentally slap myself for the responses I sent her. I'd let my mind wander and didn't think before typing either text. *Shit.* No wonder she has been distant. If our roles were reversed, I would be too.

I complimented her. Told her she was beautiful. Which is true, but could be taken out of context. Considering I define the friendship line every time we see each other, my words undoubtedly confused the hell out of her. Then I drove the nail deeper and told her I wouldn't have children without full commitment. Followed by my disinterest in serious relationships. With two texts, I went from one extreme to the other. Said something wonderful, then followed it up with distance and heartless words.

God, I am a fucking idiot. And a goddamn mess.

"It wasn't my intention to upset you."

"I know."

"Seems I can't help myself when it comes to you."

She twists on the bench, props a leg up on the seat, her knee grazing my thigh as she faces me head-on. "Like that." She jabs my arm with a finger. "You sound as if you can't stay away from me. But one false move on my part and you go cold. Feels like I can't win."

Unfortunately, she is right. No sense in denying it. No matter how many times I remind myself Shelly and I are only friends, the voice in my head, the one I stomp down often, laughs and calls me a fool for believing such hypocrisy. The number of hours I think of Shelly… I am a moron if I believe we will remain strictly friends.

But I keep that to myself.

"Sorry," I say, hypnotized by her sparkly blues. "I'm too selfish for my own good. And yours."

She opens her mouth, ready to respond, but my phone rings and cuts her off. Her lips form a tight line before she smiles and twists to face the lake.

Immediately, I hate the lack of eye contact. Hate that she shifted away.

I pull my phone from my back pocket—the number not in my contacts—and answer. "Hello?"

"Good afternoon. May I speak with Devlyn Templar, please?"

"This is he."

The woman on the other end goes into a well-rehearsed spiel. For a moment, I zone out. Don't listen to a word she says. Until I hear her say, "We'd like to feature some of your work in the exhibition. I realize it's last minute. My apologies. Another artist gave us your information and, after seeing your pieces online, we'd love to showcase your work with other local artists."

"You've piqued my interest. When is the exhibition again?"

"Saturday. In a few days. If the notice is too short, I understand."

"Count me in."

"Wonderful," she says with jubilance. "Can I send details to the email listed on your website?"

"Yes, that'd be perfect."

"Thank you, Mr. Templar. We'll see you on Saturday."

I disconnect the call and stow the phone in my pocket. Last-minute calls for exhibitions are few and far between, but they happen. When the email hits, I will read up on the exhibition. Whether or not there is a set theme. Either way, I know which pieces I will show.

And I would like if Shelly saw them.

"Do you have plans Saturday?"

She studies the lake without a word. Takes a deep breath. Tightens her grip on the edge of the bench seat.

Then meets my gaze. Left then right, left then right. Her eyes dart between mine. Seeking, hunting, searching for clues or answers to a question she has yet to speak aloud. Feels as if I know the question, but I refuse to give it a voice. I won't jeopardize time with her. I need every second she grants me.

Clamping down on her lips, she shrugs. "I work a few hours in the morning. Other than that, no. Why?"

Inviting Shelly to the exhibition with me sounds like a date. A legit date. Unlike the *friend non-dates* we share more often than not, there is no avoiding implications with this. No matter which way I spin it, asking her will suggest we are more than friends. Call me cruel or self-centered or destructive, I don't care. I want Shelly there. At my side. On my arm. To see my art on display. To decipher what she sees and feels. To watch her gravitate toward each piece. To decipher how she sees what I see.

Our friendship is still in the infantile stage, yet she consumes much of my day.

I ache for and detest how she rattles my heart. How she makes my breaths uneven. How she spins a tornado in my head. Each day, I wake up with Shelly as my first thought. It gives me life and scares me to death.

"Was just invited to display some of my work at an exhibition." I pause for two breaths. "And I'd love it if you came."

Shit. Should not have used the word *love*. Maybe she will bypass it or think of it in the general sense and nothing more. Hopefully.

"I'd like that, thank you." Her toothy smile is infectious. As is the way it lights up her eyes. Like a visual hug.

God, I want to conquer my demons, my insecurities. For me. For her. For us.

Shelly is the first woman to truly monopolize my every thought. The amount of time I spent thinking of Kelsey years back is child's play compared to the hours and days I think of Shelly. Often, I chastise my obsession with Shelly. Tell myself it isn't healthy to spend every waking—and non-waking—minute with one person invading my thoughts.

Art is how I cope with this obsession. How I release the emotions growing, building, expanding exponentially inside. The emotions I don't expose to anyone—at least not verbally.

Will Shelly pick up on the underlying emotion I don't —can't—voice when she sees my art?

Part of me hopes she sees it all. Part of me begs her to solve the big mystery. To put an end to my constant indecision. The other part of me pukes at the possibility.

"The curator is sending me the details. I'll share more when I get the email. Most exhibitions are casual. The food is hit or miss. Might be a good idea to eat before or after, depending on the showtime."

Yep, definitely making this sound more and more like an official date. While I didn't outright suggest dinner together, it won't shock me if she interprets it as an invitation. I won't deny her if she does. I will never deny Shelly.

Keep telling yourself it's her *you're not denying. You know it's* you.

"Okay." She looks back out at the lake, her smile still firmly in place. "We should head back. I smell rain."

We look up simultaneously. Looming overhead is a cluster of gray clouds, slowly drifting in from the coast and stealing the blue sky.

Rising from the bench, I wait for Shelly to lead. Her eyes scan the lake one last time as she takes a deep breath. On the way back, the rustle of leaves and clap of our shoes on the path chase away the silence. Our pace faster with the impending storm.

Peeking at her profile, I will her to speak. Will her to tell me what is on her mind.

Does she think Saturday is a date? Or just two friends hanging out, one supporting the other, while possibly sharing a meal together? Not like we haven't shared several meals or spent time together. Regardless, the list of questions grows longer with each step forward.

But I don't ask a single one. I won't ask.

Because more than anything, I fear her answer. Fear she believes Saturday is a legit date. Fear I will have to cut ties with her because being emotionally vulnerable scares the hell out of me. Fear that I feel more for her than I am willing to admit to anyone, including myself.

I care for Shelly. More than a *friend* cares for another *friend*. And no matter how hard I try to define our relationship, the lines are blurring. From where I stand, they blur more each day.

The biggest question of all… do I let those lines disappear completely? Or do I draw them sharper in the sand?

God… how I want that line to disappear.

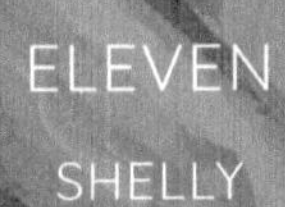

ELEVEN

SHELLY

We reach the parking lot as the first drops of rainfall.

I dig the fob out of my pocket and unlock the car. Feet away, I slow my pace. Ready to turn on my heel and tell Devlyn I will talk to him later. Before I get the chance, his fingers lightly brush my lower bicep. Curl into a firm yet gentle grip above my elbow. Stop me in my tracks.

Heat radiates from the spot where his hand touches me through the hoodie. Briefly, I close my eyes and take a deep breath. On the exhale, I open my eyes and slowly spin to face him.

"Shelly…" His voice is soft, scratchy, hesitant. His pale-green irises a touch darker and loaded with unspoken emotion.

I lick my lips and his eyes drop to follow the action. "Yeah?"

His eyes flick north as he swallows. Drizzly rain kisses our skin, yet neither of us attempts to escape it. And it is in this moment that I see it. The emotion he works so hard to keep hidden. The feelings simmering in his veins that he refuses to give control.

Since Devlyn and I fell into friendship, I questioned how he really felt. Not that I need more than he gives, but it oftentimes feels as if he holds back. Restrains himself from temptation. Resists what he truly wants. What we both want.

I have no idea what it is Devlyn wants—for himself, from me—but I wish he wouldn't fight his heart.

He scratches the back of his neck. His brows pinch together for a split second before he smooths his expression. "Come back to my place?" Of all the things to come from Devlyn's mouth, that was *not* what I expected to hear. "The weather and that call"—he tosses a thumb over his shoulder—"cut our time here."

This right here, this exact moment, is why my brain is a scrambled mess. We have hung out several times, but not a single occasion has been at my place or his. Probably his method of keeping our *friendship* in check. If we don't step into each other's personal space, the wall between friends and lovers stays upright. Solid. Permanent.

Not to be presumptuous, but him asking me to come over... did a few bricks from his highly erected wall just tumble?

"Uh..." I drop my stare to the hoodie strings near the hollow of his throat, swallow, then lift my gaze to his. "Yeah. Sure."

For someone so adamant about keeping us indefinitely in the friend zone, it seems as if Devlyn handed me an exclusive, *I never give these to anyone* invitation to the next step. I don't want to feed my inner romantic—the one currently singing and doing backflips—and think more into what all this means. But ignoring this gesture is asinine and ignorant.

"I'll text you my address. Give me an hour to clean up the house?" His fingers finally unravel from my arm and I miss the warmth of him immediately.

I nod. "Sounds good." If this was any of my other guy friends, we'd plan food or movies or games. "Need me to bring anything?" A small crease forms between his brows. "Takeout or a movie?"

He steps back, inching closer to his car and farther from me. "Nah. We'll figure it out."

Who is this guy?

Everything with Devlyn has always been on the straight and narrow. No room for deviation. Sure, the occasional misunderstanding occurs, but he is quick to put us back on the path he finds most comfortable.

In the span of an hour, the space around us feels bigger. Expansive. Ever growing. Like a new side of him has emerged. One he kept locked away. Hidden. Safe. And I am not sure how to feel about the change. Should I welcome it with open arms? Or should I remain rooted and hesitant, arms hugging my chest? I'd rather it be the former, but mentally prepare myself for the latter.

"Okay." I open the driver's side door. "See you soon."

Devlyn throws me a half smile. "See you." Then he is in his car and driving out of the lot.

Minutes go by in a haze. I start the car but sit idle in

the lot. The oak tree near my front bumper blurs into a blob of brown and green. The music on the radio fades into a low hum. Rain smacks the windshield in fatter drops, mottling my vision more as I get lost in thought.

What does this all mean?

Spending more time with Devlyn—in his home, no less—has my mind in a spiral. I don't want to overthink the invitation—to his house or the exhibition. Over-thinking is the enemy of happiness. But I need some form of clarity before taking another step.

What if this is just an extension of what Devlyn deems friendship? What if it's not?

Devlyn is a great guy. Different than anyone I have met. More reserved, but it suits him. Occasionally cold, but I think him acting distant is a front to protect his heart from whatever—whoever—hurt him. Most of all, he has this complex, sensational energy. A magnetic field that pulls you in and holds you captive.

I don't want to set myself up for heartache, but I don't want to ignore the shift between us.

My phone dings with an incoming text, snapping me from my introspection. Unlocking it, I read the message with Devlyn's address. I connect my phone to the car and map his address. *Twenty minutes.* Should be enough time to get my brain in the right headspace.

"God, I hope so."

With a huff, I put the car in reverse and back out. I make a quick stop at home. Change out of my damp clothes. Eat a few pieces of chocolate. Give myself a pep talk in the bathroom mirror as I fix my ponytail. Then, I jump back in the car and drive east, toward the unknown.

"The destination is on the right."

I park in the driveway behind Devlyn's SUV and stare at the moody blue house. In the dark, with how far back it sits from the road, I'd easily miss it. The house a single story along the front with an additional story over the rear of what I assume was once a garage. Tall crepe myrtle trees fill the spacious front lawn—minimal foliage on the branches and bare of flowers.

Exiting the car, I shoulder my purse and walk toward the front door. Along the front of a small screened-in porch is a kaleidoscope of flowering plants. Dark-pink coneflowers and sunny bright coreopsis. Vibrant orange gerbera and purple shooting stars. Behind them, fountain grasses butt against the porch and fill in the space.

Before reaching the door, I already have a new perspective of Devlyn. One I never expected. Comprised of a large house and an even larger yard. Of plants to tend to and patio furniture on the porch. It all feels… odd. But in a good way.

I lift my hand and tap my knuckles on the door. Clattering echoes on the other side of the door, followed by a *dammit*. A soft chuckle spills from my lips as I shake my head.

Then the door whips open and I remind myself to breathe.

Devlyn finger-combs his hair a beat before gesturing to the space at his back. "Come in."

I duck my chin as a rush of heat blooms across my cheeks and I step over the threshold. Entering Devlyn's space is taking a step into the inner workings of his mind. Sure, he didn't construct the house, place the walls or windows, but his touch is everywhere.

The entry is a formal sitting room. Rustic wood floors as far as the eye can see. A simple yet sleek pale-gray sofa against the right wall, several throw pillows in various colors consume most of the sitting space, a khaki throw blanket draped over an arm. A white rug with eccentric black lines parked beneath an ashy oak coffee table. On the table is a thick book of artwork, a black three-wick candle and a small vase of common daisies. Two white lattice-woven chairs with frames matching the table sit on the opposite side of the table, facing the sofa.

Moody paintings on canvas hang on the gray wall above the sofa. The images purposely staggered, but all part of the same portrait. A woman walking in the distance, trees and flowers and tall grass in her surroundings. The image reminds me of the meadow Devlyn painted in the shop, only the observer stands farther back.

"You have a beautiful home."

Devlyn shuts the door, sidles up to me, and shoves his hands in his pockets. "Thanks. My mother insisted I get more square footage than a single person needs." He shrugs. "She isn't a woman easily ignored."

I chuckle under my breath. "Yeah, I get that. I love my mom, but sometimes she can be a little too persistent."

"Can I get you a drink?"

"Water, please." I set my purse on one of the chairs and follow him to the kitchen just past the sitting room.

A framed pass-through-slash-bar connects the kitchen and sitting room. Rather than use the bar for eating, Devlyn has another vase of flowers. This one shallow and wide and filled with magnolia buds. The fragrance a gradual scent in the air.

The kitchen is U-shaped with white cabinets, black marble countertop, dark-gray marble backsplash, and stainless steel appliances. A small window over the sink at the end looks out on what I assume is the backyard. A small basket of fruit sits on the counter in one corner, a coffee-and-tea station in the other.

Devlyn pours water from a pitcher in the fridge then hands me a glass before filling his own.

Being in Devlyn's space, without the possibility of interruption, without outside means of distraction, feels claustrophobic and bizarre. Time alone with Devlyn isn't what has me worried. More often than not, our time together is spent alone.

But this is different.

There is no one to interfere. No servers or patrons or park-goers. No visual deviations such as menus or trees or walkways. And that realization adds a layer of sweat to my skin. Makes my breaths come in short bursts. Makes my pulse whoosh louder in my ears.

Devlyn sips his water, oblivious to my inner freak-out,

and steps past me. "Come on." He glances over his shoulder. "I'll give you a tour."

To say I am overwhelmed by the time we finish the tour would be an understatement. This house is *huge*.

Five bedrooms—although he showed three, the other two I assume are his bedroom and the studio upstairs—three bathrooms, living and dining room, laundry area, and the backyard. The backyard is as spacious as the front, but inhabited by a large jasmine-covered pergola over canyon stone pavers with short, fine grass between each. A slate-tiled table is parked under the canopy with eight chairs. An oak tree with a trunk too wide to hug halfway shades the yard on the left, a bench swing hanging from a thick limb. Several crepe myrtles appear strategically placed in the yard to add color, shade, and beauty.

We step back inside and I down the last of my water.

The sheer size of Devlyn's home, how he has attained a level of adulthood I have yet to, sends my head into a tailspin of questions. Has me asking where I went wrong. He has acquired so much at twenty-two and I am barely able to add to my savings each month at thirty-two.

He bumps my shoulder with his bicep. "You okay?"

Am I? Yes. No. I have no freaking clue. "Yeah." I lift my glass, then remember I have no water to quench the drought in my throat.

Devlyn takes a step and twists to face me head-on. He lifts a hand and presses the tip of his index finger between my brows. "If this spot gets any tighter, it'll never relax," he says, dropping his hand. I sigh and close my eyes.

"Relax, Shelly." His voice barely above a whisper. "It's just me. Us."

I open my eyes and meet his. There, I see something familiar yet foreign. The man in front of me is Devlyn. Complex and quiet and mysterious. Only now, a darker shade of green rims his pale irises as he holds me captive. Steals my breath and has my brain foggy.

Did a switch flip in his brain?

My voice refuses to work. Even if it did, I wouldn't know what to say. This is yet another moment where Devlyn confounds me. Says things I easily misconstrue.

So, I simply nod in response. He rewards my bewilderment with a subtle half smile.

"Let's order food. Was thinking Asian." His smile grows. "Maybe you'll also share the story I never heard over lunch at the shop?" My eyes narrow as I think back. "Why you laughed when I asked sandwiches or sushi."

"Ah." I nod with a smile. The day comes back in a flash of colors. I was so nervous to eat lunch with Devlyn that I completely forgot. "Yeah, I'll share over dinner."

Devlyn pulls up the website for a Japanese restaurant nearby. He hands me his phone, a pad of paper, and a pen. "Write down what you want."

I arch a brow. "Before I do, you should know... I order a lot. More than a lot."

With a shake of his head, he laughs. "Doesn't matter. Leftovers always taste better."

"True." I point a finger at him.

A mile-long list later, Devlyn calls in the order. He

guides us to the living room—a room he probably spends more time in, if I read the vibe accurately.

The walls throughout the house are painted the same midgray tone. Except this room. The living room is a darker gray. Cavernous with floor-to-ceiling black curtains blocking out any light from outside. Oak beams have been added to the ceiling and down the length of one wall. An oak-and-black-steel-framed bookshelf consumes the wall behind the L-shaped couch. The shelving unit decorated with small, green plants in black pots, stacked books, an eclectic wire-framed lamp with an Edison bulb, and several other statuesque knickknacks.

The L-shaped gray couch has pillowy cushions, an array of monochrome throw pillows, and a gray-and-black blanket draped over the back near the chaise. Two wooden block tables sit in the center of the room, wheels on the base, candles in the center, a drawer on one side, bolts and antique hinges and leather straps at the joints. A light tweed rug blankets the floor. Across from the couch is a black-painted brick fireplace, unburned logs on the grate, the mantel matching the oak beams. Above the fireplace, mounted to the wall, is the largest television I have seen in a home.

Devlyn doesn't strike me as someone to sit in front of the television for hours on end. But who the hell knows. We still have so much to learn about each other. Maybe Devlyn is a closet binge-watcher. Up all hours of the night, glued to endless episodes on Netflix.

Devlyn digs through the table drawer, turns on the television, then hands me the remote. "How about you find us something to watch and I'll go get us fresh drinks." I take the remote, his fingers grazing mine in the process. Heat sizzles my fingers, my forearm, my blood. No doubt my cheeks are crimson. He swallows and slowly retracts his hand. "Any requests? Water, hot tea, beer, cola."

"A beer would be great. Thanks."

The moment Devlyn exits the room, I drag in a deep breath.

Jesus, Reed. Get a hold of yourself.

Alcohol isn't something I partake in often, but maybe a beer will help settle my anxiety. While Devlyn fetches drinks, I surf Netflix. Would help if I knew what Devlyn likes and dislikes watching. I have no die-hard preferences and will give any show or movie a shot. With how creative Devlyn is, I assume the same of him.

After scrolling past far too many romantic movies, I scan the Netflix original series list and stumble upon *Dark*. Reznor, from the tattoo shop, raved about the show during one of our Sunday night gatherings.

Watching a mystery with Devlyn sounds a hell of a lot safer than anything else. *Dark* it is.

"You find something?" Devlyn asks as he walks back in and hands me a brown bottle.

Glancing down at the label, I laugh. "Interesting." His brows lift. "You just happen to have Japanese beer in the fridge. Like you planned this."

Devlyn sips his own beer as his eyes dart up in an unspoken answer. I laugh internally as I lift the bottle to my lips. The smooth, rich malt rolls over my tongue and cools my throat on the way down.

He probably planned this on his way home and stopped at the store. Don't overthink it.

"So… what are we watching?"

Oh. Right. "Since I wasn't sure of your taste, I picked something a friend recommended. *Dark.* Have you watched it?"

He shakes his head and twists to see the show synopsis on the screen. Sipping his beer, he nods. "Sounds interesting."

Next up on the list of awkward events… where do we sit on the couch?

The plush corner couch easily seats six with wiggle room. If this were my couch, I'd sit centered with the television. Which is probably where Devlyn sits when in here. I don't want to take his seat.

Should I sit in the corner spot? It's probably the most comfortable. But would I come off as distant if I sat there and Devlyn sat two seats away? Maybe I sit one off from the center. Then I appear close, but not to the point of crowding him.

Why the hell is it so damn hard to figure where to sit? Why am I overthinking couch space and seating arrangements?

Because you're in Devlyn's home. In a dark room with minimal lighting. About to have the most intimate moment between the two of you.

Ugh!

It may only be dinner and a show, but this is the *most* intimate span of time we have shared. Out in public, the looks and conversations we exchange don't feel as cozy or profound. In public, disruption is inevitable. It's easier to take a step back, to shy away from his stares when I can pretend something has caught my attention.

Here, in his home, all that disappears. The security blanket of distractions vanishes.

Devlyn takes a seat exactly where I knew he would, sets his beer on a coaster on the table, then pats the seat next to him.

Seriously, who is this guy?

"I won't bite." A smirk tips up the corner of his mouth as he fails to hide a light chuckle. "Promise."

What if I want him to bite?

Shut. Up. Shelly.

Tossing throw pillows to the side, I sit in the space beside him. Our arms inches apart, his heat hits my skin. His scent—a blend of graphite and pine and earth—hits my nose. Head forward, I close my eyes, take a deep breath, and remind myself to breathe. To not fidget. To act *normal*.

When my eyes open, I spot Devlyn in the periphery. His gaze heating my cheek more than any flush ever would.

Is it wrong to love his intensity? How deeply he studies every curve and line, dip and shadow of my profile?

I rotate my head until he comes into view. I sip my beer then pick at the label. Lick my lips. Swallow when his stare falls to watch the action. Break the spell when I lean forward and set my bottle on the table, next to his.

"Should we start the show?" I point to the screen. "Or wait for the food to arrive?"

Devlyn extracts his phone from his pocket and checks the time. "Fifteen-ish minutes until food. Let's start."

As I press play on the remote, Devlyn turns off the lamp. The room goes dark. Darker than dark. The inches between my arm and his vanishes. His heat may as well smother every inch of me on this couch, in this room.

An Albert Einstein quote fills the screen in German, subtitles listed below. A second later, ominous music follows and a man's voice floods the room. And it is all I need as a distraction. The deep timbre demands my attention. The words beckon me to listen, to pay attention.

I thank whatever instinct told me to choose this show. Because I need the diversion. Need something to grab my attention more than Devlyn.

An eerie sound fills the air from a cave on the screen just as the doorbell rings. I all but jump out of my skin. Devlyn... laughs.

"Not scared, are you?" I shake my head and he laughs again. Rising from the couch, he exits the room. "Be right back."

As my heart settles back to its normal rhythm, Devlyn strolls back into the room with two brown bags, sets them down, and rolls the two tables together. As I empty the bags, Devlyn tosses pillows on the floor between the couch and table. When I eye him, he simply says, "Makes it easier to share."

Devlyn stares at the containers in front of me as if waiting for a sign to pop up with descriptions for each. I point to each dish and tell him what they are.

"Seaweed salad, veggie tempura, bulgogi."

"Bul-what?"

"Bulgogi. Uh… essentially, it's Korean BBQ. And so good." I point to my last dish. "Yaki udon. Noodle soup with veggies and shrimp."

He glances at all the food I ordered, then looks to his salmon teriyaki, rice, miso soup, side salad, steamed veggies, and noodles. His eyes dart back and forth a few times before he looks up.

"Will you eat all that?" His voice is absent of judgment but loaded with curiosity.

I shake my head. "Definitely not. I just love all the flavors and have a hard time deciding."

A smile kicks up the corners of his lips. "Will you tell me the story behind why you laughed at sandwiches or sushi at the shop that first day I ordered lunch?"

"Only if you promise to try everything."

He tips his head side to side in contemplation. "Deal."

We dig into food. The screensaver replaces the pause point of the show, and I dive into the story.

"My best friend, Cora, loves every type of Asian food. We've known each other since elementary school and she wasn't always this way. I remember when I stayed the night at her house. She begged her mom, Elizabeth—"

"Elizabeth from the shop?"

I nod. "Yep. That's a story for another day." There I go being presumptuous. "But she always begged her mom to cook us Kid Cuisine TV dinners. She always wanted the one with chicken nuggets, macaroni and cheese, corn, and chocolate pudding. That's how it was until early high school. She loved those damn things." I laugh. "Then, one day, out of nowhere, she didn't. She wanted lo mein and egg foo young. Teriyaki and phở. Sushi and katsudon. When I asked her what sparked her sudden interest, she said her dad received a stack of gift certificates for restaurants near the beach. A few of them were to Asian restaurants. Went downhill from there."

Devlyn's lips plump as he mulls it over. Longer than a friend would, I stare at his lips. Unfortunately for me, I don't look up until he clears his throat.

Cue my virginal blush.

Someone save me from a lifetime of humiliation. I beg you.

"So, me asking sandwiches or sushi was funny because you've probably had sushi with your friend thousands of times." I nod. "Makes sense." He takes a sip of beer. "What's *your* favorite food?"

"Way to put a lady on the spot." I chuckle while dipping a piece of fried squash in the tentsuyu. "I don't know. I like variety. Picking one thing seems impossible." Tipping my head back, I stare at the ceiling. "If I had to pick *one* food, it'd probably be bread. Any kind except white sandwich bread. And fresh out of the oven." I hum, and out of the corner of my eye, Devlyn shifts his position.

What was that?

"Bread, huh?" I nod. "I'll have to remember that."

"I'll have to remember that." Why? And what does that mean?

Devlyn picks up the remote and presses play, ending the story. Our conversation may be over, but we both wear ridiculous smiles on our faces.

When our bellies are full, Devlyn puts the leftovers in the fridge. We relocate to the couch, seemingly closer than before, and watch more episodes of *Dark*. I do everything within my power to focus on the show and not how close we sit.

Inevitably, I lose the battle and it isn't long before I lay my head on Devlyn's shoulder and press my weight into him. Never more comfortable than in this moment.

TWELVE

DEVLYN

A PINCH IN MY NECK STIRS ME FROM SLEEP, BUT I DON'T dare move. Not when my senses spark to life and a scent I know all too well drifts through my nose. Jasmine, orange blossoms, and patchouli. Such a unique combination. Each note detectable on its own, but addictive when combined.

Shelly.

I crack an eye open, take in her blonde locks, then inhale deeply.

Face buried at the base of my throat; Shelly's body curls into mine. Our legs a tangled mess. Her arms sandwiched between us, palms pressed to my chest. One of my arms supports her head while the other drapes her waist.

I close my eyes and absorb the moment, the connection, the gravity we can't escape.

Oddly, in this blip of time, fear doesn't grab me by the ankles and pull me under. In fact, fear is nowhere to be found. No fear, but anxiety bubbles just below the surface.

That will never not exist when close to Shelly—physically and otherwise.

Thinking back to last night, Shelly sank into me more with each passing minute. Our bellies full after we gorged on the living room buffet. The second she laid her head on my shoulder, I closed my eyes and fought the voice of doubt in my head. The voice I heard often when it came to Shelly.

I don't want to fight what I feel for her. I also don't want to hurt again.

Question is, how do I balance what I feel for her and the self-doubt eating at my heart?

Shaking away my thoughts, I focus on the here and now. Focus on the sleeping woman in my arms. Opening my eyes to see her in a new way, a new light, close up and unrestrained. Expression soft, hair disheveled, lips slightly parted.

God, it feels good to hold her. *Really* hold her. How many times have I pictured this moment? Well, not this *exact* moment, but a similar one. One where I wrap my arms around her frame and haul her snug to mine. One where her touch provides me comfort and not unease. One where I sweep my knuckles softly over the line of her jaw, her cheekbone, her chin just before I lean in and brush my lips with hers.

Too many times. Not enough times.

A mumble leaves her lips. Something unintelligible. By her tone, I assume it was endearing or sweet, but can't be certain. She mumbles again, a soft *please* against my skin.

The heat of her breath, mixed with the weight of her plea, sends goose bumps across my skin.

Then she moves… and I freeze.

Her legs weave more with mine like vines climbing a trellis. One arm wraps around my torso and hugs me while the other fists my shirt. Her nose burrows into the bend where my shoulder and neck meet. And then she sighs. Melts into me more. Holds me physically captive. Arrests my heart. Consumes my soul.

I love and hate it equally.

I love how easy it is to love Shelly. To fall into her in ways I never did with Kelsey. To look forward to her smile and voice and presence. To feel the radiance bounding off her aura and spilling into mine. I love how her dark, starry eyes suck me in and send me soaring. Shelly makes me dream of possibilities, of the future, of a life with her.

In the same breath, I hate how easily I give in to my emotions with her. How easily I am willing to tear away the barrier guarding my heart, the one that has kept me sane and safe and whole for the last four years. The armor that shielded me from making irrational decisions based on what my heart wanted versus what my brain knew.

But Shelly isn't Kelsey.

Shelly is vibrant and charismatic, brilliant and vivacious. When she walks in a room, she brings light and laughter and love with her. More than any of that, she is wise. Wise beyond her years. Mature. She would never just drop someone because she wanted to explore life freely.

We haven't discussed our pasts—not in-depth—but

her rosy cheeks every time I toss out a compliment give her away. Tell me her experience with men isn't as vast as other women her age. She is selective with who sees her heart. If that's true, it only adds to her allure.

"Stupid thorn," she mumbles against my skin.

I bite my cheek to not laugh. For a little longer, I want this side of her. To see her in the faint, dim light creeping in from the edge of the curtain. To watch her while she sleeps. While I can look at her features without restraint, without fear of being caught. Her toffee locks with hints of sunshine. Matching lashes fanned beneath her lower lid to the apple of her cheek. The three small freckles lateral to her right eye. The soft line of her jaw and curve of her chin. And lips so soft and full and kissable.

Licking my lips, I picture what it would be like to kiss Shelly. To give in to the urge, the desire, the need to feel her lips pressed to mine.

I close my eyes and let the fantasy take over. Allow myself to daydream about how warm and supple and perfect her kiss would feel. How demanding she'd be. How demanding I'd be in return. What her moan would sound like when I drag her bottom lip between mine. What she'd taste like when she finally bloomed like a flower and let me in.

Her fingers on my lower back curl slightly, tug at my cotton shirt, and I stop breathing. My eyes fly open and I think of anything except kissing Shelly. Because fuck my life, I'm hard.

Sure, if she wakes now, I can pretend to do the same

and play it off as morning wood. This is most definitely *not* morning wood.

What is the one thing that automatically sends my mood south? Is an instant buzzkill?

My mother. Mom, Mom, Mom.

And thank god it works. Just as my erection softens, Shelly opens her eyes. She groans and leans back. A smile slowly plumps her cheeks.

Without a doubt, this is my favorite view of Shelly. Soft and unkempt and not a worry marring her beautiful face. Perfect.

Then the corners of her mouth sag. Her brows wrinkle at the middle. Pupils go wide as realization dawns. That she is wrapped around me tighter than a koala. That she is on my couch, in my house, and we fell asleep.

Before I open my mouth to say everything is okay, she bolts upright.

"Oh my god!" She looks around the room so quick it makes me dizzy. "Oh my god," she whispers and slaps a hand over her eyes.

I sit up beside her, rest my palm between her shoulder blades, and rub small, slow circles. "Shelly, it's okay. We fell asleep."

She drops her hand. "Shit. What time is it?"

Crawling across the room, I fetch my phone from the table and tap the screen. "Five thirty-eight."

A groan spills from her lips. "I need to go. The shop. I have to go home and shower and change and eat and—"

"Shelly"—I add more pressure to my touch—"it's okay. You have time. Breathe."

And she does. She inhales through her nose and out through her mouth. Then does it again.

"Better?"

She nods.

"Before you go, let me at least make you breakfast."

"I don't—"

"Please. Promise I'll be quick." Her brows twitch. "I'll even pack it to go if you want."

"Sure. Okay. But only if it's quick."

"Pinkie promise."

She gives me her beautiful smile. Warmth floods the center of my chest, my heart thumping in a new pattern. And after I rise off the couch, before my brain can stop me, I bend at the waist and press my lips to her crown.

Neither of us moves. My pulse shifts again. Beats more erratically. Fear jolts my nerves as a dose of cortisol enters my bloodstream.

I took it too far. Shit. Shit, shit, shit.

Then she reaches for my hand, lifts her eyes, and shows me her rosy cheeks. "Thank you," she whispers. "I'm just going to use the bathroom."

"Right. Yeah." I step back, give her room to pass. "I'll be in the kitchen."

By the time she walks into the kitchen, I have cheesy scrambled eggs and buttered toast ready. Immediately, I want to make her a better breakfast. One that isn't rushed and we can enjoy together. But I am getting way ahead of myself.

She tugs on her shoes and shoulders her purse. I hand her the container and a fork as we awkwardly head for the door. And because I am not ready for goodbye, I follow her out to her car.

After unlocking the car, she sets her purse and the container inside then spins to face me, the door partially between us.

I won't lie… I hate it. The barrier and the fact she has to go.

"Thank you, again. For dinner and a show. It was wonderful."

"We should do it again. I do have leftovers." I lift a brow. She opens her mouth to answer, but I hold up a hand and cut her off. "Think about it."

She rolls her eyes and chuckles. "Fine," she says on a huff. "But I really do need to go."

I want to kiss her. Right here. Right now. I want to lean forward, cradle her cheeks in my palms, and kiss her.

But I won't. Now is not the time.

Soon, though.

"Then I won't keep you any longer." I reach out, take her hand, and give it a quick squeeze. "Drive safe. I'll send you the exhibition details later."

She drops into the driver's seat. "See you."

"See you."

I close her car door and take a few steps back. Watch her back out of the driveway and wave as she pulls away. The moment she is out of sight, I pivot and jog back to the house. Weave to the stairwell off the dining room and take the stairs two at a time.

The moment I step into my studio, the moment graphite and Turpenoid and canvas hits my nose, I sag with a heavy exhale. Then I snap into action. Bolt into the closet and grab a fresh canvas. Set it on my easel then grab my brushes and paints.

In seconds, I get lost. Lost in the image of her face this morning while she snuggled my chest. Lost in the contours of her face. In the sunshine highlights in her hair. In the fullness of her lips.

Not for the first time, I transfer my memories of Shelly into art. Stroke the bristles over canvas and create the outline of her heart-shaped face. Well, half of it.

Barely a fraction into the piece, I see it all so clearly in my head. Half her profile—plump full lips, rosy cheekbone, twilight iris with a touch of gold, and her slightly arched brow, framed by her golden hair. Behind her, pink blossoms. Primrose and meadowsweet.

This is the moment—*the moment*—when it truly hits me. The moment I can no longer deny what I feel, even if it scares the hell out of me.

What I feel for Shelly isn't love. No, it is way too soon for such a deep emotion. But I like her. *Really like her.* A lot. More than I should.

I admit this, but only to myself. Our relationship is too new for verbal confessions. But I feel it all the same. In the turbulent beat of my heart. In the shortness of my breath. In the thick of my marrow.

Question is, where do I go from here?

It is too soon to put my heart on the line. To cut myself open and hand her my heart. Every instinct inside me says to trust Shelly, that she won't hurt me. But once upon a time, the same instinct existed in regard to Kelsey. I'd thought we were inseparable. Endgame. And then she crushed me. Broke me in half and left me without a care in the world.

I refuse to let that happen again. To be blindsided and thrown away.

Shelly is not Kelsey. She won't hurt you. Not on purpose.

As I paint the rich blue of her iris on the canvas, I inhale deeply. "I really hope that's true."

Surviving the breakup with Kelsey was painful and life-altering. If Shelly and I went separate ways—no matter the cause—not only would it be painful, it would be downright devastation. A crippling debilitation. Losing Shelly would be a darkness I'd never overcome. A shadowed life I'd never be able to escape. Losing Shelly… I would give up. On everything.

Shelly isn't just endgame… she is so much more.

A dangerous thought slips into the foreground. One that scares the hell out of me, but I cannot deny.

From the moment I laid eyes on her, with every re-creation of her image, I say without a shadow of doubt… Shelly is the one.

And recognizing this simple fact terrifies me more than anything.

THIRTEEN

SHELLY

I have never sweated so profusely in my life. And it's sixty degrees outside.

Devlyn picked me up for the art exhibition minutes ago. When he sent me the event details, I offered to drive myself, in case he needed to be there earlier. He insisted on arriving at my door almost two hours before the event and chauffeuring me to the exhibition.

It only took one deep breath for me to cave. To give in to his persistence. Let him take control of the evening.

Devlyn in control is one of the reasons my pores are mini waterfalls.

Please don't let me have sweat stains under my pits. I mentally put my hands in prayer position. *Please.*

The drive to Sarasota—the gallery near the college Devlyn attended—isn't far, but it's not right around the corner. The distance and the fact I don't know my way around Sarasota is another reason I let Devlyn drive.

The event starts at four and runs until six. Then, we

have dinner reservations at a restaurant near the gallery. Dinner. Reservations. As in a premeditated meal at a nice establishment.

God, this feels like a date. An expensive date.

With Devlyn, it is hard to know. My new rule with him is to never assume. Assumptions get me nowhere. After movie night the other day, and falling asleep on his couch, he seems different. More open. Closer. But assuming we are anything but friends may shut him down.

So, unless he mutters the word *date*, I will keep repeating… This. Is. Not. A. Date.

On the way, Devlyn talks more about his time at college. I lean in closer and listen with rapt attention. His willingness to share has me on the edge of my seat. Although our friendship has shifted, taken on a new persona, I don't often get this side of Devlyn. The more personal side. A deeper look into his past. Small glimpses into his life, into the way he sees the world. I soak up each new story he shares and pray it won't be the last.

My college years centered around lectures and term papers and parties. Devlyn's focused on honing his current craft, finding love in new mediums, and immersing himself in everything art related. Polar opposite lives; his ten times more fascinating.

We hit the peak of the Skyway Bridge and I stare at the bright-yellow stay cables. Blink at the strobe effect they cause as we pass at highway speed. As with all bridges, this one has history. It wasn't always this mammoth bridge supported by massive cement pillars. The old metal bridge… it had a tragic ending. It was before my time, but I remember the stories my family shared anytime we drove over the new bridge and the local history lessons taught in school.

Are Devlyn and I headed that direction? Tragedy. Not like Romeo and Juliet's tragedy. Love that deep makes me uneasy, but not fully. With tragedy, I mean more like an ending where neither of us comes out happy.

Please, don't let that be our trajectory. A one-way road of devastation.

After the other night, after waking up in his arms, I'd like to think not. But presuming anything with Devlyn is dangerous and foolhardy. A nonrefundable ticket to heartache.

I try to forget the cold shoulder moments. The instances he shut down and said the word friends for the thousandth time. Instead, I focus on the days he has shown me tenderness. Spoken sentiments friends don't exchange. Stared at my lips or neck or body with more interest than a friend.

Would it shock me if he said I read too much into any of it? No. I may be outgoing and perceptive with friends and family, but when it comes to romance, all that awareness goes out the window. It's difficult to not read between the lines with rose-colored glasses. Especially when he looks at me as if I am his world, as if I am his next breath. To say it confuses me is an understatement.

"Almost there," he says, interrupting my inner tirade.

"Are you excited?"

A smile brightens his face—the one I love more than I should—and I have my answer. "Yes and no."

When he doesn't expand on his answer, I mentally reach across the console and shake him. "Care to elaborate?"

I love Devlyn's mysterious nature. His solemnity and zen. He sees the world like no one I've known. Sees it in black and white, but also brilliant colors. Finds the beauty in all people and places and life. Depicts emotion as if it walks among us. Adds zeal to everything he touches with the flick of a brush.

And I breathe it all in.

He guides us off the interstate and my eyes zero in on the city. Most of the Bay Area cities have similar vibes and one uniquely their own. Yes, it is another coastal city with beaches and nightlife and shops, but it feels different here. More alive. Maybe because this place is new to me. Or maybe because the history of the city is different. Either way, I love the vibe.

"Seeing my work in a gallery never gets old. I don't create to have it on display, but people seeing my art opens up doors. The opportunity to sell more pieces or create custom originals."

Like most artists, Devlyn creates because the need is ingrained in him. A deep-seated urge to spill his emotions without speaking. To express himself without becoming one-hundred-percent vulnerable.

"Sounds more yes than no."

"True." He purses his lips a beat. "The downfall of these events is being in the spotlight. People asking about your personal life. Criticizing your work. Putting their two cents in. I don't necessarily mind criticism from peers or people I look up to. They give me new perspective. Help me improve who I am as an artist. It's the snooty folks who think, because they have art hanging in their house, they know what *good* art looks like."

I reach across the console and touch his bicep. "Ignore them."

Briefly, he glances down at my hand on him. I pull it back and drop it to my lap before I spot the slight uptick of his lips. "I do my best. Isn't always easy." I don't miss his brief glance at my hand again, and I wonder if he enjoyed the small physical connection.

Since the other morning, Devlyn and I haven't touched. Friends don't share intimate touch. And until I know how movie night and the morning after makes him feel, I am doing my damnedest to stay on my side of the friendship line. Keep our physical contact to arm bumps and the occasional hooked elbows. We don't hug hello or goodbye like I do with my other friends or family. No teasing slaps on the arm or ruffling of hair. And we both know why.

To form a stronger connection—to touch easily, without second thought—our friendship would morph into more. Evolve beyond pizza lunches and walks in the park. Move beyond movie night with takeout and awkward mornings the next day. Blossom into something neither Devlyn nor I am prepared for, if I am honest with myself.

We haven't talked much about our pasts, but I know someone hurt Devlyn. I see it in the way he fights his feelings. The hidden stares followed by cold shoulders. The invitation to spend time together accompanied by the reminder of that ugly line drawn in the sand.

Hurt bruises my heart that a past relationship shook him so deeply, he refuses to let it happen again. Refuses to let love in. By choice, he shelters his heart—well, he attempts to shelter it. I do and don't understand, mainly because the subject has never come up. So, I grant him all the time he needs. Let this—us—be whatever it is while it exists. Let Devlyn set the pace. Allow him to set the tone and shape our relationship.

But I see the small cracks in his exterior. Notice how his stares last longer. Hear the undercurrent of desire and longing in his voice. Feel his warmth and impulsive need for physical contact when we exist in the same space. All of which weighs more heavily since my limbs tangled with his and he didn't let go.

Is going at Devlyn's pace fair? Not when I don't know where his head is at.

But I like Devlyn, more than he'd deem comfortable. I enjoy our time together. The brief chats as well as the lengthy conversations. The fleeting lunches and hours strolling in the park. If we remain only friends, I consider myself lucky to have him. If we become more... loving Devlyn would be sublime.

When it comes to this complex man, I set no expectations.

He parks the car, exits, and jogs around to my open door. I open my mouth to ask what he is doing, but when my eyes meet his, I zip my lips and smile at the gesture. His chivalry may be unexpected, but I refuse to depreciate the moment. Not with the way my heart flip-flops in my chest.

This is not a date.

We walk into the gallery, elbows hooked, and are bombarded. The event doesn't open to the general public for another thirty minutes. All the people flocking to Devlyn's side are peers and professors and fellow local artists. People who have seen or heard of his work. His fan club.

Although Devlyn doesn't care for the spotlight, he smiles and laughs and boasts about other artists whose work is *better*. Watching him here, now, I get another new side of him. He isn't necessarily more outgoing, just more himself. More comfortable in his own skin around those who share the same passion.

I love this side of him.

After a few minutes, he introduces me to the group. He doesn't introduce me as his girlfriend, but he also doesn't introduce me as a friend either. Just Shelly. A low hum whirls beneath my diaphragm. A new layer of perspiration dampens my skin. I work to not let the moment go to my head. Much. Easier said than done.

"Want a drink before the doors open?" he asks.

"Please." Lord knows I need something to temper the heat in my veins.

Drinks in hand, Devlyn guides us to the start of the exhibition. Tonight, there are seven local artists on display, including Devlyn.

Offering his elbow, my favorite smile of his makes an appearance. "Shall we?"

A fresh wave of heat blankets my skin as I hook my arm with his. I swallow past the thick swell of emotion in my throat and nod. "Yeah," I say, voice hoarse and low. Clearing my throat, I try again. "Yes."

The first showcase is Tomas Suarez. His medium of choice is watercolor and, as I gaze at each canvas, I am already at a loss for words. I never knew watercolor could be so bold. So evocative. Pops of bright blue and fuchsia. Subtle greens and soft yellow. Powerful yet subdued. Tomas paints landscapes, and this one reminds me of the meadow Devlyn painted in the shop—*my meadow*—but with softer lines. As if out of focus. We study his other pieces, digest their beauty, then move on to the next artist.

Kanesha Winston. Her three-dimensional art on canvas has me utterly fascinated. Oil paintings with book pages or paper-mache or origami added, then painted to blend in. I have never seen anything like it. The art is literally in my face, screaming to be seen. Begging me to reach out and run my fingers over it. Shifting left and right, I look at each piece from a different angle, a different perspective. See it come to life in its own way.

Akira Yamamoto and Leonard Denver are the two sculptors on display. The clay artist has softer appeal. A profile bust of a man in mourning. An ancient warrior mask. A mosaic of a woman in a garden. Each beautiful and mesmerizing in their own right. The metal pieces have harsher lines and are made of scraps. A humming-bird on a flower. A bionic cat. And my favorite—the softest of the metal pieces—is the embracing couple. Two human forms from the waist up, holding each other. One of them shiny and without imperfections. The other a mix of chain mail and luster with minor cracks.

Devlyn and I stare at this piece the longest. As if it represents us. Soft and rough. Smooth and harsh. Solid and broken. When I peek at him from the corner of my eye, I want to ask what he is thinking and feeling as he stares at the piece. If he sees the uncanny resemblance of us in the art. The strength and instability.

For now, I keep the thought to myself.

The last two artists before we reach Devlyn's work are Justine Thomas and Harrison Beaufort. Their charcoal pieces are remarkable. The art world is still so new to me, but it blows my mind how people create such beauty with paper and charcoal.

One piece, dubbed *Blue Woman*, is easily life size. Drawn on a six-by-three-foot paper scroll, the *Blue Woman* hides behind messy strands and a large sweater. Without question, the term blue depicts her mood. And I don't know why, but I *feel* her pain, her despair. So much it has me on the cusp of tears.

As if he senses my mood shift, Devlyn leans into me more. Gives me more heat and weight. Soothes the sting with his natural balm. Dropping his chin, his breath heats the skin of my earlobe and just beneath. "On to the most embarrassing moment of the night," Devlyn says, and I shiver.

He rests his free hand on my forearm and gives it a slight squeeze. For a split second, I stare down as if imagining things. The lingering sensation of his breath on my skin. The warmth of his hand on my arm. It isn't weird or uncomfortable, but it is different. New.

Without second thought, I lay my hand over his. Allow his warmth to blanket my skin and seep into my veins. Let my heart pound viciously, my lungs inhale erratically, and my nerve endings light on fire.

This feels more like holding hands. Forming an entirely new bond. A connection miles past the friendship line. Because friends don't hold hands. Not unless they are drunk or exhausted or injured. And I am none of the above.

"Don't be embarrassed," I say, voice unsteady as I peer up at him. Eyes on mine, he swallows and nods.

I tighten my hold on our connection, close my eyes for two breaths and savor how perfect this feels. Then I let him lead the way.

Ten steps and several rapid heartbeats later, we stand in front of a collage of pencil drawings. Two on larger pieces of stock, five on smaller pieces and surrounding the two larger.

I step closer to the images and Devlyn steps with me, not relinquishing my arm. My eyes graze over the first smaller drawing. Fingers, the top of a hand, a wrist and forearm, the start of a bicep. The limb feminine, soft, shaded, intimate. I swallow as heat blooms in my cheeks. A sudden sense of voyeurism hits the center of my chest. As if I am invading an intimate moment.

Taking a deep breath, I shift my gaze to the next small piece. The supple curve of a shoulder and border of the throat. Extra shading to emphasize the collarbone and subtle dip of the hollow spot at the base of the throat.

Jesus. Is it hot in here?

How does he make simple body parts, parts we see on people every day, so striking? Something you can't not take pause to stare at, to absorb, to get lost in. Something that makes your pulse race and your breath catch.

The next is the profile of a neck and jaw. I assume the muse for all the pieces is the same due to the feminine depiction. I want to ask Devlyn who she is. If she is the person who has him scared to move forward. To open himself to another.

But I don't ask. I fear his answer. Fear whoever this woman is, he will never move past her.

The last two smaller pieces depict a shadowed profile of her face and a pair of eyes. The eyes tug at something inside me, beg me to open my mouth and ask questions. Dark irises with the occasional shimmer resembling stars.

My eyes narrow as I step closer. Study the irises more critically. The occasional shimmer in the darkness makes me think of my sister-in-law, Peyton. How she calls my brother starlight. Because of his eyes. The same eyes that match my own.

And suddenly, I can't breathe.

My heart rattles in my rib cage. Bangs in the hopes of escape. And I do my best to settle the irrational thoughts and emotions surging inside. I don't *know* this is me, and should not assume as much. For all I know, these drawings are years old. Depictions of the woman that broke his heart. Someone he once loved, but who is no longer in his life. Someone other than me.

I try to collect myself. Calm my racing heart. Normalize my breathing. Not stiffen my arm looped in his. Focus on the rest of the images—the two larger ones I have yet to see. All while not letting on the path my mind has taken.

When I shift my gaze, when I take in the last two pieces, I stop breathing all over again.

Confused. I am so damn confused.

One is the back of a woman. Light wavy strands down her back. The edge of her profile on display as she looks off to the side. The second… it is the same woman. In a meadow. A meadow strikingly similar to the one painted inside Petal and Vine.

I don't know what to think. What to say. How to feel. How to function.

Devlyn leans into me, his breath warm on my ear as his body presses into mine. I might have a heart attack in the middle of this gallery. "What do you think?" he whisper-asks.

What do I think? What a loaded question.

My eyes roam the drawings as I ponder how to answer his simple yet complex question. A question so heavy, I'm not sure if there is a right answer. Right or wrong, I think Devlyn feels much deeper for me than he realizes. Either that or he refuses to accept how he feels.

"I… uh…" I close my eyes and swallow. How do I act myself, act as if everything is still the same, after seeing these? How do I go on pretending we are just friends?

Because this—these drawings—screams more than friendship. This is passion and longing and heartache. Beauty and fantasy and hunger. These aren't just depictions of an elegant woman, they are intimacy and affection and hope. A desperate cry for more. Of what, I can't be sure.

No doubt they took weeks to draw. Weeks. Our friendship was only weeks old.

What rattles me most is that Devlyn *chose* this collection to display tonight. Purposely selected these drawings for hundreds to see. Is all but silently telling everyone we are more than friends. That I don't just occupy his thoughts, but also his heart.

Friends don't draw provocative, intimate angles of another friend's body. Friends don't focus on eyes and lips and freckles. Friends don't invite friends to see how much they think and feel and desire the other. Lovers do.

And in this moment, it feels as if Devlyn has always thought of me as more than a friend. Whether he wants to admit it or not.

"They're beautiful," I say after a long pause.

His breath wafts my hair and I close my eyes. "Couldn't agree more."

When it comes to this man, this beautifully broken, soft-spoken, timid man… I am screwed. No matter where we go from here, no matter if we remain friends or take the next step, I am, without a doubt, screwed. After all I have seen tonight, my heart no longer wants to fight what it feels. The only problem with that… Devlyn might not be ready to reciprocate. His walls may be slowly crumbling, but I doubt they will ever fully fall. Not anytime soon.

Devlyn may not be ready to confess his heart, but I am willing to push his boundaries. Willing to cross the line with him. For him. No matter the outcome, at least he will know where I stand.

Best buckle up and enjoy the journey. While it lasts.

I MUST BE HAVING AN OUT-OF-BODY EXPERIENCE. IT'S the only logical explanation as to why I have practically erased the line between me and Shelly.

As often as I tell myself we are just friends, that we will *only* be friends, my actions and thoughts and feelings toward Shelly supersede that of a friend. I am a walking contradiction. Saying and doing things more like a lover than a friend. The subtle touches that come off as normal, but are far from it. The whispered words close to her ear as I inhale her intoxicating scent. The constant need to be closer to her, to feel her warmth and weight.

Worst of all, I don't stop myself.

I no longer *want* to stop myself.

"Am I underdressed?" Shelly asks as we pull up to the restaurant.

I stare out the windshield at the glass-front brick structure. The restaurant gives off fine dining vibes, but is quite casual. Online reviews raved over the food, atmosphere, and service. I studied the menu long enough to learn it had decent variety. So I set a reservation.

"You look great. The website didn't mention dress, so I wouldn't worry."

She laughs under her breath. "Easy for you."

And I wonder what she means. Why would it be easy for me and not her? If anything, Shelly outshines every-one. Me? I'm the scrawny, quirky guy at her side. The person everyone will look past to glimpse her.

I park the car then jog to the passenger door to help her out. Not that she needs help. Shelly is a strong woman. Capable of standing tall on her own.

But having her at my side and on my arm tonight was a new, unfamiliar high. Something I never expected. Something I want more of. Her warm hand wrapped around my bicep, her eyes on my art. Nothing has ever felt so right and perfect and exhilarating.

Am I walking a dangerous line? Yes. I have never been on a slope this slippery. Do I care? At the moment, no. I'd tread the steepest incline for her.

When was the last time I felt a connection like this? When was the last time someone *wanted* me? It had been too long. Scary as it is, I crave Shelly. More than my next breath.

Instead of fearing what may happen, I offer my arm once more. Lock onto my favorite constellation and wait for her acceptance. And she does not disappoint. I don't think it's possible for Shelly to ever disappoint. At least not me. She hooks her arm with mine, wraps her dainty fingers near my elbow, the digits giving a gentle squeeze. I live for that squeeze. For any near or intentional touch she bestows. Each has my breath more erratic. Each little reassurance says she enjoys being on my arm.

I am so fucked. *We* are so fucked. In the best way.

We step into the restaurant and I give the hostess my name. She escorts us through the restaurant, toward a table in the back near another set of large windows that looks out onto the Gulf. Shelly takes her seat, then I take mine across from her. As much as I would love to sit closer, to be within easy reach of her hand or knee, I love this unobstructed view. To see half her face aglow from the setting sun and the other half from a candle at the heart of the table.

There are a million and one ways to take in Shelly. To catalog her features in a new light. To discover a new angle of her delicate profile. A new light to absorb the beauty of this woman. Taking the time to learn them all has my body abuzz. Shoots thrill through my limbs and to the center of my chest.

I want to view all million and one.

"Devlyn." My name is soft and worrisome on her tongue. I snap out of my Shelly-induced daydream, lower my menu and lock onto her wide eyes. She curves the menu to the side of her face to shield our conversation from other tables. The gesture is cute. "Did you look at the prices on the menu?"

I give her a half smile. "Didn't cross my mind."

Her eyes go impossibly wider. "You may want to."

To appease her, I stare down at the menu. See a thirty-dollar chicken dish and don't think twice. Not that I eat at places with price points like this on the regular, but it wouldn't be the first time. Not with all the fancy dinners and fundraiser events I attended with my parents as a child.

Mom always has to have the best. Be the best.

Cue mental eye roll.

Since living on my own, most nights I cook at home or get takeout from small, local places. Nothing pricey or lavish. I tend to not dine out often since crowds aren't my thing.

Tonight is an exception. Tonight is a special occasion. My art in a gallery—without the help or influence of my mother—warrants celebration. And there is no other person I would rather share an overpriced, intimate meal with than Shelly.

"It's fine, Shelly. Tonight is a special occasion and I'd like to indulge. Order what you'd like and don't worry about the cost."

She shifts the menu so it hides her eyes. After a few deep breaths, she nods and scans the menu again. Thank goodness she doesn't fight me on this. On the price of a meal. Yes, the cost of dinner here is more than I typically spend. But tonight is worth every cent. *She* is worth every cent and much more.

The server comes to the table, tells us the chef specials for the evening, takes our drink order and gives us another moment to decide. Before either of us sets our menu down, the server returns with two glasses of red wine and takes our order.

Shelly stares out the window at the fire-tinged horizon.

Studies the skyline, sips her wine, and sighs. I don't hide my stare. Don't hide my eyes as they trace the arch of her brow, slope of her nose, and plump lines of her lips. I drink her in more than ever. Get drunk on her and not the wine. Love how at ease she is in this moment, at a table with me, sharing a meal after an evening on my arm.

Our easy connection has me dizzy. The comfort she gives has me wobbly in my chair.

The entire night—the drive, the gallery, dinner—is more than I expected. With Shelly, I set zero expectations. But she shocks me at every turn, with what she says and the feelings she stirs up from deep, hidden places.

The more time Shelly and I spend together, the more I want to open myself to her. Give her pieces of myself I have given no one. Not even Kelsey.

Over the last two months, Shelly has wiggled her way in. Not with her wit or charm or beauty—although, I love these traits too—but with her magnetic energy and gravitational pull.

In our minimal conversations, we communicate more with silence and body language than most do with words. Our quiet chats reflect my introversion more than her natural disposition. Shelly lights up a room with her exuberance. Being the center of attention has never been my cup of tea, but I want to test the waters. Dip my toes in, ask the questions on the tip of my tongue, and learn more about Shelly Reed.

And share more about myself.

"Do you visit the beach much? When it's warmer, obviously."

She inhales deeply then shifts her gaze from the setting sun to me. "Not as much as I did years ago. This adulting business is bullshit."

I laugh, far louder than I should, but it can't be helped. Thinking back, I can't recall many occasions when a curse slipped between Shelly's lips. Not that I pictured Shelly as a complete saint.

"Couldn't agree more. Whoever came up with the idea you had to pay to live, to exist… I'd like to have a word with them."

Now, it's her turn to laugh. Head slightly back, hand over her heart, lips and eyes tipped up at the corners. I love how effervescent the sound is. Like carbonation and sunshine. A gust of wind on a still day. Her laughter is one more thing to like about the woman sitting across the table.

"What about you?" she asks. "Do you visit the beach much?"

"I actually enjoy the beach when it's cooler. Not the water, but bundled in a blanket on the sand with my sketchpad. A unique creativity sparks when I'm out in the elements. It challenges me in a fresh way. Changes how I interpret what I see and feel on paper, or canvas later. It also depends on my mood."

She nods then sips her wine. Before either of us gets in another question, the server returns with the appetizer—ricotta-stuffed figs with a balsamic reduction. I gesture for Shelly to taste one first.

"What's your favorite color?" The question is generic.

One I probably know the answer to, based on her wardrobe, but I ask anyway.

"Pink." Correct. Shelly may not be decked out in pink daily, but she incorporates the color in her life. Polish, hair accessories, jewelry, lip gloss, pins. I see each touch, each shade and variation.

"Favorite foods? Aside from bread." We both laugh under our breaths.

"That's a little more difficult." She taps her lips with a finger and my eyes magnetize to the action. "Household staples… I *love* cashew butter. Too much for my own good. Slap it on crusty bread"—her frame wilts slightly as a dreamy look fills her eyes—"and I'm in heaven." Her exaggeration of the word love makes me chuckle under my breath. "Prepared foods, especially ones I don't cook"—we both laugh—"bulgogi. There's more, but those rank highest."

Flashes of the other night, of Shelly in my house, eating dinner with me in front of the television, pop in my head. Followed by waking up with her wrapped in my arms. I want another night with Shelly. I want another morning with her snuggled against my frame.

"Still can't believe I'd never eaten it before the other night."

"Right? I'll make it your favorite too." She winks and the corner of my mouth instantly lifts.

With simple ease, we slip into a more intimate space. One I learn to love more each time it happens. One that doesn't put me in panic mode. Doesn't have me fleeing the scene like I committed homicide. I never want to be scared at the ease flowing through my veins, at the comfort I feel being with Shelly. Ever.

After years of letting heartbreak rule my heart, I decide it's finally time to push all the negativity aside and bask in this woman. Indulge in the way she makes me feel. Give over to my heart and ignore the hushed voices of warning in the back of my head.

The more we talk, the more I let loose. Shelly pumps life into my veins. Makes me laugh more and lean in closer. Makes me smile so much my cheeks sting. She is the light I have missed all these years. A light I never want extinguished.

When our meals arrive, we eat and talk and enjoy the evening. Worry evades me and I give merit to the idea of Shelly being more than a friend. For a minute. Only a minute.

Four and a half years have passed since I relished the company of a woman. Let it swallow me whole and never let go. When Kelsey ditched me for frat boys and the *college experience*, I shut down. Closed myself off from emotion and intimacy and anything that would hurt me further. I became numb. To everything.

With Shelly, I never want to let go. Never want to spend a day without seeing her or speaking with her or knowing her. Is this healthy? Probably not. No form of addiction is. But Shelly... her brand of drug is exactly what I need. What I never knew I needed.

As our plates empty, the server comes with a tray of desserts. Shelly ogles them with wide eyes and her lips trapped between her teeth. Much as I'd like to trap her lips with my own, now is not the time. Instead, I agree on her choice of dessert, a thick slice of chocolate ganache cake with fresh whipped cream and berries, to share.

All I will say about dessert... I have a new love for chocolate cake that has nothing to do with the taste and everything to do with watching Shelly eat it.

Oh, how I wish to be that cake. Sweet and warm on her tongue. Eliciting the most provocative sounds.

After I settle the bill, we walk to the car, arms hooked at the elbow. The drive to Shelly's apartment is a blur of quiet music, good conversation, and our arms a breath apart. Hushed as we are together, our talks flow with more ease now. As if we have known each other for years and not months. And I want more.

More of her. More time. More of whatever she will let me have. More *us*.

I park in the guest spot near her building and walk her to the door. The cool November night grows hot and thick and edgy. There has always been this unspoken familiarity between us. An energy that brings us closer. Since day one, I fought the sensation with every molecule I control. Little by little, I've slowly let it take over.

"Would you like to come in for coffee or tea?"

At her question, that stupid voice in the back of my head speaks up. Tells me to say no. Tells me to get in the car and drive home. To leave and not take another step toward her front door.

I hate this voice. Hate that it still creeps in and tries to sway my life in one direction or another. Tries to keep me from moving forward and moving on. Eerie as it is, I hate this voice even more because it suddenly sounds like my mother. Full of acid and judgment.

Tonight has been perfect. More than perfect. If I leave now, will it end perfect? Or will I wake up in a cloud of regret? Miserable from not doing what *I* want versus listening to the *no one will ever love you* voice in my head.

I am not ready for tonight to end. The more I have Shelly in my world, the more I want to exist in her bubble. Breathe her in. Share my life. Make her mine.

A new voice storms forward and tramples the doubt. The voice of selfishness. Soft and lovable and coaxing. She whispers, *"Go inside. Spend more time with her."* And without a second thought, the selfish part wins.

"I'd like that."

A timid smile pushes up her flush cheeks. Shelly unlocks the door and steps aside to let me in. The apartment is small but quaint. Enough for one person. Cozy enough to entertain guests. The vibe and appearance simple, but very much Shelly.

Ivory walls with occasional family photos and framed print art. Soft-pink sheer curtains accent standard blinds. A beige sofa with throw pillows to add a pop of color and a knitted blanket slung over the back. An ivory-shaded lamp on a side table farthest from the door. A rectangular, cherrywood table sits between the couch and a small entertainment center with a television, DVD player, and streaming device. Fuchsia and taffy and blush flowering buds in a vase on the table.

"Make yourself at home," she says as she hangs her purse on a hook behind the door. "Coffee or tea?"

"Tea. Please."

"I'll be back in a moment."

Shelly walks to the left, past a small dining space, and into a kitchen big enough for just her. The dining has a small, round table with two chairs. Another vase, this one smaller, with the same array of flowers rests at the heart. A chandelier fixture that doesn't match Shelly's style, and probably what comes standard with the apartment, hangs above the table. The kitchen, from my position in the living room, has stainless steel appliances, oak cabinets, and dark countertops. The kitchen appears to be the darkest part of the entire space.

I sit on the sofa, run my fingertips over the fabric, the throw pillow and blanket. Soft. But not as soft as Shelly. So much of her is woven into this small place. Although it isn't vast, it casts a warm energy. An energy I recognize any time Shelly and I exist in the same space.

While I wait, I breathe it all in. Fill my lungs with her floral and patchouli scent. Fill my heart with her kindness and radiance. After tonight, everything will be different. Everything. Yes, inviting her into my home was huge. Sitting beside her in my living room was heart stopping. Falling asleep curled up beside her was unreal. Waking up with her wrapped in my arms was life altering. But tonight... it feels... more.

"Hope you like chamomile."

I open my eyes as she rounds the couch and hands me a mug. "Chamomile is perfect." Because I need something to calm the buzz swirling in my head and beneath my diaphragm. Going from zero to one hundred may be exhilarating in a car, but with my heart…

We sip our tea and sit in silence a moment. A silence vastly different than any other we have shared. Why? Because it's in her home. Her most sacred space. And for the first time in minutes, I realize just how close we are. That her knee brushes my lower thigh. Her lips a mere foot away.

She sets her mug on the table and I mirror the action. Was I this nervous when she came to my house? No, not to this degree. Sure, I was hyperaware of Shelly the second she set foot in my home, but her presence soothed me otherwise. Maybe it's the size of the space. How, in her apartment, I feel like I am on top of her.

"Do you want to watch something? A movie," she clarifies.

Without checking the time, I know it's late. Easily after ten. A movie would keep me well past midnight. Much as I want to entertain the idea, I probably shouldn't press my luck. The temptation is real, though.

"No, I—"

She cuts me off. Frames my face with her hands and brings her mouth to mine. Then everything goes dark as my eyes roll back. Dark and warm and euphoric.

Her lips move against mine in gentle strokes. Sweet and soft and pink. On the second wave, my lips move with hers. Perform a dance they haven't in years. I tilt my head to the side, change the angle of the kiss, and she shifts too. My hands reach for her, land on the curve of her hips. Glide up either side of her rib cage, skirt the length of her collarbones until I trail up her neck and take her face in my palms.

I need to taste her. See if she is as sweet as I have imagined.

Parting my lips, I lick the seam of hers. Like the blooming petals of a flower, she opens up and invites me in. Lets me sweep my tongue over hers. Tangle it with hers. Taste her.

And I am done.

Lost with no desire to be found.

Lost in her warmth. In the electricity. Her earthy-floral scent. Her sweet and succulent taste. Lost in the high that hits my bloodstream with my lips on hers. Obliterated by the volatile rhythm she teaches my heart.

I kiss her as if I never will again. As if she is my last supper and I am a starved fool.

You are a fool.

A ping sounds in my brain. A system override. A trip-wire. An alarm telling me to abort. To stop kissing Shelly because we can never be anything more than friends. Because emotional attachment beyond friendship only leads to heartache. To pain and suffering. To an inevitable end. Because one day, she will decide she no longer wants me. No longer needs me. Doesn't want me at her side to touch her or hold her or give her whatever she needs.

She will throw me away.

Just like Kelsey did.

I break the kiss and scoot away from her. Eyes downcast, I shake my head and hold up a hand. "No." I shake my head again. "No, I can't. We can't. I can't do this."

Finally, I meet her gaze and see the tears already rimming her eyes. "I'm sorry."

Fuck.

I hate myself. Hate that kissing a woman I want, a woman who wants me, a woman I *trust,* ends in catastrophe. More than anything, I hate that my brain is wired this way. Ready to ruin everything good.

It's bullshit, but I already lit the fuse.

I need time to think. Time to figure out how to fix the messed-up shit in my head. Time to make myself worthy of Shelly. She deserves better than this. Better than me.

Rising from the couch, I look everywhere but at her. Mutter my apologies over and over as I slowly make my way to the door.

I need to get out of here. Away from her. Before I lose the strength to go.

"I shouldn't have… I'm sorry, Devlyn. You don't have to go. Please, I'm sorry." She is off the couch, taking slow, deliberate steps in my direction. Approaching me like a scared, wounded animal.

She can't touch me. If she touches me, I will cave. Lose all willpower and give in to her pleas. And I can't. Not yet. Not now. Not until I unscramble my warped brain. Otherwise, I will just make it worse. Hurt her worse.

I meet her eyes again. Take one last look at her glassy, veiny, twilight irises. "I can't," I whisper. "I wish I could, but I just…" Two more steps and I grab the knob. Twist and take another step, this one outside. "I'm so sorry."

And then, I leave. Dash to the car, start the engine,

and drive home in a fog. In my pocket, my phone vibrates over and over. Without fishing it out, I know who it is. Know that Shelly is texting or calling. And I want to answer her. Want to tell her how I feel. Want to confess how much I care for her. Explain what just happened. Why I reacted the way I did.

Just as I closed her door, I saw the first bout of tears glide down her cheeks. And now, it will be all I see when I think of her. Her pain and misery and regret. And I deserve that to be my reminder. I deserve to only see her suffering. Her pain is my punishment.

I reach a red light and pull out my phone. Thirteen text messages, all from Shelly and all various forms of an apology.

"I'm sorry too. You don't know how much." I look at the screen and shake my head. "God, I wish it was that easy. I wish I could give you more. But I can't. Not yet."

And then I power off my phone, stow it in my pocket, and finish the drive home.

Tonight started out as one the best nights in a long time. Correction, tonight was *the* best night of my life—the second being Shelly in my house, in my space. Leave it up to me to ruin it. To ruin her. To ruin us.

I fucking hate myself. But dammit, I will do whatever it takes to fix myself and make things right between us. Because Shelly… I *need* her.

FIFTEEN

SHELLY

HAVE YOU EVER FELT LIKE YOUR LIFE HAS BEEN ONE major clusterfuck of an amusement park ride? The more time passes, the more I feel this all too deeply. And it just fucking hurts. A bone-deep ache that won't go away.

Night after night, I stare at the romance books on my shelves. Scan their worn spines and tattered covers. Books I have read over and over. Others waiting for me to pick them up. And I just can't do it. I refuse to let myself get swept up in some happy fairy tale where everyone ends up with their happily ever after. Meanwhile, I'm over here plucking the occasional gray hair, developing wrinkles at the corners of my eyes, and contemplating if I should buy one cat or ten.

Not like I don't want to experience those "all the feels" moments in my own life. For my heart to rip apart the cage holding it captive. For my lungs to burn when I forget to breathe. For my skin to heat and dampen with just his eyes on me, his body near mine. To feel each and every one of those don't-ever-let-me-go moments.

God, do I want them. *Really* want them. I thought I had them—some of them—for a blip of time. A very small blip. But I was wrong.

And now… I am exhausted. Utterly spent. Out of gusto.

So tired of faking happy twenty-four seven. Tired of contributing one hundred percent to everything and getting shit on constantly. Tired of being paired with the other single friend in our circle, Erin, because we don't have someone on our arm.

During get-togethers—like Autumn's baby shower today—they seat Erin and me together. Why? Because we have singledom in common. Because we haven't found someone to sweep us off our feet. Because we are lepers when it comes to love. At least, that is what it feels like.

Gah! I want to fist my hair, scream at the top of my lungs, and rip the strands from my scalp. I want it to hurt more than the unyielding pain beneath my breastbone. Physical pain, I can handle. Gut-wrenching emotional pain…

Autumn unwraps and opens a box wrapped in black-and-white baby farm animals. Since she and Jonas don't know the sex of the baby yet, everything has been neutral. Light and soft tones. Khaki, gray, cream. No pink or blue, yellow or green. The gifts, the cake, the decor. All of it is just… neutral. Plain. Simple.

My life is plain. Neutral. But not simple.

I wish it were simple. That I didn't spend most of my

time each day trying to fix what I broke. To mend fences with Devlyn. Unfortunately, some things can't be fixed. Not when only one person does the work and two are required.

God, I miss him.

I took our friendship for granted. Got swept up in the moment. In his earthy, artsy scent. The way his smile only popped up on occasion and not for just anyone. I only ever saw him smile at me and Elizabeth. And the smile he gave me was not the same he gave her. And I miss the contrast between his dark, floppy hair and pale-green eyes.

His eyes still linger. When I close mine, I see them with such clarity. Staring back at me. Haunting me. Crushing me. Which is why sleep has been shit recently. Distracting yourself while you dream is a bit difficult.

Why did I have to mess things up? Why did I kiss him?

No, I am not the only one to blame for all of this. I felt it. The way he gravitated toward me any chance he got. The subtle, unspoken hints of something more than *friend-ship*. Always wanting more time together. That night and morning at his house…

"Shh, shh, shh," Cora shushes as baby Clara starts fussing. "Someone's hungry." After a few wiggly moves, Clara latches onto Cora's breast and suckles.

Everyone in the room watches in awe. Everyone but me.

I love my best friend and niece fiercely. Would do anything for either of them. But watching them share this intimate bonding moment makes the backs of my eyes sting. Forms a lump in my throat. Makes the ache in my chest more pronounced.

Rising from the couch, I wander out of the room and mumble, "Be right back."

I step into the bathroom, shut the door and lock it, then slide down the back until my butt hits the cold tile. Silently, I weep into my sweater sleeves. Cry long enough to get it out, but short enough to not let my face puff up. Then I get up, take a deep breath, use the toilet, and rinse my face with cool water.

Minutes mimic days as I stare at my reflection. As I question my life, my past, my way of thinking. Question what the hell is wrong with me. Question why two weeks and hundreds of text messages and phone calls from me to Devlyn go unanswered.

Why? What have I done to warrant this level of extreme solitude? What karmic rule did I break to receive this overflowing spoonful of loneliness?

I love people. Family, friends, strangers. I do right by others. Help out whenever possible. Give back to those less fortunate in the community. Always contribute if possible. I care for others. Am loyal without question.

But it never seems enough, and I don't know why.

Someone, please tell me why.

Hell, the fact that I haven't given up my *virtue* should count for something. Give me bonus points in someone's book. Not that being a thirty-two-year-old virgin was a goal, but here I am…

Why won't he talk to me?

My hands hurt from wiping them so long with the towel. I hang the cloth back on the bar, give myself one last glance in the mirror, take a deep breath, then turn for the door.

Back in the living room, the crowd has thinned. Guilt seeps into my veins and rattles me.

How long was I in the bathroom? I didn't get to say goodbye.

After a deep breath, I sit in the same spot on the couch and try to pick up on what I missed. Which proves difficult because no one says a word. When I survey the room, all eyes are on me.

Great. Just fucking great.

"Shell, what's wrong?" Cora asks, her tone treading lightly.

Much as I don't want to dump my lackluster life onto my friends, I refuse to lie. Especially to Cora. She leaned on me countless times in the past. To deny her the truth would make me a hypocrite and a horrible best friend.

If only the truth didn't throb painfully in my chest.

Eyes on my lap, I tuck my hands and fingers in the sweater sleeves. Hide them from view, so no one sees me pick at my cuticles. The room goes quiet, too quiet, but the stares I feel burning my skin scream deafening tones. And I just want the silent questions and eye-piercing volume to stop.

"Remember the guy at the shop last year?" I don't need to elaborate. Cora knows who I mean. It's not often I talk shop… or guys.

"*The artist* who did the mural?" Cora questions.

"Yeah."

"Sort of. I remember Mom talking about him. Only saw him briefly during a visit. I remember him being there, but not *him*." She rises from her chair and sets Clara—who fell asleep while I was in the bathroom—in her carrier. Then she parks next to me on the couch. "Is he the reason you're down?"

This is so weird, awkward. Maybe because guys don't stick around past date number two. Maybe because I have never had a long-term romantic relationship. Not that Devlyn and I are—were—long term or romantic anything. But he is the first person I connected with on a profound level.

Then I ruined everything with a stupid kiss.

What a great kiss it was, though.

"Yes and no," I say with a shrug. "He was back at the shop, touching up the outside mural and painting a new one inside." I drag in a deep breath and exhale loudly. "He was there daily for weeks and we talked. A lot. When he finished, we started hanging out. About a month and a half. Nothing serious. Guy friend stuff."

I pause and close my eyes. Fill my lungs with fresh air and swallow past the lump forming in my throat. I peel my eyes back open, but keep them on my lap and trudge forward.

"A couple weeks ago, I kissed him. He was into it. Really into it." I lift my gaze to Cora and see the wince already building on her face. All it does is amplify the pain in my chest. A pain that just won't quit. I press the heel of my palm to my breastbone and get no relief. "Then, he freaked. Couldn't leave fast enough. And I haven't heard from him since."

The spear pushes straight through my heart and lets every drop of life puddle at my feet. When did I become this woman? An emotional wreckage pile. The woman who lets the idea of a guy rule her life.

Cora scoots closer as Autumn presses her weight to the opposite side. A hand swipes my cheek. Wipes away the tears I hadn't realized were leaking from my eyes. Which makes me cry harder. Then, I am swathed tighter than a newborn. Surrounded by arms and warmth. Friendship and love. Family.

And I let it all go. Cry as if my ducts hadn't been used in years. Weep as if I lost the love of a lifetime. And I don't stop until my eyes are puffy and cheeks are hot.

"What did I miss?"

Cora, Autumn, Peyton, and Penny lean back. A whoosh of cool air smacks my face as Elizabeth steps closer. When she wasn't in the room when I returned, I assumed she left. Guess she was in the kitchen or off doing something with Clementine.

"Nothing, Mom," Cora says. "Shelly's just been a little down. So, we were giving her some love."

Elizabeth regards her daughter, then me. She may see me more times a week than Cora, but I haven't mentioned anything to her. Just kept my head low and hands busy at work. But I see the questions in her eyes now. See her motherly armor slip into place.

"Devlyn?"

All she asks is his name. She doesn't need to elaborate. The woman isn't oblivious. Although she appeared to not notice my interaction with Devlyn at the store, she didn't miss a thing. Maybe it is her motherly intuition. Or perhaps, it is the wisdom that only comes with time and life experience. Either way, she knows. And it eases the pain a little.

At least it's Elizabeth and not my own mother. Mom's mission to see me married with children is *not* what I need right now.

I nod. "Yeah."

"Oh, sweetheart." Without hesitation, she steps closer, takes my hand, hoists me up from the couch, and gives me the best mama bear hug. A fresh batch of tears spill down my cheeks. Dampens my shirt and hers. It only makes her hug me harder. Tighter. Longer. "I got you," she says as she softly strokes between my shoulder blades. "Get it all out."

And I do. For the longest time, Elizabeth embraces me with a fierceness only mothers possess. She strokes my hair and shushes my cries. Whispers reassurances and motherly love in my ear. When my ducts run dry, we pull apart and she holds me at arm's length. Gives me a gentle smile that soothes the pain. A little.

Elizabeth and I take a seat among the others. Heat crawls up my neck to my cheeks as guilt swirls in my veins for stealing the spotlight during Autumn's baby shower. For making my personal problems more of a focus than Autumn's impending delivery.

"Sorry," I mutter, then abandon my spot on the couch

to refill my glass of water. When I return, I *feel* more than see everyone's stare on my face.

"What are you apologizing for?" Autumn asks.

I park on the couch, sip my water then set it on the table, but keep my eyes trained on the glass as I lean back. This isn't my day. No one is here to celebrate me or a child I am bringing into the world. And it feels ten kinds of wrong to steal the spotlight from Autumn.

"Nothing. Can we talk about something else, please?"

"Nuh-uh," Cora says with a shake of her finger. "You've been up and down a lot recently. Then, you cry your eyes out for almost an hour. Baby talk can wait a few. Am I right?" Cora looks to Autumn, who nods.

"I'd like to talk about something other than pregnancy and babies, thank you very much," Autumn states as she purses her lips. She rests a hand on my forearm, the touch soothing yet serious. "You matter, too, Shell."

I peer down at Autumn's hand before meeting her dark-amber eyes. All I see is love when I look at her. Not an ounce of anger or frustration or jealousy that her baby shower has turned into some form of a Shelly Reed soap opera. A fresh sting bites the backs of my eyes and I tip my head back, blink a few times and swallow past the lump in my throat.

How did I get this lucky? To be surrounded by such wonderful women who support me regardless of what is happening in their own lives.

"Thank you." I sniffle. "Still don't want to be the center of attention." I laugh without humor.

"Well, then, you best get it all out now. Tell us everything weighing you down."

"Might need something stronger than water."

Autumn rises from the couch and waddles toward the kitchen. "I've been saving this ginger beer for a special occasion, but…"

Laughter fills the room, even from me, as she returns with brown bottles of ginger beer. She pops the lid off one and hands it over. I take the first sip and go into a coughing fit.

"Jesus." I cough into my elbow. "Is that just liquid ginger?"

She shrugs. "Don't know, but I love it and so does the little one." She rubs her belly.

Over the next hour, I spill my heart out to my friends and family. Tell them about every day or evening Devlyn and I spent together. Our minimal conversations and how I never knew so little could mean so much. How he always looked at me more than a male friend looks at a female friend. How he went out of his way to do nice things for me. That he always wanted more time together. And was the one that pushed us in the direction we ended up in.

"He never wanted to get me those drinks in the morning," Elizabeth chimes in. "But he did so it wouldn't look like he was showing his affections toward you."

I narrow my eyes at her. "What makes you say that?"

"Just because I've been married most of my adult life, doesn't mean I am blind to flirting and gestures."

I shake my head in disbelief. "No, he was just being nice."

"Keep telling yourself that, if it helps you sleep. But that young man sees you, sweetheart. Not just the woman on the outside, but what's here, too." She presses a hand to her heart. "He just doesn't know how to express that verbally."

Elizabeth has a point. Devlyn hasn't opened up much since I have known him. Not that I expect his entire life story after knowing me a minute. Those six-plus weeks were the best. Each week, I got a fresh glimpse at Devlyn. A new side to him. Some days, he was so deep in thought while he painted, I could've screamed and he wouldn't have flinched. Other days, we were so in tune. The slightest look my direction and it heated my skin.

The night at his house… the next morning… those memories strike the hardest. Hurt the most. Everything about that memory feels like a lead-up to the kiss.

He wanted me there. In his home. In his space. Alone with him. Inches away in the dark. Snug to his body as we slept. He made me breakfast. Didn't want me to leave. At the car, I saw it… he wanted to kiss me too.

But maybe Elizabeth is on to something.

"Yeah, you're probably right." I sigh and stare down at the fumbling fingers in my lap. "What do I do now? He doesn't answer my calls or texts." Tipping my head back, I stare at the ceiling and huff. "I hate how bereft I feel."

Cora wraps an arm around my shoulders and tugs me into her. "Wish I had the right answer. The one to put a smile on your face. But everyone operates differently. Especially Devlyn, from what you've told us." She gives my shoulder a squeeze and I peer up at my best and longest friend. "You either need to give him patience or…" Her eyes dart between mine for two breaths. "Let him go." My shoulders drop and Cora's lips turn down at the corners. "You don't want to, I'm sure. But you need to do what's best for you."

The backs of my eyes sting for the umpteenth time today. "Why does this have to be so hard?" I garble out.

Autumn embraces me from the other side. "Because you obviously have feelings for him. Beyond friendship." A palm rubs up and down my back. "Jonas and I went back and forth so many times because I wanted to do what was best for Clementine. Little did I know, what I was doing wasn't best. But I had to learn that in my own time." Autumn leans her head on my shoulder. "What's meant to be will play out. But don't stop living because he won't own his feelings."

I nod, absorbing Autumn and Cora's words. Letting them sink deep and fill me with the strength I need to get past this. More than ever, I am grateful for the wonderful women in my circle. All my family, none by blood. Lucky is an understatement. I take their love and support and harness it as armor. Feel their courage pass to me as I wipe the tears from my cheeks.

"Thank you," I say as I glance at each of them in turn. "Thank you for always being there."

Cora squeezes me a bit tighter. "Wouldn't have it any other way." Her arm drops from my shoulder as she gives me a smile. "Now, let's talk about something else. Since none of the guys are here, let's talk shit about them and laugh when they get here later."

Everyone laughs, including Elizabeth, and I love how the mood in the room became ten times lighter. And for the next few hours, life is normal. Happy. Loaded with jokes. When the guys show, we make plans for another get-together. Karaoke or bowling. Something in addition to our Sunday gatherings.

I leave Jonas and Autumn's house with less weight on my shoulders and a warmer heart. Now more than ever, I need to spend time with people who make me whole. Who bring me joy.

Which is why what I am about to do is more important than anything else. I have to do this if I want to move on. If I want out of this dark place.

Parking the car in my designated spot, I cut the engine and stare at my front door. My apartment has been occupied with the energy of that night. *The night.* The night when I kissed Devlyn, and he reciprocated long enough to give me hope. Only to squash it just as quickly.

Tonight, I am detoxifying my space. Lighting sage, opening the windows and letting all the negative vibes out. Time to make it mine again. To make it a place I love.

Exiting the car, I walk to the front door with a straighter spine. I insert the key, turn the knob, and step inside. Plopping down on the couch, I fish my phone from my purse and pull up the text history between me and Devlyn. After two deep breaths, I tap out the most diffi-cult seven letters of my life, then hit send.

A tear splatters on the screen and the word *goodbye* blurs... just like my life. But I am taking my life back. After this final cry.

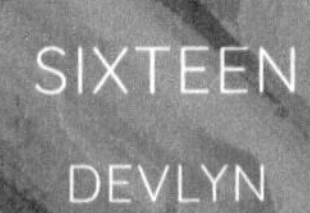

SIXTEEN

DEVLYN

MY PHONE LIGHTS UP ON THE TABLE, THE MESSAGE ICON on the notification. Without leaning for a closer look, I already know the text is from Shelly. Over the last two weeks, she has texted and called more times than I care to admit. Although I haven't responded to a single call, voice mail or text from Shelly, I listen to and look at each one. She is none the wiser since I disabled my read message receipts.

Yep, I have become *that* guy. The biggest asshole in the Bay Area.

And I detest the person I have become. Hate that I hurt her. Hate that I led her on then flipped.

I opened myself up to her, let her in the slightest bit, gave her a glimpse of who I want to be, that I want *her.* Then I smashed it all with a foolish mistake.

Kissing Shelly was *not* the mistake. Losing my shit and walking out the door was the mistake. Not responding to her daily texts and calls was—is—a mistake. Sitting on this couch instead of driving to her apartment and apologizing in person is a big. Fucking. Mistake.

Now I fear it's too late to repair the damage.

Fuck. I hope it isn't, but I feel stuck. Unsure what to do to fix myself or how to make things between us right.

Memories of the kiss drift back in—not that they ever leave. Shelly's lips pressed to mine, so soft and warm and inviting, knocked the air from my lungs. The memory of it still does, each and every time. As does the searing pain at my epicenter. The pain that never leaves. The pain I deserve, not Shelly.

If I were the only one suffering, I would willingly take a dagger to the heart. Let it twist over and over.

But Shelly is suffering too.

Her pain spills across the screen with each word she types. Is evident in the crack of her voice when I play back her messages. Hearing—*feeling*—her pain is ten times worse.

Ignoring the nature documentary in the background, I pick up the phone, take a deep breath, and open the message.

Shelly: Goodbye

Goodbye? What the hell does that mean?

I stare at the screen until I lose focus. Until my eyes glaze over and my thoughts swirl into a vicious hurricane. One after another, I take a deep breath. Try to settle the erratic line of my thinking. Sending a text with only *goodbye* in the message could translate a hundred ways.

Goodbye, I no longer want to speak to you.

Goodbye, I never want to see you again.

Goodbye, we were obviously never friends.
Goodbye, you're an asshole.
Or the one I don't want to think, but can't ignore.
Goodbye world.

I shake my head at the last one. Shake off the dark direction my thoughts took. Shelly and I may not have shared everything, we may not have fully exposed our pasts, but I don't picture her harming herself. Not with her sunny disposition. Not with the brilliant smile she flashes the world. Not with the long line of people who love her. She would never hurt herself. Right?

Fuck.

Why can't I be a better person? Why can't I step up and own what I feel? Tell this woman, this phenomenal woman, how I feel about *her.* Tell her she invades every waking moment of my life. That the kiss we shared is all I think about. That I still feel her lips on mine when I close my eyes. Still see her starry eyes. Still picture her in my home, in my arms, nestled against my chest. That I still smell her in the couch fabric and haven't slept in my own bed since that night.

Why haven't I told her any of this? Why haven't I acted?

Because I am a fucking coward. A chickenshit. A pathetic excuse. Rather than opening up and letting her in, I cower in the corner and shut out the world.

Any chance I had at a friendship with Shelly in the future has flown out the window. Because Shelly just cut ties with one word. In a text message, no less, because I won't speak to her. I shut her out and she locked the door for good. Threw the key in the landfill.

A red, hot dagger pierces between my ribs. I smash the heel of my palm to my sternum and curl my fingers into a fist. I drop the phone to the floor, drop my head to my knees, and rock in place on the couch. Fist my hair and tug until the pain steals my vision. Gasp for the breaths that refuse to fill my lungs.

"Aaaah!" I scream until my vocal cords strain. Then I scream again. Louder. Not giving a damn what the neighbors hear or think. I bolt up from the couch, scoop my phone from the floor, and throw it at the wall. I grab the next thing in reach, then the next, and throw them across the room.

Pain and anger are poison in my veins. Seeping slow and steady into my bloodstream, the marrow of my bones, every atom and cell. Turning everything black. Dark. A shadow of its former self. And I let it. Allow it to consume me. Swallow me into a never-ending abyss. I deserve nothing less.

I dash up the stairs, taking them two at a time. Enter my studio and scan the room. Study the countless drawings and paintings along the walls, on the floors, on my desk and easel. Each and every one of them inspired by the same person. The woman I wouldn't open up to because of past insecurities I refuse to face.

"Fucking idiot," I scream into the room. "Dumb. Fucking. Idiot."

Stepping farther into the room, I stand inches from the canvas on the easel. Stare at the stormy, dark-blue backdrop, the strategic gold splatters, the fine, faint white lines forming a half face. My Andromeda.

No, not yours. Shelly was never yours. She never will be.

I fist my hair and scream at the canvas. Scream at the pain I inflicted on Shelly and myself. Scream until my vocal cords shrivel and my lungs exhaust themselves. Then, I take the canvas in my hands. Grip the wood frame until it bites my skin. Rotate it in my hands, lift my foot from the ground, and crack the frame over my knee. The canvas doesn't tear, which only serves to fuel the flames of my anger.

Stomping to my tools, I dump them on the floor, drop down on my knees, and dig for the spackle knife. The wooden handle grazes my fingertips and I grip it until my knuckles whiten. I lay the floppy canvas on the ground, hold the edge with one hand, raise the blade in the other, and freeze.

The room blurs. My lungs quiver. The hand harnessing the blade trembles.

I don't want to do this.

Goodbye.

But I have to.

Goodbye.

Have to erase every piece of her.

Goodbye.

Have to let the idea of her go.

Goodbye.

I brought this upon myself. Opened us both up to heartache. Heartache Shelly doesn't deserve. But I do.

Goodbye.

Tipping my head back, I close my eyes and let the salty tears spill down my cheeks, my temples. "Give me her pain," I croak out. "Give me her sorrow, her heartache, her anguish. I deserve it. Not her."

I drop my head to the floor, grip the tattered canvas in my hands, and crowd it around my face. Again and again, my heart spasms. I accept the pain. Absorb every strike without complaint. Beg for more if it means Shelly feels none.

With each new hit, I rise to my feet. Take my pencils, my brushes, my oils and throw them across the room. I rip the drawings from the wall. Tear them down the middle twice and toss them in the air like confetti. I swipe my arm over the shelves and spill everything to the floor. Punch my fist through one painting after another until my fist meets drywall. My foot connects with the trash bin and scatters debris in a wide radius.

I stop and stare around the studio. Stare down at my fist and watch in fascination as a thick layer of crimson drips from my fingertips. Gaze at the chaos, the shredded sketches, the demolished canvases, the splattered paint. The sight should throw me off balance. Should have me in hysterics. Eager to put everything back in its rightful place.

Instead, I laugh. A delirious, maniacal sound spilling from my throat. I bend at the waist and grip my knees. The hysterical laughter transitions into an unsteady wheeze. I take in the disaster that is my studio and a fresh wave of panic hits. Punches me in the gut and knocks the air from my lungs.

"Damnit."

I drop to my hands and knees. Grab the tattered drawings on the floor and try to match them up. Try to salvage them and make them whole again. I put all the pieces in a pile. Then create another pile of the decimated paintings. Frantic hands sift through the first pile, trying to match the images and edges like a puzzle. When none of the pieces fit, I move to the next pile. Try to right my wrong.

But I am too late. Just like with Shelly.

Goodbye.

I fucked up and now I am paying the price. "Stupid, selfish idiot. Why did you do this? Why are you ruining every good thing in your life?"

Crawling across the floor, I grab a blank canvas from the stack. Rise to my feet and pad over to my easel. Gingerly set it on the stand. My eyes dart between the debris and the blank canvas, an idea developing.

Much as I should eliminate all reminders of Shelly from my life—most of which are locked in my memories— I simply can't. So, this is my punishment. To live with mental photographs and videos of her. To paint or sketch her likeness until my digits and limbs no longer work. To torture myself, day after day, because I deserve nothing less. I deserve pain and anguish—mine and hers.

I sift through the catastrophe on the floor, locate some brushes and a handful of paints, and then I start anew. Use bits of the drawings I shredded and add them to the new project. To twist the knife deeper in my chest, of course I recreate Shelly. If this is the only way I can have her, so be it.

Parked on my stool, I paint the canvas a blue so rich, it appears black. Using the scraps, I adhere them to the damp canvas. Create a mosaic of sorts. I rummage through the room and look for other bits I can add to the canvas, tools to add other forms of texture and dimension. Before returning to the stool, I turn on music. Play something other than the typical classical music I listen to in this room. Tonight, I need something to match my mood. Beats and lyrics filled with irritation or fury. Music with grit and rage. Songs to scream and thrash and smash objects to without concerning the neighbors. In the short time I have lived here, they have adapted to the weird guy in the neighborhood.

Loud, violent rock music spills from the speaker. The growly vocals against the fast tempo crowd the room. The hairs on my arms stand on end. The bass vibrates my bones. And the noise steals all potential space for thought.

This… this is what I need.

To not think. To get lost in something. Anything. To forget about what I lost and the pain I caused us both. This may not be the cure, but it will help the time pass easier. Help ease the pain, if only the slightest.

Goodbye.

The seven-letter word will be one I never hear or say in the same context again. I hate it had to be said in the first place. I never wanted to say goodbye to Shelly. Part of me hoped, after enough time passed, we would find our way back to each other. As friends.

Yes, I want to be more than Shelly's friend. No sense in denying the truth now. If I felt the cosmos collide when we kissed, she felt the intensity ten times stronger. I am not emotionless. I simply feel on a different scale. A scale tipped closer toward numb. Void. But not completely.

"Goodbye." The word singes my throat and burns my lips. Leaves a rancid taste on my tongue.

I swipe up a piece of a charcoal drawing. Home in on the thick black lines. Without question, this is Shelly's brow. An arch I memorized weeks ago, when the sun shone on the lateral edge. I brush the tip of my finger over the line. Swallow the pooling saliva in my mouth. Blink and look away for two breaths. Bite the inside of my cheek until a metallic tang hits my tongue.

"Wish we could've been more. Wish I was strong enough to be who you want. Who you *need*." I close my eyes and shake my head. "You're always in here, you know." I tap my temple. "That'll have to be enough, for now." A half-hearted laugh spills from my lips. "Maybe one day, I'll get my shit together. Maybe one day, I'll be strong enough, good enough, for you."

No! No, no, no, no, no.

Get your shit together, Templar. Now. And make this right. Quit wallowing in self-pity and fix this.

My eyes drift around the studio, take in the disaster once more, then land on the fresh canvas. "I fucked this up," I say to the canvas as if it is Shelly. "Now... I need to make it right. Hopefully, you'll forgive me. Hopefully, I'm not too late."

Because this pain... I won't survive it. Not for long.

SEVENTEEN

SHELLY

Sleep evades me as I lie in bed and stare up at the hints of moonlight slipping through the blinds. And for the hundredth time since I sent the *goodbye* text hours ago, nausea rolls in my belly.

If letting go of Devlyn was the right thing to do, why am I sick to my stomach?

The urge to rip my phone from the charger and type out a new message hits me like a freight train. I want to delete the message. Rescind it. Pretend like the thought never crossed my mind.

In its place, I want to send my longest apology. An extensive plea for him to forgive me for crossing the line. To beg him to take me back as his friend. Something. Anything.

God, I am such a fool.

How many times did Devlyn tell me he could only be my friend? So many times, I hate the word more than moist. Did I listen and respect his boundaries? No, but with good reason.

There is no possible way I read him wrong. Right? In our last week together, he threw one hint after another. Showed me his interest with small gestures and sentiments. His romantic interest. By no means can I professionally read people, but I picked up every hint and smile and longer-than-normal stare he sent my way. Honestly, I thought it was his way of telling me he wanted more without using words.

Obviously, I am an idiot. And supremely horrible at body language and gauging others.

"Ugh," I huff out, throwing the comforter and sheet from my body. I sit up and stare at the clock on my bedside table. The dull-blue numbers stare back and mock me—3:21. "Fuck you," I whisper to no one as I rise from the mattress.

Maybe a steaming mug of chamomile will settle my mind enough to allow sleep. Even if only a few hours, some sleep is better than none.

The electric kettle comes to a boil just as I hear something outside. Flipping the switch to off, I abandon the kettle and tiptoe to the window near the door. Slowly, I inch back the curtain and part a slat of the blinds to peek out. A gasp leaves my lips.

Why is Devlyn on my porch?

Hands shoved in his hoodie, he paces back and forth in front of the door. Every other direction change, he stops and looks at the door. In the artificial light, I watch the lines of his forehead scrunch and flatten then repeat. It's obvious he wants to knock on my door, but refrains from following through.

After watching him pace the same ten feet several times, I close my eyes, drop my hand from the blinds, and take a step back. Part of me wants to ignore Devlyn outside my door. Ignore him and hold firmly to the goodbye I sent earlier. He hurt me when he left here without explanation. He hurt me when he ignored my obsessive texts and calls.

Until I sent the one that hurt him.

Much as I want to ignore the upset man on my porch, I also want to fling the door open and give him a chance. Allow him the opportunity to explain why he flipped. Let him grovel and beg for forgiveness. Not that it would take much for me to forgive Devlyn. My feelings for him would override any stint of torture my mind wanted to inflict.

My fingers wrap around the door handle as my lungs take one last deep breath. *Give him a chance.* After I unbolt the lock, I twist the knob and swing the door wide.

Devlyn stops his trek past my door, his back to me goes rigid. Then his head drops, shoulders cave, and his entire frame deflates. Neither of us speaks, but the tension between us is a living, breathing entity. Harsh energy radiates off him and spills over me, causing a shiver. Devlyn is angry, but it isn't directed at me. Perhaps that is why he hasn't faced me yet.

Minutes pass before he lifts his head. Measured and hesitant, he spins around and meets my waiting gaze.

Translucent-green irises hold my blues. He takes a step in my direction, eyes darting between mine, silently asking why. Then with another step, he stands inches away. It's now that I notice the red veins hugging his irises. The puffiness around his eyes. The dampness on his lashes. The permanent valley between his brows.

"No," he whispers, his eyes holding me prisoner.

My brows bend in the middle. "No?"

He shakes his head slowly. Steps impossibly closer. Slips his hand around mine and holds it like I am his lifeline. "No goodbye."

I open my mouth to rebut him. To tell him I won't be the recipient of mind games. That I won't always wait in the wings while he melts down and abandons people who care about him—including me. That I won't let him break my heart because he is too scared to feel or own what he wants.

But I say none of those things. Don't even get the chance.

Devlyn lifts his free hand and cups my cheek. Captures my eyes with his as our breaths turn ragged. Then, ever so slowly, he leans forward and presses his lips to mine. I freeze at the initial connection but melt when he lightly sucks my bottom lip between his.

Warmth spreads through me as our lips dance together. His hand abandons my cheek as his fingers weave through my hair. I fist his hoodie, walk backward and drag him inside. The door shuts behind us and I assume he kicked it. He lifts our joined hands between us, between our hearts, and trails kisses along my jaw, my ear, my neck.

"So sorry," he mutters between kisses. "Such an ass."

At this, I chuckle. His lips break free of my skin, eyes meeting mine. "I want to explain. Please, let me explain."

I drop my forehead to his and sigh heavily. His thumb on my hand draws lazy circles while the fingers of his other hand massage my scalp. The hurt side of me wants to pull away and drag out the agony. Make him feel an iota of what I felt after he ran off. But the sensible side shakes her head and tells me to hear him out. Let him talk. Let him share the pieces he keeps hidden from everyone else.

Sensibility wins.

Nodding, I pull back. "Okay." I drop my hand from his hoodie. "I was making tea. Would you like some?"

He presses his lips to my forehead. "Thank you." Why does this kiss feel more intimate? "I'd love some tea."

I head for the kitchen while Devlyn takes a seat on the couch. Filling two mugs with hot water from the kettle, I deposit chamomile in both and let them steep as I watch Devlyn.

His head falls back on the sofa. Eyes closed, he looks as exhausted as I feel. The last two weeks have obviously tormented us both, yet neither of us did anything to rectify the situation. Well, not until I sent the most recent text message. That was all it took to truly rattle Devlyn to the bone. To wake him up from whatever dream—or night-mare—he'd abandoned me for.

Whoever hurt him in the past… I have never been a violent person, but I want to strangle them. Then maybe thank them. Devlyn wouldn't be who he is now without them, but I hate that he was hurt.

Setting the mugs on the table, I take a seat beside him on the couch. He rolls his head my direction and opens his eyes. And for a minute, we sit in suspended animation. I read his every movement, every unspoken word scrawled in the worry lines of his face. See his apology in the redness of his eyes, in the defeat of his posture.

I want to comfort him. Tell him I forgive him. Let him know we will be okay.

But I won't say a word. Not until he gives me more. Explains what made him panic.

He extends his arm closest to me. Lays it palm up on his thigh. An open invitation for me to take his hand. To twine our fingers. To connect us physically while he exposes himself emotionally.

Without hesitation, I take his hand. His eyes drift shut as a heavy breath stutters from his lungs. A sad smile on his lips.

"Sorry will never be enough," he says as his eyes open and capture mine. His thumb glides up and down in gentle, measured strokes over my skin. "But it's a start." He sits taller. Scoots an inch closer. "And I promise to make it up to you. Every day of forever, if necessary."

Forever. The word holds a heavier weight than imaginable. And I want to let it pin me down. Blanket me in comfort.

He brings the mug to his lips and takes a sip before setting it back down. His gaze fixes on our joined hands. The fingertips of his free hand lightly dance over the top of my hand. Draw invisible lines permanently etched in my soul.

"When I think back, the reason I'm so closed off seems childish. Immature. The result of a young love lost. Something millions have dealt with, but overcome with little struggle."

He shakes his head, again and again, as if he can't believe he let someone from his youth disrupt his life with such severity.

Bringing my free hand to his cheek, I brush my knuckles over the line of his jaw. "Devlyn," I say in a hushed tone. He leans into my touch, but keeps his head down. "Your feelings are valid. Justifiable." He tips his head to the side. "Just because you were young, it doesn't mean what you felt was inconsequential. It was real. It mattered. *You matter.*"

At this, he lifts his head. Glassy eyes meet mine, unbelieving. Full of questions. I cup his cheek and stroke the stubble with my thumb. He closes his eyes and leans into my touch again, parallel tears painting lines down his cheeks.

"I don't deserve you," he whispers into the darkened space. "Your heart. Your..." His eyes pinch tighter. His head gently rocks in my palm as he swallows. "Your love."

I sweep my fingers beneath his chin and lift. "Look at me," I whisper a breath from his lips. His eyes pop open, dart between mine, flash me with worry and fear. My stare doesn't deviate from his as I lick my lips. "Devlyn, you deserve so much more. And I'll spend every day of forever proving it to you." I use his words from earlier to tell him I am in this with him.

To seal my promise, I lean in and press my lips to his. The kiss chaste, but equally potent.

I may not have long-term relationship experience, I may not be the person people go to when they need relationship advice, but I will do whatever it takes to help Devlyn heal. To show him that what we have is not the same as his past. That what he felt then and what he feels now are similar and yet completely different.

Everyone has experienced young love—whether it be a crush, deep infatuation, or heartfelt love. The only difference between the love we feel in our youth versus what inhabits us in adulthood—wisdom. And wisdom only comes with time and experience.

I may not have long-term relationship experience, but I have dated my fair share of men. From sweethearts to assholes, I have dated them all. But none of them *felt right*. None of them made me feel alive. None of them made my palms sweat or my knees weak. And none of them made me want more than a simple meal a time or two.

None except for the man next to me.

Devlyn may be young, he may be inexperienced at life and love and hardship, but he has an old soul. He sees the world through a unique filter. And I should be so lucky as to sit at his side and let him see me. Let him love me.

"I'm here. Always," I say, then kiss his lips again.

EIGHTEEN
DEVLYN

The next couple of hours on Shelly's couch are filled with me telling her about Kelsey. From the start of our relationship to its abrupt end. And the entire time, Shelly sits beside me, her hand encased in mine, in silent support.

How am I worthy of this woman?

"Thank you for telling me," she whispers, eyes closed as she rests her head on my shoulder.

I kiss her forehead. "Thank you for listening." I tighten my hold around her waist and inhale her sweet and earthy floral scent. "Should get some sleep," I mumble as my eyes drift shut.

Shelly curls into my side, fists my hoodie above my heart and snuggles into my neck. "You too."

I startle awake, Shelly nestled in my arms. Without waking her, I dig my phone from my pocket and check the time. Quarter to seven. Must have drifted off. Thank goodness it's Sunday and Shelly doesn't work today. Neither of us is mentally capable of much right now.

Shifting on the couch, I scoop an arm beneath her knees and haul her into my lap. She groans slightly and I bite the inside of my cheek to resist laughing. Rising from the couch, I walk down the small hall and step into her bedroom. A space that suddenly feels more intimate than a place to rest.

With the curtains drawn and a small amount of light peeking through the blinds, it's difficult to make out the intricacies of her space. But the energy radiates Shelly the farther I step inside.

Sidling up to her bed, I lower her onto the side I assume she sleeps on since the covers are pulled back. The moment I set her down and remove my arms from around her, she reaches for me.

"Stay," she says in her groggy state.

The single word weighs heavy on my mind the more it sets in. I am in no condition to drive, but I don't want to invade her privacy.

Bending over, I kiss her cheek. "I'll be on the couch," I whisper in her ear.

Her head moves side to side in slow motion. "Don't be silly." She yanks at the covers on the opposite side of the bed then pats the sheet. "Lie with me." When I don't move for a beat, her eyes crack open. "Please," she adds and gives my hand a gentle squeeze.

Sleeping. You're just sleeping.

"Okay," I acquiesce.

Once she frees my hand, I move to the other side of

the bed and sit. I toe off my shoes then ditch my hoodie and shirt. Something as simple as removing clothes has never felt this rousing. Heady. Potent. Although I hear the soft cadence of Shelly's breathing as she drifts off to sleep, every nerve ending in me is wide awake. Ready to feel and consume every physical touch shared.

Considering we slept on my couch weeks ago, I shouldn't be this antsy. Shouldn't feel this on edge.

But Shelly isn't just anyone. And as much as I wanted to keep things between us black and white, Shelly showed me how vivid and glorious and breathtaking life can be when you fill it with color.

We have spilled our pasts. Exposed our hearts. And now… we move forward.

I slip beneath the covers and turn on my side to face her. The moment I stop moving, she shifts from her side of the bed. Scoots impossibly close and curls into me, face to face, like the night on my couch. I wrap her in my arms and snuggle her closer. Breathe in her scent and tangle my legs with hers.

Not a minute later, her body relaxes completely. Her breathing slows and quiets. Her palms on my chest lax and leg between mine slack.

With one last kiss on her forehead, I let go of every worry and drift off to sleep with the most incredible woman in my arms.

THE REST OF SUNDAY IS SPENT ON SHELLY'S COUCH with takeout and more episodes of *Dark*. With Shelly curled into my side, I have never felt more comfortable in my own skin or life. By no means is my life perfect, but she makes each day better than the previous.

Shelly tells me about the upcoming classes she and Elizabeth will offer at Petal and Vine in the new year. Nothing elaborate, maybe five to ten people, and only once a month.

"Do you have plans for the holidays?" she asks around a mouthful of fried ravioli.

I shake my head with a laugh. "Not yet, but I'm sure my mother will text the day before and demand my presence." I aim for it to sound like a joke, but with the way Shelly stares at me in the periphery, I must not have succeeded.

I love my mother. I do. But sometimes—okay, a lot of the time—she can be a bit much.

As a child, I never paid attention to her insistence. Never put much thought into her need for perfection. Honestly, at the time, I admired her desire for everything to be in its place or exactly how she wanted it. Friends would come over and describe her as a neat freak or controlling. I shrugged it off and said she just didn't like dysfunction or disorganization.

Now, as an adult, I see her differently. Especially after college and living on my own, making new friends and meeting their parents, I have a new perspective.

My mother isn't just a perfectionist. She isn't your classic control freak. There is more to it. I picked up on it the first month home after college graduation. She invited colleagues from the museum to dinner. Hours before their arrival, she walked into my bedroom, went straight to my closet, plucked clothes I only wore for dressy occasions from the hangers and handed them to me with a sour look on her face.

"We have dinner guests this evening," she'd said. "You will wear this and be downstairs no later than five thirty. You will be well-groomed and behave like a proper young man. Do not speak unless spoken to. Do not say anything untoward or questionable. They are not coming to hear your opinions. They are coming to talk about the museum and what I'm doing."

That night, I saw my mother in a whole new light. She'd spoken to me like a disobedient child. As if I never used manners. As if I didn't grasp common courtesy. At first, I played it off as nerves. Gave her the benefit of the doubt. These people must have been important. Probably on the fence about donating funds or art to the museum and this dinner might seal the deal.

But as I dressed that night and combed my hair, one piece of her tirade stuck out. Playing on repeat and unnerving me in a way unlike any previous occasion.

What I'm doing.

Since that night, I paid closer attention to our conversations. The more I listened, really listened, the more I heard it. The constant me, me, me. Anytime Mom called to "catch up," she led the conversation. Talked about everything driving her crazy, followed by the incompetence of everyone around her. Anyone not doting on her or lifting her up or making her life easier was unworthy in her eyes, and she voiced as much during our one-sided conversations.

As it stands, I ignore most of her calls. Let them go to voice mail. Listen to them when I am mentally prepared. Call her back when I have the energy but cut her off after thirty minutes. My mother isn't just an energy vampire. She is something entirely different. And after hours of research, I gathered my mother is a narcissist. Or something along those lines, since she hasn't been professionally diagnosed. Unfortunate for me and everyone who encounters my mother, we will never live up to her standards. And my father—sweet man that he is—is her enabler.

"My mom can be a bit much too," Shelly states. "Before my brother Micah started dating his now wife a little more than a year ago, Mom wanted to start having these regular family dinners." She sips her wine. "At first, we both thought it was no big deal. Just our parents missing us."

"Why do I sense a but coming on?"

Shelly laughs without humor. "They did miss us. But Mom also wanted to pester us about our love lives, or lack thereof."

"Ouch."

"Yeah." Her lips kick up in a meh half smile. "Nothing like sitting down for dinner and your mother asking if you've been dating or plan to give her grandchildren before she dies." Shelly rolls her eyes then twists in her seat. "What if I don't want kids?"

"Then that's your choice."

She spears another ravioli and eats the edges off before stuffing the rest in her mouth. "Have you ever thought about it? Having kids, I mean."

If any other person would have thrown this question at me, I'd probably fly off the handle. But with Shelly, I know this is her curiosity. Us still getting to know each other.

For a split second, I remember the texts I sent when her friend had a baby. What a damn fool I was.

"Honestly, I haven't given it much thought. Like I said that day when you texted from the hospital, I'd have to be in a serious relationship before the idea ever crossed my mind. And since I avoided relationships—until you—there was no sense in thinking such things."

Shelly nods. "I get that. The guys I dated before, none lasted past date two." The look on her face says there is more, but she doesn't add anything else. She shrugs and pokes at her dinner.

"Why does it feel like you want to say more?" Her cheeks stain pink, a color I haven't seen on her in weeks. There is more. "You don't have to tell me if you don't want to."

Her lips tip up at the corners. "I appreciate you saying that." She takes a deep breath and exhales slowly. "But I'm going to say it anyway."

She grabs her wineglass and downs the remaining half glass. *Whoa.* "Shelly, you don't—"

"I'm a virgin," she blurts then smothers herself with a throw pillow.

Wait, what?

No way I heard her right.

By the way she is actively trying to cut off her oxygen, I'd say I heard her perfectly fine.

How is that even possible? I mentally roll my eyes. Okay, I *know* how it's possible. But how in the hell does someone as stunning and magnificent as Shelly reach her early thirties and not lose her virginity? Not that I have loads of experience, considering Kelsey is the only sexual partner I've had.

I reach for the pillow and pull it away from her face. She resists me at first but finally lets me take it.

"Shelly…" I encase her hands in mine. "You have nothing to be ashamed of or embarrassed about." She tucks her lips between her teeth and rocks her jaw side to side. "If anything, the trait makes you more attractive. Not because of some male need to claim you. It says more about your character. Defines you as particular, selective. That you associate the act with love and not physicality. That you don't just hand your heart or body over to anyone who shows interest."

She releases her lips and looks up. "No one ever felt right. Not before."

"Not before." I will not overanalyze Shelly's words. Will not read into them and conjure up my own fantasies. But I also won't leave here tonight until I ask what she means.

"Not before?"

Her cheeks turn crimson, but she doesn't try to hide it. "I make no assumptions." I narrow my eyes in question. "About you or me or us."

I nod. "Neither do I."

"And…" Her hands fidget in mine. "With you, things lean that way." I tilt my head and beg her to elaborate. To shape her thoughts into words. "They feel… right."

I free her hands and bring mine to her cheeks. Before she gets another word in, I pull her to me and press my lips to hers. Kiss her gentle and slow. When a moan spills from her lips and down my throat, I deepen the kiss. Wrap my arm around her waist and drag her onto my lap. Fist the hair at the nape of her neck and hug her body flush to mine.

The kiss lasts forever and not long enough before I break it. Before both of us gasp for air.

It is in this moment that realization hits. This very blip in time that I finally believe. In paths and fate. That everything happens for a reason. The struggles of our past align us for the beauty of our future.

Kelsey may have been my first love. The teenage girl I pictured with me for eternity. Although she broke my heart, although she threw my life into a tornado, I wouldn't be in this very moment if none of it happened. I wouldn't have Shelly or this constant swell beneath my sternum. I wouldn't appreciate and reciprocate the emotion spilling from my heart without first experiencing the cracks and aches.

If I bump into Kelsey one day, I will thank her. If it weren't for her need for freedom, I wouldn't have stumbled upon the woman in my arms. If it weren't for her selfishness, I wouldn't have fallen in love. Real love.

Yep, I said it. In love. Although, I may just keep that to myself a little longer.

NINETEEN

SHELLY

Lights twinkle from every direction. Red and green, blue and white. Rainbows and blinking and solid strands. Some wrapped around tree trunks and limbs. Others clinging to bushes and rooflines. Animals on lawns with robotic animation. Blow up snow people—because actual snow doesn't happen here—and cartoon characters on the grass and rooftops.

Each year, the amount of holiday decorations people add to their homes is mind blowing. Every Christmas, I ooh and ahh over the displays. Drive slowly down my parents' street to glimpse each setup. Note the new additions from the previous year. Hem and haw over my inability to put up exterior lights, with the exception of my small porch. Complain how I wish I had a blow-up reindeer or Santa to put outside.

I love Christmas. Well, I love all holidays. They all have their own kind of magic. Christmas just happens to be the one I go the most bonkers over.

But this year is a bit different.

This year, the lights twinkle brighter. Candy canes have a little more zip in the peppermint. Balsam firs smell fresher and more piney than any previous year. And the slight chill in the air puts a smile on my face.

During the holidays, I add a minimal amount of decorations to my tiny apartment. A small artificial evergreen. Citrus and clove-scented candles as well as balsam fir. Strands of white fairy lights. Garland made of evergreens and cranberries. An evergreen wreath on the door with blue thistle, white berries, eucalyptus, holly berries, and lightly wrapped gray ribbon. Festive bouquets on the coffee and dining tables as well as the kitchen and bathroom counter. Festive towels hanging from the oven door.

If I had the space, my home would be a holiday mecca.

Every year, I purchase gifts weeks before the holiday. Lug the bin out from under my bed and riffle through rolls of festive paper and ribbons and bows. Play cheery Yuletide music and sip hot cocoa as I write jolly messages in cards. Decorate the tree and light candles.

For years, this has been my ritual. Not down to an exact science, but pretty damn close. This year, everything changed.

A month ago, things with Devlyn went haywire. Out of nowhere, I kissed him and he kissed me back. Then, he panicked and disappeared for two weeks… until I sent a text that scared him more. The night he paced outside my apartment, I had no expectations of what would happen when I opened the door. I definitely didn't expect our relationship to manifest into what it is now.

Devlyn has shifted himself out of the friend category and sits firmly in the boyfriend category. And over the last few weeks, we have been solidifying that new status. Spending every free moment together. Kissing… constantly. And losing track of time.

Which is why, two days ago, I was frantic. One of those berserk people in Target searching empty shelves for the perfect gift. I scored a few small gifts but caved and bought gift cards for the rest. Gift cards are not my style. They feel so impersonal. But I'd rather give a gift card than nothing at all.

"Hallelujah," I whisper as I park next to Peyton's car in my parents' driveway.

I love my parents. Really, I do. From time to time, though, Mom gets a little pushy. Not in the way Devlyn described his mother. Mom has a big heart and means well, she just gets a bit overwhelming here and there. The only thing Nicole Reed wants is for her children to have a happy life. Unfortunately, her version of a happy life includes the perfect spouse, the perfect house, and babies.

I have none of the above.

With the newness of my and Devlyn's relationship, I don't assume to have any of the three in the near future. At this point in the game, I go with the flow. Marriage and picket fences and offspring don't necessarily equal a happy life. Happiness comes from a deeper place. One I have barely started to discover but am eager to explore.

From the moment I witnessed it on screen and read it in romance novels, there has only been one thing that matters when it comes to the future. Love. Deep, hungry,

I can't go a day without seeing you love. One that steals the air from your lungs, whisks you off your feet and has your heart banging out of your chest.

Above everything else, I want that type of love. If the other things follow in love's wake, so be it. But without love, the other three don't matter.

Walking under the row of icicle lights, I step onto the porch and pause in front of the door. A fresh evergreen wreath with red berries hangs on a hook. My hand hovers over the knob as I inhale the earthy pine scent and let it relax me. "It's Christmas. Mom won't nag me. Not today," I mumble. I nod as if to reassure myself, then twist the knob and step inside.

Three things hit me at once. Deep, booming laughter, mouthwatering baked cheese, and the clanging of pans.

I toe off my shoes in the foyer, set my purse and bags down, and tiptoe toward the kitchen. Peering around the corner, I spy my dad and Peyton seated at the breakfast bar. Tears roll down Dad's cheeks as he presses a loose fist to his mouth. Peyton clamps down on her lips, her cheeks and neck blotchy, as she tries not to laugh.

Across from them, in the heart of the kitchen, are Mom and Micah. My dear, sweet, occasional pain in the ass brother is decked out in Mom's *I love to rub meat* apron. Mom is at his side, coaching him as he sautés carrots in one pan and stirs gravy in another. Sweat beads his forehead and temple. His tongue peeking out between his lips as he shifts his weight left then right.

To most, this sight would be endearing. A son helping his mother cook Christmas dinner. Lovable as the moment is, Dad's tumultuous laughter when I walked in the house now makes sense. Because Micah in the kitchen is equal parts frightening and hilarious. I love my brother, but his ability to cook is null. Mom refuses to give up on him, though. Has him over or goes to his house once a week and shows him something new. Before Peyton, Micah burned water. Now, he successfully cooks five full meals without supervision. This is the first holiday meal he has cooked, and I am proud of him.

"Look at you," I say as I enter the kitchen. "Keep this up and you'll be cooking all the holiday meals."

He shoots me with wide eyes and a slight shake of his head. "Ha ha. Best not push your luck."

Stepping around Micah, I hug Mom and kiss her cheek. Dad and Peyton slide off their stools and pull me in for hugs next. Since Micah is too focused on not burning dinner, I wrap my arms around him and squeeze until he taps my arm.

"You're doing great, big brother," I whisper so only he hears. "Proud of you."

He sets the spoon on the rest, spins around, and hugs me properly. "Thanks, Shell." He kisses my crown then releases me. "Means a lot."

The stove timer buzzes and he goes back to work. I fill a glass with sparkling cranberry-apple cider—a Reed family tradition—then join Dad and Peyton. Micah and Mom put the final touches on dinner while we all catch up. Mom declares dinner is ready and we all file into a line with plates in hand.

I pile my plate high with herb and citrus roasted duck,

potato gratin, baked macaroni and cheese, sautéed carrots, cranberry-orange relish, balsamic Brussel sprouts, and a homemade roll. The next ten minutes pass in silence as we savor the meal.

"Starlight, this is the best yet." Peyton beams at Micah. "You might have to cook some of this again. Soon."

My brother glows from her compliment. And as if they were alone, he takes her elbow, tugs her closer, and kisses her. Not a sweet peck on the cheek. Nope, this is my brother we are talking about. He kisses his wife as if his parents and sister are nowhere in sight. When the kiss breaks, Peyton's cheeks pink.

I doubt her flush is darker than mine.

Public displays of affection don't bother or embarrass me. I adore seeing people so happy and in love. It reminds me true love exists. The heat on my cheeks comes more from picturing myself in a similar situation. Caring for someone—Devlyn, perhaps—so deeply, I can't not kiss them. Regardless of who is around.

The last month plays like a movie in my head.

The night I took Devlyn's face in my hands and kissed him. What it felt like when he kissed me back. The splendor in that first kiss. How perfect the moment was. All the romance novels I'd read finally made sense. The rapid pulse and shortness of breath. It all made sense because I felt them too.

Until Devlyn pulled away. Until I saw the fear on his face. The dread. The regret. I now know why, I understand it, but it still hurts.

Fast forward two weeks later. The text. His appearance at my front door in the middle of the night. Hours of apologies and shared history and heartache spilled between us. In less than twenty-four hours, Devlyn and I had become somewhat inseparable. And over the last three weeks, our need to be with each other has magnified.

Now, we just need the balls to share our relationship with everyone else. We aren't intentionally hiding our relationship, are we? Maybe. I don't know.

A sharp sting on my shin snaps my eyes across the table. Micah winces, his silent apology for kicking my leg. "You okay?" he mouths.

I nod, subtly.

"Liar," he mouths before taking a bite.

Great.

It isn't a lie. I just haven't figured out how to tell him the truth. I have a boyfriend.

God, I feel his brotherly wrath and see his macho chest slaps already. Someone preemptively saves me from my brother.

We decide to save dessert for after gifts.

For the last five years, my parents have told us no gifts. Micah and I refuse to give them nothing. So, we coordinate. We both buy them a card and gift certificate for their favorite restaurant. The first year, they smiled and accepted the gift. Since then, they invite us out for dinner and take us to the restaurant. The first time they did this, Micah and I argued with them and tried to pay our part of the bill. We were unsuccessful. Now, we pick somewhere everyone likes and add more to the gift price, so we are still paying for ourselves.

Mom and Dad graciously thank us for the cards and gift certificates. Micah surprises Peyton with a photo album full of pictures of their first year and a half together. Since falling for Peyton, my brother has become such a romantic. He isn't all goo-goo eyes and flowers every week, but he is more affectionate than I have ever seen him. Hand-holding, whispering in her ear, subtle touches on her cheek, neck or shoulder. And the occasional flower delivery from Petal and Vine.

I envy what they share so openly. Fingers crossed, one day in the near future, that will be me. Giggly and doe eyed and curled into Devlyn's side while we spend time with loved ones.

"Here, Shelly," Mom says as she hands me a gift.

I take the large, thin rectangular package. As I peel back the paper, I wonder if my parents framed our family photo from last Christmas. Wouldn't be abnormal. With each passing year, my parents get more sentimental. Valuing time together and photographs over anything else.

I discard the paper and flip the frame over, prepared to plaster on my fake enthusiasm for an oversized family photo I won't hang. Instead, my jaw drops and my heart stammers.

"Wha-What is this?" I mumble as the backs of my eyes sting.

"Isn't it beautiful?" Mom asks as she leans into Dad. "A friend at work gave me the link to a local artist's website. She wouldn't shut up about his work. So, I went on and found this. The moment I saw it, I knew I had to get it. Like it was drawn for you."

Not for me, I want to tell her. *This* is *me*.

Framed in light oak is an up-close view of a woman's face. From just above the brow to the edge of the top lip, from the bridge of the nose to the lateral edge of the eye. The piece is in pencil with no color. Impeccable detail over every inch. A constellation mapped out in her eye.

The only pieces I have seen of Devlyn's are what he painted at the shop and those from the gallery—which were also me. Perhaps that is why he didn't let me into his studio while touring his house. Would it freak me out? Are there more images of my likeness in his studio? On his website? Something tells me there is a lot more where this came from.

"Let me see," Peyton says.

I close my eyes briefly and swallow. The second Peyton takes in the image, she lifts a hand to her mouth and gasps. Micah may not pick up on the connection as quickly as Peyton. He doesn't stare at his eyes like she does. Plus, Peyton was at the baby shower when I spilled my heart out about Devlyn.

"It's…" She pauses and bites her bottom lip a moment. "It's stunning."

I restrain the tears begging to roll down my cheeks. Last thing I need is for Mom to think I don't appreciate the gift. I do love it. More than any other gift I received.

Mom gifting this to me feels like another sign. A broadcast alert that my relationship with Devlyn is bigger than either of us realizes. How big exactly? I have no clue.

"It is," I garble out then clear my throat and look to my smiling parents. "Thank you, Mom, Dad."

Dessert goes by in a blur of apple pie and light chatter. The melodies and baritones of voices echo in my ears, but I miss everything said. My eyes continue to drift to the drawing in the oak frame.

When did Devlyn draw it? How long would it take to draw something with this level of detail? Days, maybe weeks. Plus, listing it online, processing the sale, shipping. Did he draw this shortly after coming back to the shop? Are there more drawings or paintings of me in his studio?

I shake my head to dispel the endless questions I have no way of answering. Instead, I zero back in on my family. Listen to Mom prattle on over the new client her firm attained. Listen to Dad tell tales of strange client stories as they buy an insurance policy. And listen to my brother and Peyton as they regale all the wonderful parts of married life.

Scooping apples, crust, and fresh whipped cream on my fork, I smile and respond and laugh at the appropriate times. Inside, I scream for the night to be over already. I pray to walk out the front door any second, so I can call the one person with the answers. And to ask Devlyn for a tour of his studio.

I'D RATHER GO TO DEVLYN'S HOUSE THAN JONAS AND Autumn's. Less than forty-eight hours have passed since we were together, and every opportunity to see or speak with each other gets squashed by someone else. Not that I don't want to spend time with loved ones, but I want time with Devlyn too. So I plaster on my best smile and trudge through each moment. Take deep breaths, remind myself to be grateful and that I will see Devlyn soon.

Our call when I left my parents' house was short lived due to his mother pestering him in the background. Plus, if I don't show at Friendsmas, my phone will blow up with unmerry threats and promises to come get me.

Over the last few hours, I've stared at the drawing gifted to me from my parents. Art with such precision and detail had to take Devlyn a while to draw. Weeks, possibly a month or more, to finish. The more I study it, the more intimate it feels. Like Devlyn spills his secrets through his art. The biggest secret of all… how he feels about me.

Artists don't paint or draw the same person over and over or with such delicacy without a reason. What is Devlyn's reason? When did I become his muse? Although it feels as if a lifetime has passed since October, our relationship beyond the friends stage is still so young. It's difficult to imagine him creating such a piece months ago. Is this—his art—it can't be… *love*.

Dizziness consumes me with the possibilities.

My heart has her hands in the air, hips swaying, as she screams *yes* at the top of her lungs. My head, on the other hand, has calculators and spreadsheets and pro/con lists out. A scale on the desk, weighing emotions versus life. And I hate that my brain steals this moment of joy.

With the purchase of Petal and Vine a year out, my

focus has been prepping for the business handoff. Getting all my financial ducks in a row. Albeit a good one, Devlyn has been a distraction. The type of distraction I haven't had to deal with in the past. The type of distraction I need to learn how to balance in my life.

Hopping up from the couch, I take a few cleansing breaths. Close my eyes and hum with my inner zen master. Tell myself I am strong, I am capable, and I can accomplish anything I put my mind to. When I open my eyes, relief filters in.

I got this.

After a bite to eat and a shower, I dress in my comfiest jeans and long-sleeve V-neck pink sweater. I blow out my hair and dab on a light coat of natural makeup. Satisfied with my appearance, I slip on my matching pink Vans then grab my purse and gifts.

I arrive at Jonas and Autumn's just after five. Several cars are parked out front, but not everyone is here yet. Unbuckling, I exit the car and scramble to the passenger side. Snag the gifts from the seat and head for the door with full arms.

When we all asked to bring something for the food, Jonas and Autumn insisted we leave it to them. So, aside from gifting them a small houseplant and matching fuzzy socks for everyone, I got them a gift card for the grocery store. Seeing as they pay for the majority of our gatherings, this is my way of contributing. I told Cora my idea and she agreed to buy them one too.

Spartan greets me at the door with paws to the chest

and attempts to lick my face. Jonas apologizes profusely and I laugh.

"For some reason, he's a little extra today. Probably because we spoiled him yesterday," he says as he hugs me around the gifts. "Let me take that off your hands." Jonas takes the gifts and parks them under the tree. He points a finger at Spartan. "Leave it."

Spartan grumbles then trots off in search of Clementine, who lets him get away with more.

"How was Christmas?" I ask.

He leads me to the kitchen where everyone lingers around the island. "Good. Spoiled my girls more than ever." The brightest smile lights his face. "How was dinner with the parents?"

"Good. Mom was less invasive than usual." I keep the news of the artwork gift to myself. Sidling up to Cora, I hug her side. "Hey, you. Merry Christmas."

She twists to face me head-on and hugs me tight. "Merry Christmas."

Her hug lingers longer than normal and I wonder if everything is okay. She releases me, but the soft sadness on her lips tells me she wanted to hold on longer. "What's wrong?" I ask.

The lines of her forehead deepen for a beat. Had I blinked, I would have missed it. Her eyes dart over my shoulder then back to mine. She either looked to my brother or Peyton. My guess… Peyton. And judging by her extended hug and careful attitude, she knows about Mom's gift last night.

Really don't want to talk about Devlyn with everyone here.

At the baby shower, I told every woman here that I was letting Devlyn go. Although I did when I sent the text, things are different now. And on Friendsmas, I get to bring them up to speed. No doubt the guys will overhear and jump in on the conversation.

SOS. This gal needs help.

"If you need to talk, I'm here."

Closing my eyes, I let out a huff. It's now or never. If I don't speak up and tell her Devlyn and I are no longer on the outs, Cora will be hurt I kept it secret. We share everything—even the painful stuff. For the longest time, I was her shoulder to cry on. Now, she wants to be mine. It would be wrong of me to let her believe I needed one.

"Thanks, but…" I throw her a look, one we have shared over the years. *There's more. Just wait a minute.* She nods subtly.

Once I give everyone a hug, I fill a plate with holiday-themed snack foods and a glass with wine. I sit in the end seat at the dining table and munch while I wait. Cranberry-peach glazed meatballs, cheesy-herb pull-apart bread, ham and Swiss pinwheels, four-cheese sausage quiche, and rosemary-garlic hasselback potatoes. There is plenty more I didn't grab, but I will save them for later.

The chairs closest to me drag against the floor and fill a moment later. Without looking, I know it is the ladies, each of them with a plate and drink of their own.

"Sorry," Cora mumbles, and I look up.

"No need. Never apologize for being thoughtful." I bring the glass to my lips and take a sip. "Things have changed since the shower."

"Changed how?" Cora asks before stuffing her mouth full of green beans and potato.

Looking around the room, I see everyone else chatting or otherwise occupied. After a deep breath, I explain what happened after I sent the infamous text to Devlyn. How twisted up I felt inside. How I couldn't sleep. And the fact that Devlyn was on my porch in the middle of the night. At this, Cora and Autumn gasp.

Then, without spilling the intricate details of Devlyn's past, I tell them about our talk. How Devlyn confided in me and explained why he shut down. The more I shared, the more my friends got dreamy eyed.

Did I tell them about the kiss? Of course, but more from a *it made me melt* point of view. They don't need all the dirty details.

I share how much time Devlyn and I have spent together these last three weeks. How wonderful it has been to get to know each other better. And for some reason, as the words leave my lips, my stomach twists in knots. Somehow, this moment reminds me of high school. How others teased me for not having a boyfriend. How hungry I was for the inside scoop on all the things boys, but never asked in fear of embarrassment. The girl of my youth rejoices that she is finally experiencing those moments. That she gets to brag to her friends. But the woman I am now wants to zip her lips and keep Devlyn to herself.

Cora rises from her chair and hugs the air from my lungs. "So glad you're happy. It's about damn time."

Couldn't agree more.

"When do we get to meet him?" Autumn chimes in just as Jonas sidles up to her and says it's time for gifts.

Halle-freaking-lujah!

The gift exchange goes down with much enthusiasm. Spartan and Clementine play with the packages and wrapping paper. Jonas and Autumn frown at the number of grocery gift cards we all gifted. Between everyone, they accumulated over three hundred dollars. Plants and ugly sweaters, gag gifts and graphic tees. Smiles and laughter abound in this more relaxed holiday celebration.

As I look around the room and take in this wonderful group of people that are the best family I know, my heart wobbles a little. So much has changed over the years, but we are still together. Through thick and thin. Our lives full and bountiful.

My only wish… for Devlyn to be here too.

Then I ask myself if he'd want to be here. Would he want to sit with this colossal group of people and share a piece of himself? Would he want to insert himself in my life, with my family? Devlyn belongs here. With me. With us. He may be timid and quirky, but I easily picture him fitting in with us all. I easily picture everyone loving him as much as I do.

It may be too soon, and I may have read too many romance novels, but I think I am in love with Devlyn. But how will I know if he is in love with me?

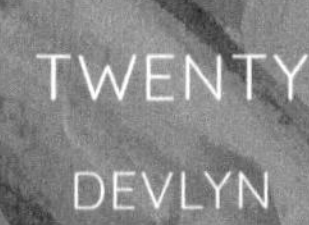

TWENTY
DEVLYN

Holidays and birthdays have never been big on my to-do list. Growing up, my mother turned every occasion into a lavish party. No matter the event, she was the center of attention—even when the party wasn't for her. Over time, I grew to despise celebrations. Avoided as many invites as possible.

Until now. Until today.

Spending New Year's Eve with Shelly sounds like the perfect way to kick off a new year. Considering I have never watched the ball drop or made a list of resolutions, I look forward to doing both with her.

Petal and Vine closes early today and doesn't reopen until January second. I get a full, uninterrupted day and a half with her, and I have never been this damn nervous in my life.

Last night, after she spent an hour in the kitchen making the most amazing pasta carbonara and garlic bread, I asked her to come to my place for New Year's.

Without hesitation, she said yes. Then, as I fisted my napkin beneath the table, I asked her to stay the night.

Considering we have spent the night together a few times now, asking her shouldn't flip my stomach upside down. But the previous times we slept in the same space were different. The first was accidental. The second, we were both exhausted. But the third, and most recent, didn't happen from falling asleep on the couch or pure exhaustion. Shelly said she was tired, took my hand, and walked me to her room. The action felt so normal. A natural progression in our relationship.

That said, we haven't broached anything beyond spooning or kissing in bed. No bare flesh or fondling through clothes. To some, our relationship may appear clean or innocent, but the truth is we are both waiting for the right moment. That unspoken word to say we are ready for more, for the next step.

Me asking Shelly to stay over—preplanning a sleep-over—carries the heaviest weight yet. Pushes us to the next level of seriousness in our relationship. A step I think we're ready for, but I don't want her to think I have assumptions about what will or won't happen.

My goal in asking her to stay isn't about sex. Not that my thoughts haven't drifted to the fantasy of what it'd be like to connect with Shelly in such a powerful way. More than any other reason, I asked Shelly to stay because I hate when she leaves. I love her in my space and in my arms. Her in both at the start of a new year… I can't think of anything more right.

Parking at the grocery store, where everyone and their

mother is shopping for last-minute party goods, I head inside, grab a cart, and wind through the aisles. The plan for tonight is to cook instead of order takeout. A chef I am not, but I have some meals down to a science.

After I load the cart with ingredients for tonight, essentials, dessert, and movie snacks, I head for the checkout. Four brown bags and way too much money later, I pack the groceries in the back of the car and leave. Traffic is heavier than usual with people driving to parties or beachside hotels for the fireworks.

I make it home before Shelly arrives and put everything away except the ingredients for dinner. As I toss the chicken breasts in a resealable bag with marinade, there is a soft knock at the door.

She's here.

With a simple knock, I grow dizzy. My steps wobbly as I walk to the front door. Breath stuttering as I unbolt the lock and twist the handle. Heart hammering as I open the door and see my favorite smile. Skin dampening as I take in the larger than normal bag on her shoulder.

This is really happening. Shelly is here and staying the night. In my house. In my bed.

I swallow past the nervous lump in my throat. "Hey." Stepping back, I make room for her to enter then close the door.

"Hey," she says, voice softer than usual. "Where can I..." Her question trails off as she lifts the bag from her shoulder.

Taking the bag from her, she toes off her shoes before I slip my hand in hers and start for the bedroom.

When I gave Shelly a tour of the house on her first visit, there were two rooms I intentionally left out. The studio and my bedroom. The studio because I didn't want her to panic at how often she inspired my recent work. And my bedroom because I didn't want to insinuate something or make her more uncomfortable on her first visit. After all, we were just friends then. At least, that is what I told myself a thousand times a day.

The notion of *just friends* never really stuck.

I lead her into the bedroom and set her bag on the bed. As best I can, I hide the tremor in my limbs. With our romantic relationship still in the early stages, the last thing I want to do is give Shelly the wrong impression. That I only have one goal in mind. Sex. And although I want to experience everything with her, sex is not what drives me to be with her.

But I am a man.

More times than I care to admit, I've fantasized what it would be like to have Shelly beneath me. Aura a blazing red as my mouth devoured hers. Skin damp with sweat, her nails in my back. Heels digging into my ass as I rock my hips forward. My name whispered from her lips as we reached euphoria.

Needless to say, my soap supply has depleted much quicker since meeting Shelly.

But I won't pressure Shelly into anything she isn't ready for. This woman… she is worth waiting a lifetime for. I want every other part of her too, not just the physical. Her heart. Her trust. Her soul.

"Your room is not what I expected," she whispers into the dimly lit space.

I twist to face her. Take in her inquisitive eyes as they roam the space. "No?"

She shakes her head. "Don't laugh." Heat pinks her cheeks. "I expected to see more color. Paintings on the wall and sculptures on the dresser."

I bite the inside of my cheek and fight the smile on my lips. "Not laughing. Promise." I let my smile loose. "However, I do find it cute that you'd think my room would be vibrant."

Shelly shrugs. "You're a hard man to read sometimes."

Every now and then, I felt the same about her—that she was difficult to read. Simple things that made Shelly happy were easy to see—her love for minimalism and simplicity, her food and drink preferences, the way she regarded flowers as she placed them in paper or vases.

What I wanted to learn were the things that made this beautiful woman tick. Where to touch her with fingertips and lips that would make her back bow and lungs gasp. The sights that captivated her, so I could take her to each one and memorize the way her smile lit up the sky. What quenched her soul, so I could gift it to her more often than not.

I lace my fingers with hers. "You haven't seen it yet, but my studio is kind of chaotic. Organized chaos, if you will. Which is why my bedroom is the complete opposite." I stare around at the bare pewter-painted walls. Scan the pale oak dresser free of clutter. Glance at the two nightstands in the same pale oak; soft light glows from selenite lamps on both. Then I take in the king bed with cream bedding, four pillows and nothing more. "After spending all day in a kaleidoscope of color or deep in thought, I need a blank slate. A way to reset myself."

"Never thought of it like that, but it makes sense."

Walking toward the door, I lead us back out to the main part of the house. "C'mon. You can help me make dinner." Back in the kitchen, I set Shelly up to chop and assemble salad ingredients while I work on root vegetables for roasting.

By no means am I a pro in the kitchen, but I watched too many shows on Food Network in college and some of the easier meals stuck. Bless my dorm mates. At the time, I hated how often I heard about mincing garlic and dicing carrots. They used it as background noise while working on projects. And after weeks of it, I grew to love the channel too. Not just for the distractions I desperately needed, but also the skills it taught me.

We work in silence and it's as comfortable as every other moment with Shelly. Every now and again, I glance her way and watch her work. Her precision with a knife reminds me of how intricately she assembles a vase of flowers. Arranging is her version of art, and it is so damn mesmerizing.

Once the chicken and vegetables are in the oven, I clean up. Shelly finishes the salad then pours the ingredients for a vinaigrette into a mason jar and shakes. While waiting for the food in the oven to finish, we head to the living room and set up the table and television.

When the timer buzzes, I remove dinner from the

oven. After plating the chicken and vegetables, I carry the plates and salad bowls to the living room and we park ourselves on cushions on the floor. Food and wine and episodes of *Dark* on the screen. It all feels so natural and sublime and effortless.

When our plates and bowls are empty, I take them to the kitchen and leave them for later. On my return, I bring the wine bottle and two slices of black forest cake I snagged from the grocery store bakery.

"This looks so good," Shelly says as she twists the plate left and right to inspect the slice enough for two.

"Wasn't sure what you liked, but these looked too good to pass up."

She twists in her seat and gives me the smile I love too much. "Good choice."

We devour the cake in no time then move up to the couch and I flip off the light. Shelly curls into my side as we continue another episode. When this episode ends, the plan is to flip over to the broadcast of the ball drop.

The closer it gets to midnight, the louder the neighborhood gets with fireworks and party cheers. And the more my stomach wrings with nervous energy. A sensation that has become more familiar in recent weeks. A ball of chaotic energy just beneath my diaphragm that, if I tried to translate it on canvas, would look like a maddening swirl of blue and red and yellow. Bright and vibrant and begging for attention.

Shelly's breath heats the skin of my neck as the room goes black at the end of the episode. Much as I want to relish in the feel of her so close, I pick up the remote and switch the television to the channel broadcasting the festivities.

With less than a half hour to midnight, the crowd in Times Square is so boisterous I feel their excitement. For the first time, celebrating a holiday feels significant. All because of the woman in my arms.

"Hey," I whisper, unsure if Shelly is still awake. All I get is a low *hmm* in return. "I'm going to clean up in the kitchen. Need anything?"

Shelly uncurls herself from my side and I immediately miss her warmth and touch. She lifts a hand to cover her mouth as she yawns. "No. Might go splash my face so I don't fall asleep early."

With a light chuckle, I press my lips to her forehead. "Take your time."

While Shelly heads for the bathroom, I clean up in the kitchen. It doesn't take long to rinse the dishes, put them in the dishwasher and start the load. With a glance at the clock on the stove, I note it is seven minutes to midnight. Uncorking another bottle of wine, I wander back to the living room and stop when I reach the threshold.

In the corner of the couch, Shelly is curled up with the throw blanket, eyes closed and chest rising and falling at a slow rhythm. I take in the sight of her, inhale deeply, and tiptoe toward the couch. Setting the bottle on the table, I gingerly sit next to her, hoping not to disturb her from sleep. But the moment my weight shifts the cushion, her eyes pop open.

"Did I miss it?" she asks, voice thick with exhaustion as she scoots up to a seat.

"No. A few minutes to go." I tuck a stray lock of hair behind her ear. "But we can head to bed."

She sits straighter and shakes her head. "It's almost time. No backing out now." Shelly drops her head to my shoulder. "Sorry I dozed off."

I weave my fingers with hers and rest my head on her crown. "Don't apologize. It's been a long day."

On the television, the crowd grows restless as midnight draws closer. The clock in the corner of the screen drops under the minute marker. I pour enough wine into our glasses to toast the new year and hand Shelly hers. Thousands of crystals and lights change color on the screen as the final ten seconds count down.

Cheers and fireworks erupt outside the moment midnight strikes. Shelly and I clink glasses and take a swig of wine as we stare at the countless people on the screen kissing. With each new camera shot, a new couple flashes their smiling faces together in a lip lock.

Is this what couples do on New Year's to celebrate? I wouldn't know. But without a second thought, I take Shelly's glass from her hand and set it on the table with mine.

"What are you—"

I frame her face in my palms and crash my lips to hers. Startled by the sudden gesture, she doesn't kiss me back immediately. When I pull her bottom lip between mine, though, she melts into me, fists the bottom hem of my shirt and returns the kiss with heat and intensity.

Time and noise vanish as our lips dance and tongues tangle. Color dances behind my eyes as I taste the wine on her tongue and breathe in her sweet, earthy scent. When her nails graze my abdomen beneath my shirt, I drag in a sharp breath and inch back from her.

Her eyes flash open and lock on mine, worry etched in the lines of her forehead. "Sorry, I—"

I press a finger to her lips and shake my head. "Don't apologize." I wrap her hand in mine, rise from the couch and tug for her to follow. She untangles herself from the blanket and scoots off the couch. I guide her out of the living room, shutting off the television as we pass, and walk us to the bedroom.

It takes less than a minute to reach the bedroom, but my heart bangs in my rib cage the entire time. The moment we cross the threshold, Shelly grips my hand tighter. When we reach the foot of the bed, I stop and turn to face her.

Damn, she steals the air from my lungs.

Reaching up, I wrap a lock of her hair around my finger. "Hey," I whisper in the dimly lit space. Her eyes lift and rob me of my next breath. "If all you want to do is sleep, we sleep." I press my lips to her forehead. "More than anything, I just want you here with me. Okay?"

Her fingers curl in the cotton of my shirt again and drag me closer. Lips inches apart, she whispers, "Okay." Then she eliminates the remaining space between us, presses her lips to mine and picks up right where we left off in the living room.

My hands fall to her hips and hold her flush to my frame, the bulge in my pants undeniable. Her hands draw parallel lines up my torso, snake around my neck and skate up the base of my skull. Every impulse in my hormonal makeup fights the urge to strip her bare and mark her as mine. Fights the urge to be less than a gentleman and tender boyfriend.

Of the few times I had sex in the past, I never once was aggressive. Never once had the *impulse* to rip clothes and imprint skin with nails and teeth.

Right now, with Shelly flush against my erection and her lips ravaging me as if the opportunity won't come again, fighting my base instincts proves more difficult. I *want* to claw at her skin with nails and teeth. Taste every inch of her on my tongue. Inhale the perfume at her neck and the pheromones between her legs. Watch her body react as I tease her flesh with fingers and licks. Listen to her soft cries and throaty moans as I give her pleasure and drive her to ecstasy.

Her fingers tug at my hair, lips skirt along my jaw and teeth nip at my ear. My jaw falls slack as a gravelly moan escapes.

God, I want her. Desperately.

But physical intimacy with Shelly isn't just about what I want. She has to guide us along the path she wants us to take. Say when she wants more. Tell me when to stop. Because at this rate, I won't stop. Ever.

I drag my hands up the sides of her torso, beneath her shirt, along the warm curves of her body. At the base of her bra, I clutch her rib cage and drop my lips to her ear. "Shelly." My voice husky and foreign. "Tell me what you want." The tips of my fingers curl in slightly and dig at flesh and bone. My tongue darts out and I lick the shell of her ear. "Tell me."

She frees my hair, slides her palms down my chest and fists my shirt. I inch back and lock our gazes. Her eyes shine as they look up. All I see is every star in the night sky, burning hot and bright and intense. I lick my lips then swallow, on edge while waiting for her response.

Her lips part as she pushes up on her toes. "I want *you*, Devlyn." Her eyes drop and trail the length of my body before they slowly make their way back up. "*All* of you."

My eyes drift shut as her words sink in. My grip on her tightens as I stroke beneath the base of her bra with my thumbs. I drag in a deep breath then drop my forehead to hers. "Are you sure?" The question a soft stutter on my lips. Subtly, she nods and my body sighs. I press my lips to hers and kiss her softly. "I want that too."

TWENTY-ONE

SHELLY

Heat blooms low in my belly at his whispered words on my lips. His next kiss is softer, more tender as his fingers knead my skin. Trace lines between my ribs. Unclasp the closure at the back of my bra. Free my breasts beneath my top.

I break my lips from his. Gasp as his hands roam the length of my spine without interruption. Slide my palms lower to his waist and dip them below his shirt. Close my eyes as my fingers trail over the ridges and valleys of his abdomen.

I may not have had sex, but I am not virginal in all things. My experience is minuscule, but I have gotten to second base with a few guys. Of course, they got a little too handsy when the kiss deepened, going from light, over-the-clothes petting to trying to strip me bare. Needless to say, I cut things off and never saw them again. If someone won't respect voiced boundaries, who knows what else they'd push past.

Right now, this moment, is different.

Tonight is the first time I want to explore and be explored beyond impassioned kisses and hands fondling parts through clothes. Tonight, I want to be more than the woman Devlyn can't take his eyes off of. More than the woman he holds in his arms. I want to be the woman he can't get enough of. The woman he never lets go of.

His kiss travels from my lips to the line of my jaw. Every press of his lips to my skin, along my jaw, down the column of my throat sends a ripple of heat and leaves an unfamiliar, but desirable tingle in its wake. Each kiss sears me, brands me, marks me in a new way. And I love every single one. Yearn for the next kiss he gives.

With a gentle tug, Devlyn inches up my top and bra, peels them away and drops them to the floor. My breath comes in short bursts as goose bumps blanket my exposed flesh. On instinct, I cross my arms over my chest. Hide my bare breasts as my line of sight drops to Devlyn's still clothed body.

He paints his fingers along my jaw then tips my chin up. Warm affection greets me in his gentle green eyes. "Please don't be embarrassed. Not with me." His lips press mine and vanish too soon. "You ravish me, Shelly." *Kiss*. "Rob me of sight and sound and thought." *Kiss*. "Inspire me more than anyone or anything." *Kiss*. "And as hard as I fought against this—against being yours, against you being mine..." *Kiss*. "Subconsciously, I knew we'd always be more than friends." *Kiss*. "So much more."

Fire licks my skin as my arms fall away. Devlyn steps closer, cups my cheeks in his palms, and kisses me slow and deep. As his tongue tastes mine, I take the hem of his shirt in my fists and slowly push the fabric up and over his head. The moment his chest is bare, he molds my body to his. Snakes an arm around my rib cage. Digs his fingers in my hair. Tilts my head and devours every whimper bubbling in my throat.

It's too much and not enough.

Devlyn drops his hands to my hips and guides me until my legs bump the mattress. I trace his hip bones with needy fingers. Move to the dip on either side of his spine just above his waistband. Journey up his back and memorize the corded muscles beneath my touch.

The kiss breaks as I drop to the bed. Eyes locked, I press my hands into the fluffy comforter and inch back on the bed. Beneath my breastbone, my heart rattles my rib cage while my lungs beg for air. Devlyn leans forward, his hands on either side of me on the bed as he kisses the curve of my neck.

"Beautiful," he whispers, breath hot on my skin.

His lips travel to the hollow of my throat, kissing me once, twice, three times before drifting lower. An arm comes around my waist, his palm in the middle of my spine, and then he leans into me more. Guides me to lie on the mattress. Shifts me up the bed and near the pillows. Crawls up my body and cages me in.

Then his lips drive me wild again.

My eyes drift closed as each sensation stirs new life in my veins. I fist his hair as he paints my skin with his lips. Kiss by kiss, his mouth deviates from my midline. Leaves a trail of tingles as he moves toward my left breast. A rush of adrenaline spikes my bloodstream as my heavy breaths fill the room. My fingers in his hair curl tighter.

"Breathe, Shelly." He inches up the bed and pins me with his gaze. One breath at a time, my breathing settles. His greens dart between my blues a moment before he swallows. "Didn't think it was possible, but I'm more lost in your starry eyes." Eyes wide open, he presses a heady kiss to my lips. "My Andromeda."

Caught off guard by the reference—or perhaps, nickname—I tilt my head and study him a beat. A smile kicks up the corners of my lips. "Ruler of man, huh?"

Devlyn shrugs as his own smile appears. "Ruler of man. The only constellation I see when I look in your eyes." His face grows more serious. "Ruler of my heart."

"Devlyn…"

He captures my lips with his and rocks his hips against mine. "It's true," he says, cupping my cheek. "And I admit it without shame."

Heat radiates from the center of my chest as I lift off the mattress and kiss him. Trailing my fingers down his abdomen, I pause at his jeans. Trace the tip of my finger along the hemline, hip to hip. Relish in the shiver of his body and stutter in his breath at my touch.

Then I unbutton his jeans. Drag the slider down the teeth. Separate the fly and expose his cotton-covered bulge. Palm his thick erection, go wide eyed at the length and freeze.

Devlyn rears back enough to catch my gaze. "What's the matter?"

I shake my head. Embarrassment heating my cheeks as I bite back my words.

"If you want to stop…"

"No." My headshake grows panicky. "I want this. You. Us."

He presses a chaste kiss to my lips. "Please tell me what's wrong."

My pulse quickens for an entirely new reason. "It's just…" Devlyn doesn't push me to speak. Hovering above me, he gives me a moment to formulate the words to explain my suddenly tense muscles and obvious anxiety. I rotate my head slightly, enough to lose eye contact. "Nerves. It's just nerves." I swallow and close my eyes. "Then I… felt how big you are and I freaked out," I mutter in a rush.

The room goes quiet. Too quiet. Silence with Devlyn has always been comfortable. Soothing. A balm I never knew I needed. But now, his silence feels like a bomb ready to detonate. An explosion of disappointment and concern. Something I have never felt with anyone.

"Look at me, Shelly." I take a deep breath and roll my lips between my teeth. "Please." His voice barely audible.

On another deep breath, I open my eyes. He takes my chin in his fingers and brings me back to his line of sight. And what I see in his eyes is the complete opposite of what I expected.

Warmth and hope and something akin to love. I swallow and pray he doesn't hear the action.

"All of this is new for you." His knuckles graze my cheek. "Hell, it's practically new for me." I furrow my brow and a subtle smile pushes up his cheeks. "I may not be a virgin, but my experience is minuscule." He kisses the tip of my nose. "Is it weird that I kind of love how uncoordinated we'll be together?"

Out of nowhere, I laugh. And then Devlyn laughs.

"Seriously, Shelly. You have nothing to fear or be embarrassed about with me. Ever." His finger twirls in my hair. "I love that I get to be your first. Not because your virginity is a trophy or something to conquer. But because it means no one mattered before me. Even with my broken parts and odd view of the world, you chose me over everyone else."

"Wasn't really a choice," I say softly.

"Couldn't agree more." He lightly traces a finger along my jaw to my chin, his eyes following the movement. "So if you want to stop, I'll understand. I won't be upset. Promise."

I shake my head. "I don't want to stop."

He stares at my lips, hungry. "You're sure?"

"Yes."

"Thank God."

His lips crash on mine, kissing me like a starved man. With deft fingers, he unbuttons my jeans and parts the zipper. Tugs the snug denim at my hips and drags the material down my thighs, my calves, then tosses them on the floor. Crawling up my body, he stops when his eyes land on my panties and I internally berate myself.

I had no expectations of staying the night at Devlyn's house. Okay, that's a lie. I assumed we would probably fool around. Maybe grope each other under our clothes.

Which is why it never crossed my mind to wear my prettier underwear. The baby-pink lacy thong and matching bra.

Instead, I wore the cotton thong with a hole near the hip and a fading floral print from too many washes. What bra had I even been wearing? The dingy white one. *Ugh. Kill me now.* I mentally slap my forehead.

I peer down at Devlyn as he hovers a place no one else has been. The longer he remains frozen, the more embarrassment claws at my insides.

Then his eyes track up my body until we connect. A subtle half smile kicks up his lips. "You know, I love these." I want to roll my eyes, but then he traces his fingertip above the waistband and I forget all thought. "That you didn't *dress* for the occasion." His finger dips below the elastic and brushes the thin strip of curls. "That I see you how you are naturally and not what you think I want to see."

His hands land on my hips. Fingers hook beneath the elastic. Slowly, ever so slowly, he peels the cotton down, down, down; eyes locked on mine the entire time.

When my panties join my jeans on the floor, he is back at my center. Breath hot on my skin. Thumbs drawing circles on my hips. Hovering. Waiting. Panting between my spread legs. I don't dare move. Don't dare say a word. I simply wait for his next move while reminding myself to breathe.

Devlyn runs the tip of his nose up my center and inhales deeply. Strengthens his grip on my hips. Kneads my flesh with his fingers. Breathes heavily over my mound for one, two, three breaths. Then his mouth meets my lower lips. A gentle, wet kiss. Followed by another. And another. Then his tongue darts out and flattens against my seam as he slowly licks up my center.

"Oh god," I moan out as I fist the comforter.

He groans at the junction of my thighs then releases my hips from his touch. In a swift move, he sweeps his arms under my legs and rests my thighs on his shoulders. His hands cup my butt and tug me closer. Bringing my center to his mouth. And then his tongue licks up my lips again. Tastes me with unmatched hunger. Flicks at the small bundle of nerves.

I squirm beneath him. Moan without restraint. Curl my fingers in his hair and tug when he hits *the spot* that has me begging for more. Grind against his mouth without shame as he inserts one finger then another and slowly pumps in and out of my core. Fist the comforter until my knuckles sting as fire and power and ecstasy swirl low in my belly and spill out of me in the form of euphoria.

Blinding light illuminates behind my closed eyes as I float in the heavens. And before my feet hit earth again, the mattress dips as Devlyn crawls up my body. His lips kiss a slow trail up my midline, stray left to suck my aching breast and pert nipple between his lips, followed by the right. Releasing my breast, he kisses and licks along my collarbone. Nips at the length of my shoulder, the curve of my neck, the column of my throat before sucking my earlobe between his teeth.

"Please tell me you're sure," he whispers in my ear then rubs his bare length along my center.

When did he remove the last of his clothes? Most likely when I was in a trance, blissed out by what he had done to my body.

"Yes, I'm sure." I lift my hips and rock against him. I don't miss the audible shake in his next breath. Or the way his fingers bruise my hip.

"Need to get a condom." Devlyn shifts his weight off me and reaches for one of the nightstand drawers. He fumbles with the box, still wrapped, and glances back with a wince. "Sorry."

I giggle under my breath. "The fact that you have to unwrap the box is more than okay." To some, this would kill the mood. Waiting while their partner fumbles with the cellophane and breaks into the box. But me? I find the action sexy. Yes, Devlyn said he hadn't been with anyone in years—not that his sexual history changes how I see him—but watching his dexterous fingers maul the box of condoms while he pins his lips between his teeth… I have a front-row seat to his inexperience. A fact that calms my jittery nerves a little more.

"Halle-freaking-lujah," he mutters as he takes a square from the box. I want to giggle again, but stop myself the moment our eyes connect.

In a microsecond, the seriousness of what is about to happen hits me full force. A fresh wave of anxiety blooms in my chest, kicks my heart into fifth gear, has my lungs begging for oxygen. Everything moves in slow motion as Devlyn tears the wrapper open, removes the condom, fumbles with it slightly then rolls it down his thick length.

Holy shit!

I shouldn't have looked. Shouldn't have watched. Shouldn't have stared at the size of him. Because my anxiety amplifies tenfold. My skin feels tight on my body. A hand wraps around my heart and squeezes, tighter and tighter. And for the life of me, I can't remember how to breathe. My sight blurs as my ears fill with white noise.

What was I thinking? I thought I was ready. Thought I could go through with this. But right now, it feels like death is swallowing me whole. Death by embarrassment. Death by panic attack because this thirty-two-year-old woman is scared to have sex for the first time.

What was I thinking?

And then he is there. Devlyn. Body pressed to mine and face a breath away. Still blurry, but slowly coming into focus as he strokes my cheek. His lips move, but his words hit my ears in a garbled mess. Then he kisses me — my lips, my cheek, the spot beneath my ear.

"Breathe," he says, soft and slow. Another kiss heats the skin beneath my ear. "I've got you." He shifts to meet my gaze. "Just breathe."

Then I take the deepest breath of my life as Devlyn rocks his hips forward.

TWENTY-TWO

DEVLYN

I never want to let her go.

Forehead pressed to hers, I tighten my hold on Shelly. Our heavy breaths mingle in the air and further dampen our skin. Still inside her, I shift us onto our sides and band my arms around her more securely. Hold her impossibly closer and kiss her forehead, the tip of her nose, her cheek, her lips.

My fingers comb through her hair as our breathing settles and the room grows still. I close my eyes and bask in the hormonal high my body is on. Relish the heat and sensation of Shelly in my arms, bare and natural and uninhibited. Cherish the subtle touches she gives as her fingers paint small circles on my lower back.

"That was…"

"Incredible," I finish for her.

"Incredible," she repeats wistfully.

Sex—making love—with Shelly was more than incredible. Once I calmed her, once the sharp sting of my invasion faded, we fumbled with our rhythm. But it didn't take long for the lack of coordination to fall away. In its place, we figured out the perfect tempo. Learned when to rock our hips at the perfect time. Discovered which position or angle made each other moan. And then she let go.

Watching Shelly come undone beneath me is a sight I will never forget. A sight I will mentally revisit time and again. The moment her orgasm peaked, it was like watching the most beautiful flower open its petals and come to life. A magical sight to behold. Her skin blotched in various shades of pink and red. Shades I will only associate with her.

But making love was more than just a physical act with Shelly.

When her starry blues locked on mine as we let go, an inferno of emotion burned beneath my sternum. The shimmering stars in her eyes sucked me deeper. The connection we shared from the start tightened its grip around my heart. And it was in that singular moment, in that infinite blip of time, I knew I would never spend a day without Shelly in my life.

Is it too soon to confess such bold statements aloud?

Minute by minute, I grow more flaccid inside Shelly. Much as I don't want to break the physical connection, remaining like this isn't ideal. So I reluctantly withdraw from her. Press a kiss to her forehead and excuse myself to dispose of the condom.

When I crawl under the sheets, Shelly is softly snoring on my pillow. I don't wake or move her. Instead, I adjust myself to mold my body to her frame, wrap my arms around her waist, and whisper good night against the skin beneath her ear.

I WAKE TO COLD SHEETS WHERE SHELLY FELL ASLEEP IN my arms only hours ago. The smell of bacon and fresh bread float through the house and my stomach grumbles in response. I press a palm to my stomach to quelch the feisty organ.

Arms above my head, I stretch the sleep from my muscles. As I scoot toward the edge of the bed, I pick up Shelly's scent on the pillow. I roll over, press my nose to the space she abandoned not long ago and inhale the scent distinctly Shelly—sweet and floral and earthy. Fisting the pillow, I smother myself with her perfume.

How will I ever sleep without her in my bed again?

Now is not the time for such questions or answers. I may want Shelly in my bed—not strictly for sex—every night going forward, but that doesn't mean she is ready for the same level of commitment. Last thing I need to do is scare her off. Doesn't mean I won't skirt the subject and put out feelers.

Out of bed, I dig a pair of sweatpants from the dresser, step into them, and presumptuously grab a condom from the nightstand and pocket it before wandering to the kitchen. At the end of the hall, the kitchen comes into view and I freeze. My breath catches in my throat as I take in the view.

Screwed. I am so screwed when it comes to this woman. Without a doubt, my heart is hers.

With her back to me, I survey the scene unannounced. Shelly has her toffee-blonde locks securely piled on her head; a few stragglers tickle the nape of her neck. She wears the shirt I wore last night, and only the shirt. Her bare legs go on for miles. I swallow and try to temper the thoughts causing my sweats to tent.

Moving away from the cutting board, she spots me in her periphery. A hand slaps her chest as she gasps. "Holy shit." I amble into the kitchen as she catches her breath. "You practically gave me a heart attack," she says, smacking my bare chest as I snake my arms around her waist.

I kiss her lips. "Sorry." *Am I, though?* "Actually, I'm not sorry. I rather enjoyed watching you a minute."

My favorite smile lights up her face. "Yeah, you do have a thing for watching me."

So she has noticed the way I can't look away from her. How *long* has she noticed?

"Is that so?"

"Mm-hmm." Her finger draws circles on my pec. "Don't think I didn't notice you at the shop. Or in the museum. Or the park." She licks her lips. "And every other time before we decided to be more than friends."

Part of me is embarrassed she noticed every time I studied her face longer than normal. No wonder she was confused. My words constantly told her one thing while my actions said the complete opposite. The other part of me is delighted that she read the signs the way she did.

That she didn't shove me away, that she gave me room to breathe. To figure out how to move forward with her. To clear some of my past demons and make room for her light.

The back of my knuckles brush along her cheekbone. I kiss her forehead, the tip of her nose, her lips. Press my forehead to hers. "Glad I didn't scare you off." Another kiss to her lips; this one deeper, potent, ravaging.

"Never." Out of nowhere, she straightens her spine. "Shit," she hisses and breaks free of my arms. She bolts to the stove, fiddles with the knob, and stirs what I assume are eggs. "Oh, thank goodness."

I step up behind her and peer over her shoulder. "All good?" My lips drop to her neck.

"Yeah." She melts into my touch. "Breakfast will be done in a few, if you want to set up a place to eat."

I kiss her neck again. "On it."

The dining room rarely gets used, but today I want to sit with Shelly and share a meal at the table. Add touches of her to yet another room in the house. Maybe after breakfast, if I gather up enough nerve, I will walk her up the stairs and show her my studio. The only space she has yet to see, for good reason. Weeks ago, the sight of my studio—her face and likeness on several pieces of canvas and stock—may have sent Shelly running for the hills. Now, she may accept my obsession with more grace.

Shelly walks into the dining room with two loaded plates, sets them down, and turns back for the kitchen. Before I get the chance to ask if she needs help, she returns with two mugs of tea.

"This looks wonderful." I scan the plate of cheesy southwestern scrambled eggs, bacon, tangerine segments, and toast with sliced avocado. "Thank you for making breakfast."

Heat pinks her cheeks as she shrugs. "No big deal. Just wanted to do something nice for you." With both hands, she brings the mug to her lips and sips her tea. "Plus, I might be in love with your kitchen."

It is on the tip of my tongue to invite her to use my kitchen every day of the week. But jumping on that bandwagon prematurely probably isn't the best idea. Still, I open my mouth and abbreviate the idea.

"You're welcome to use it whenever you like."

Her eyes drop to her plate. *Shit.* Stepped over the line anyway. *Dammit.* But then I catch the corners of her mouth as they tip up. That small action steals every worry I felt seconds ago and fills me with jubilation.

I devour each bite, and it isn't long before I pat my stomach and push my plate away. "So good. If you're not careful, you'll cook all the meals."

Shelly rolls her eyes. "Ha ha." She sips her tea then sets her mug down. "Aside from the occasional *when will you get married and give me grandchildren* moments, my mom is pretty great. She's no kitchen guru but made sure we knew basics before moving out. Her lessons stuck with me, but not so much with my brother."

"So what you're saying is the kitchen is his arch-nemesis."

She laughs. "Once upon a time, yes. But since meeting his now wife, he's putting in the time and effort to learn."

We sit in silence for a beat, both of us letting our full bellies settle while we sip tea. And I can't help but think how much I love this. Sitting here, across the table from Shelly, eating breakfast, sipping tea, having casual conversation, enjoying each other's company. I also can't stop thinking about how I want this with her more often than not.

"I want to show you something," I say, eyes on hers.

"Okay. Just give me a minute to clean up."

"No." My chair legs scrape the wood floor as I rise to my feet. "Leave it. We'll clean up after."

I offer my hand and she takes it, standing from her seat. "O-okay."

With a deep breath, I walk to the left and up the staircase. There is only one room when you reach the top. My studio. And I am about to expose the biggest piece of myself to her. Something I have never done with another soul.

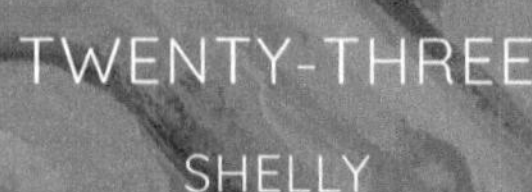

TWENTY-THREE

SHELLY

Slowly, we ascend the stairs. With each step up, Devlyn's breathing quickens. His grip on my hand tightens. This isn't just his studio he is leading me up to. This *is* Devlyn. The inner workings of his mind. Him expressing all the things he can't find a voice for.

We reach the landing and the massive space comes into view. There is no door to separate the studio from the stairwell. The only door to this room is at the other end of the stairs. To the right, a large window brightens the space naturally. A second smaller window sits on the opposite wall higher up. A skylight in the center of the ceiling.

My eyes dart in every direction as I absorb the chaos that is Devlyn's studio.

A closet with an open barn door is packed with canvases in various sizes. Some painted, others blank. One wall of the closet is lined with shelves. Implements and brushes, cleaning supplies and rags, pencils and more sit on the shelves—many of them unopened.

A bathroom with a stall shower, toilet, and double sink with a black countertop is brightened by a small window. Hand towels hang from the bar. A bottle of mineral oil and bar of soap sit between the sinks. The faint splatter of paint from washed hands in one of the bowls.

The main room of the studio has a drafting table at one end, a cart and shelves beside it. In the heart of the room is a large table covered in used rags, large coffee cans with brushes sticking out, various-sized glass jars with dripped paint on the glass, and an abundance of paint tubes in different states of use.

Canvases lean against walls and each other. Drawings lie scattered on the floor and pinned to the walls. Some in color, others monochrome. But there appears to be a theme with several of them. A theme that doesn't shock me after seeing Devlyn's work at the exhibition or the piece my parents gifted me for Christmas.

Me. I am the theme.

Considering our romantic relationship is fairly new, this should bother me. Shouldn't it? Some women might think an artist's obsession with one person—their muse— is awkward or disturbing. But as I scan the room and take in all the various ways Devlyn has reconstructed my image, a warmth builds in my chest.

Devlyn may have difficulty expressing himself with words, but the art in this room says more than any words ever will. *Devlyn is in love with me. Madly.*

"Wow," I breathe out.

I haven't met his gaze since we entered the room, but his eyes sear my profile. His silence begs for me to expand on my single-word response. To tell him if I love it or never plan to return.

"Is it weird that I love seeing myself in so many different ways?" I ask this to lighten the tension rolling off him. And it works.

A soft chuckle leaves his lips, growing louder with each breath, and soon I join in. As our laughter fades, he gives my hand a squeeze.

"Does it freak you out?" He waves his hand around the room. "Seeing all this. Seeing how much you inspire me."

Turning to face him, I bring my body flush with his and lock my fingers behind his neck. His hands automatically find my hips. "Nope." I press my lips to his. "Maybe because of the images at the exhibition." Another kiss. "Or maybe because my parents bought one of your pieces and gifted it to me for Christmas."

Devlyn jerks his head back. "Really?"

I nod. "Mm-hmm."

"Was it the iris drawing?" I nod again. "Funny enough, I thought maybe it was someone related to you. But I'd never heard you mention a George."

"Ah. That would be my dad. Mom uses his cards to shop online."

"Gotcha." Devlyn brings his lips back to mine. "Seriously, though… you're not bothered by all this?"

I shake my head. "Is it weird that my face might be on someone's wall? Sure." I glance around the studio for a beat. "But I love that you can't get me out of your head."

His hands drop beneath the hemline and dip under the

cotton of my shirt, inching up the material. One arm bands around my waist while his other hand traces up my spine.

"I don't sell paintings or drawings where the image is noticeably you. Those, I keep." Leaning in, he devours my lips. When the kiss breaks, fire and passion brew in his eyes. "Can I paint you?"

Confused by the question, considering he has painted me countless times, I narrow my eyes. "Um, yes."

The corner of his mouth kicks up and my stomach does somersaults. Before realization dawns on me, Devlyn is peeling the shirt over my head. Pushing my panties to the floor. Exposing me completely with a wicked grin on his face.

"Uh, Devlyn." The urge to slap an arm over my breasts and lady bits is strong. "I don't know if I'm okay with you putting my nude body on canvas."

His smile widens. "Good thing that's not what I'm doing." He takes my hand and walks me over to a metal stool, the seat splattered in every shade of the rainbow and more. "Sit here."

I park myself on the stool, shiver as the cool metal meets my skin, hide my breasts behind my forearms, and cross my legs. My heart pounds in my chest while Devlyn roams the studio, picks up a tube of blue paint, then pink, then yellow. I lose focus as he continues, oblivious to my mini panic attack.

I may not be the shyest woman in the room most days, but the idea of having my naked body on display—even if it never leaves this room—has me in crisis mode.

"Breathe," Devlyn says in my ear. His hands come up from behind and take hold of my biceps. He kisses along my shoulder, the curve of my neck, up my throat. "Trust me." His words hot and soft on my skin.

My entire frame sags as he peels my arms away and lets them fall to my sides. Stepping around the stool, he parts my legs and positions himself between them. With a finger under my chin, he tips my head back and presses his lips to mine. The kiss starts off slow and gentle with light pecks. But with each kiss, it grows more intense. Impassioned and hungry.

We roam each other's bodies with our hands. A moan spilling from my lips as a growl builds in his chest.

Something slick coats my skin when he palms my breast. I tear my lips away and look down. A hand-sized streak of magenta paint smears my skin. Adds a pop of contrast to my pale, bare flesh. And that is when it clicks.

"Can I paint you?"

Did Devlyn mean he wanted to put paint on my actual body? Not paint my likeness on canvas? By the questioning look in his glass-green eyes right now, I would say yes.

Off to the right, I stare at the tray of paints squeezed out. Dipping two fingers in the dark green, I swirl the paint onto my skin. Then I bring them to Devlyn's chest, look him square in the eyes, and streak his skin with the pigment.

Hunger and need darken Devlyn's green irises. Before I make a joke about him asking for it, he strips off his sweats. Kicks them aside. Grabs the paint tray from the table then wraps an arm around my waist and sits us both on the floor.

Time evades us with each laugh, moan and fondle as we paint each other. Our paint-coated fingers roam and clutch and bruise. Our mouths crash together while our lips and tongues taste. After the majority of our bodies are paint slicked, Devlyn pulls a condom from the pocket of his sweats, rolls it on, and eases his thick erection between my legs. I fist his hair as he clutches the nape of my neck. My legs wrap around his waist as his hips rock at a steady, delicious tempo. The paint on our skin swirls in a kaleidoscope of colors and it isn't long before my orgasm vibrates every nerve ending in my body. Then Devlyn is right behind me, jaw slack and body trembling in ecstasy.

Minutes pass and we don't move. Our breaths calm as Devlyn props himself up on his forearms, then kisses me deeply.

"Thank you for christening my studio. Work will never be dull again."

I slap his arm and laugh. "Painting me will never be dull."

The same hunger from earlier ignites his eyes. "If by painting you, you mean this"—he glances between our bodies—"damn right. Given the chance, I'd paint you every day."

Heat crawls up my neck to my cheeks, but the paint disguises most of it. "I'd like you to paint me every day. But only if I get to do the same."

Devlyn drops his lips to mine as his hips start to rock. I am about to mention something about the condom needing to be replaced when I hear a noise from downstairs.

Breaking the kiss, I ask, "Did you hear that?"

"Hear what?" He kisses my stained skin.

"Devlyn?" a woman calls from downstairs. "You home?"

Above me, Devlyn freezes and goes wide eyed. "Shit." His eyes slam shut. "Shit, shit, shit."

A new dose of panic floods my veins. "What's wrong? Who is that?"

"Devlyn? Are you upstairs?" The woman sounds closer than she did a moment ago.

Devlyn pulls out quickly and I wince. "Sorry." He fumbles for his sweats, my shirt, and panties. "Here." He hands me the garments with a pained look. "Give me a minute, Mother," he shouts. "I'll be right down."

Oh. My. God. Oh my god!

Devlyn's mom is here. Downstairs. Right now. There is no possible way for either of us to skirt past her without her seeing us. And with the paint covering both our bodies, literally, it won't be difficult to surmise what we were doing.

Kill. Me. Now.

He removes the condom, tosses it in the trash, then steps into his sweats. I slip the shirt over my head and pull on my panties. As I straighten, he steps into me, frames my face with his hands, and presses a gentle kiss to my lips.

"Wait here a minute. I'll see if I can get her to leave."

I tuck my lips between my teeth and nod. "'Kay."

"Be right back."

Devlyn dashes down the stairs, paint smeared over ninety percent of his body, and greets his mother. I move closer to the landing and try to listen in on their conversation without being seen.

"What in the world, Devlyn?" Her tone blade sharp. "Why are you covered in paint?"

"Hello to you too, Mother."

"Don't be smart with me." Her shoes clap the floor and grow quieter as they move away.

Hesitantly, I go down a few stairs and listen for further movement.

"What brought you by?" Devlyn doesn't hide the curtness from his words. The sharp tone so different from what I am used to hearing from him.

Devlyn has told me about his parents, but not in in-depth detail. From what I do know, she sounds like a lot to handle. And by the way she speaks with Devlyn now, I don't disagree with that opinion.

"Well," she huffs out. "I came over to ask you to lunch, but with the state of your appearance, that isn't happening." Her shoes clap the floor again. This time, they grow louder and I panic. "Your father and I have planned a post-New Year's party at the house for next Saturday. It's more than enough—"

She stops speaking the moment my foot slips on the top stair and I fall on my butt.

"Shit," I whisper as I scurry up into the studio. There is nowhere to go, nowhere to hide. So, I dash over to the table and sit on the stool. At least I can hide my bare legs.

Clap, clap, clap.

With each step she takes up the stairs, my heart shrivels a little more. When she reaches the landing, looks around the room, and spots me, a snarl displays on her face. Albeit brief, I still catch it.

The woman eyes me with disgust as Devlyn darts past her and comes to my side.

"Devlyn, who is this girl?"

Girl?

"Mother." Devlyn wraps an arm around my waist then kisses my temple. "This is Shelly." His eyes home back in on her. "My girlfriend." She grinds her jaw. "Shelly, this is my mother, Karen Templar."

If the tension were any thicker in the room, we would all suffocate.

Without a word, she turns on her heel and stomps down the stairs like a pouty juvenile. When she reaches the bottom floor, she shouts up the stairwell. "Devlyn, a word downstairs. Now."

He doesn't answer her. He doesn't move from my side. Instead, he frames my face and holds my stare. "We'll talk when she leaves. But please, don't let her bother you." He kisses my lips, my nose, my forehead. "Let me get rid of her, then we can talk."

Speechless, I nod.

Devlyn darts down the stairs and I stay put on the stool. From my seat, I hoped to not hear what his mother would say next. Sadly, I hear every seething, ugly word.

"That girl will ruin your career. She will tarnish the

Templar name. I bet she only wants your money. Have you gotten a good look at her?"

All the ugly words twirl in my head like a cyclone gone astray. One by one, her words cripple me. Douse me in fear and hurt. Steal the happiness from my soul.

Then Devlyn pipes up. "Enough, Mother!" he booms. "Enough."

"Don't you dare—"

"No, Mother, it's my turn to speak. That *woman* upstairs is brilliant and wonderful and kind. More than I could ever ask for or deserve. Without hesitation, she gives me her heart. More than you ever have."

"I've heard enough."

"No, you haven't. Because you never listen." Her shoes clap the floor and get quieter. "She matters to me. A lot. And if you can't respect her or my feelings, I suggest you don't stop by unannounced. Ever."

My heart races in my chest. Tears well in my eyes. Not that no one has ever stood up for me, but this is different. This is someone I love putting me first. Over their family.

"How dare you speak to me with such disregard."

"How dare I? *How dare I?*" Devlyn laughs without humor. "I'm done, Mother. Done. Don't call or email. Don't reach out at all. I'll be changing the code to the door as soon as you leave."

"You can't just get rid of your mother, Devlyn. It doesn't work that way." The house goes eerily quiet a beat. "When that girl trashes your life, when you have nowhere left to turn, you'll beg for my forgiveness."

Dear god. What the hell is wrong with this woman?

She obviously thinks of herself as holier than thou, while everyone at her feet is shit.

"Get out!" he screams. "Get out now!"

"How dare—"

"Now!"

A moment later, the door slams. Then Devlyn screams at the top of his lungs.

Immediately, I want to run down the stairs and go to him. Comfort him. See if he needs anything, even if it is time alone. But I also don't want to crowd him. Make him think he doesn't have the space or time to process what happened on his own. Be a nag or pest when what he needs is solitude and quiet.

I don't want him to think I'm like *her*.

Sliding off the stool, I tiptoe to the landing, then down the stairs. The house is quiet. Too quiet. When I reach the bottom floor, I peek around the doorway. No sign of Devlyn. I pad across the room, look left into the living room then right into the dining room. Still no Devlyn. I round the corner, walk past the kitchen, and step into the formal sitting room at the entrance of the house.

There, on the floor, near the front door, Devlyn is curled in on himself, back to the ceiling. Slowly, I pad across the room, come to his side and crouch down. I don't say a word. Instead, I gently rest a hand on his back. He startles at my touch. A breath passes between us and then he twists, wraps his arms around my waist, and clings to me as if I am the air he breathes.

His frame shakes as he sobs into my lap. I bend over

him, blanket him with touch, and kiss along his spine. "I got you." I hug him tighter. "No matter what."

He grips me impossibly tighter, his fingers bruising my flesh. But I don't care. "I need you, Shelly. Always."

"You have me."

Wiggling free, he sits up and frames my face. "Promise?"

I lift my hand and stick out my pinkie. "Promise."

He hooks our pinkies then drags me onto his lap. "Never letting you go," he says before smashing my lips with his.

Good. Because there is nowhere else I want to be.

TWENTY-FOUR

DEVLYN

Life has never been this exhausting.

When I cut ties with my mother two weeks ago, it felt like she sucked part of my soul out. Knowing her, she probably did.

Although life feels less weighted with her absence, my body is still recovering from our screaming match. Not just my physical self, but my mental and emotional self too. Dumping toxic people from your life, especially family, isn't as simple as saying goodbye. You don't just get to wave a hand and be done with it. Because, as expected, my mother has continuously tried to keep in contact. At this point, I am ready to block her. Put a ten-foot cinder block wall around my home and shut out the possibility of her knocking on my door again.

Thank goodness I have Shelly. The only light in my life. The sole reason I wake up each morning and roll out of bed. In the last two weeks, we haven't spent a night without each other. A couple of times, she has hung out

with her friends after work. As soon as they all went separate ways, Shelly came to me.

"Ready?" she asks as she exits the bathroom.

With each night she stays in my home, she adds more
pieces of herself. Occasionally, we stay at her apartment,
but more often than not, she walks through my door.
Cooks in my kitchen. Curls into me on my sofa. Eats
meals at my table. Spoons with me in my bed.

And I don't want it any other way. Well, I would
rather call them *ours* instead of mine, but that is a conversation for a different day.

"Yeah, I'm ready."

Tonight is a big deal. Tonight, I am meeting her friends
at their weekly Sunday gathering. But not just her friends,
I also get to meet her brother and sister-in-law. The whole
situation has me sweaty and itchy.

From what little Shelly has told me about her brother,
he sounds pretty protective of her. I mean, I get it. Shelly
means everything to me, so I am pretty protective of her
too. In a different way. But since Shelly asked me to join
her at the Sunday night gathering, I haven't been able to
shake the jitters from my limbs.

As if she senses my unease, Shelly wedges herself
between my legs at the edge of the bed. Bringing a hand to
my cheek, she wipes away any discomfort with the soft
brush of her thumb.

"I know crowds aren't your thing, but I promise this is
a low-key gathering. Just friends hanging out and
catching up." I nod as my arms band around her waist and
haul her closer. "It's usually a little odd when someone

new comes, like when Micah brought Peyton the first time, but I promise everyone will resume normal conversation in no time."

Being the odd man out has never been something that bothered me. Throughout my middle and high school years, I had been the subject of bullies. People who thought I was weird because I didn't dress the same or socialize the same or join all the clicks. So, instead of getting to know me, they said hurtful things, threw food at me in the cafeteria, or rigged my locker. After a while, it simply became a part of who I was and I accepted it.

When Kelsey came along, I often questioned if she was truly interested or if befriending, then eventually dating me was a prank. It took months for me to believe she cared. When she ended our relationship, the questions came back again. Nothing but heartache came from our breakup, so I brushed the idea under the rug where it belonged.

"As long as you're there, it doesn't matter how strange everyone acts." I hug her to me, bury my nose in the hollow of her throat and inhale. "Meeting new people is always uncomfortable. But these people matter to you, so I want to know them too."

I hold on to Shelly for three breaths, then let her lead me from the bedroom. After we stop in the kitchen to grab the Crock-Pot of sweet-and-spicy meatballs, we get in my car and drive toward the party. On the drive over, Shelly gives me small tidbits about everyone who will be in attendance. When she starts talking about the seventh person, my mind goes numb.

She said a lot of people would be there, but I didn't think it'd be more than a dozen. Jesus.

My heart runs rampant as the whooshing of my pulse fills my ear. I take a deep breath. Then another. And just like she always has, Shelly settles the craziness inside. She grips my hand a little tighter. Rubs her thumb in small circles over my skin. Tells me everything will be okay, that she won't leave my side. Reminds me that everyone at the party is cool and fun and can't wait for us to arrive.

I steer the car into the neighborhood and take in the homes on the street. Most are two-story and look to be built in the last twenty to thirty years. Simple yet clean and elegant. Yards with tall trees and manicured land-scapes. Flower beds and wind chimes and welcome signs. Strategically placed lights to illuminate sturdy magnolias and clustered palms.

I park on the street two houses down and take the Crock-Pot from Shelly when we exit the car. She laces her fingers with mine and guides us toward the house. "They'll love you," she says softly, kissing my cheek.

Not bothering to knock or ring the doorbell, Shelly twists the knob and walks us inside. Just as the door closes, a husky gallops around the corner with a little girl hot on its heels.

"Sparty!" she shouts over the music and chatter. "No, sir." The girl's bossy tone says she is not to be messed with. Before the dog collides with our legs, it screeches to a halt like a speed skater on ice.

Not releasing my hand, Shelly squats down and the

dog steps up to lick her face. "Hey, Spartan. This is Devlyn."

Woof, woof, woof. He cocks his head while looking up and assessing me.

Shelly rises and ruffles the fur on his head. "Be a good boy."

The little girl reaches us and wraps her arms around Shelly's midsection. "Hi, Miss Shelly. Sorry if Sparty was a jerk."

With a laugh, Shelly says, "He's just being himself. Clementine, this is my boyfriend, Devlyn." Shelly wraps her free hand around my bicep and molds herself to my side. "Devlyn, this is Clementine, Autumn's daughter."

Autumn. She and Jonas own this house. They also are expecting a baby any day now.

I untwine my fingers from Shelly and offer Clementine my hand. "It's nice to meet you, Clementine." The girl looks at my hand as her forehead bunches into crooked lines.

About to ask Shelly if I did something wrong, Clementine wraps her arms around me as if we have been friends all her life. "Nice to meet you, Mr. Devlyn."

Shelly leans into my ear. "She's a hugger." I chuckle and return Clementine's brief hug.

Minus the unexpected hug, everyone else greets me with the same enthusiasm as we walk deeper into the house. One by one, I put faces to the names of people Shelly told me about. Some of them are how I pictured them in my mind's eye, others the complete opposite. When Shelly introduces me to her brother, Micah, and sister-in-law, Peyton, I half expect to get the big brother lecture. But Micah surprises us both with a brief hug and big smile.

As the night wears on, I learn why Shelly is so bonded with these people. Her people. Every person here has been kind and wonderful and accepting of me. They smile my way and spark up conversation as if we have been friends just as long as anyone else here. They ask about my work and I ask about theirs. The easiest conversations are with Rex and Reznor from the tattoo shop. They show me pictures of pieces they have done and I show them my art too.

And before the night ends, I feel as if I am just as much their family as everyone else in the room. It stirs new meaning to the term family in my life. Studying the face of each person, I home in on the connection they share that is nothing like what I have ever known as family. Love. Consideration. Tenderness. Friendship.

When it is time to say good night, every hug and promise to see them again is heartfelt and genuine. Nervous as I was before we arrived, every person here made me feel as if I belonged. As if I were their family.

We load into the car and I drive us home. Our fingers laced together and resting in her lap.

"Did you have a nice time?"

I lift her hand to my lips and kiss her knuckles. "I did. Thought I'd be more overwhelmed, but everyone was very welcoming."

She leans across the console and rests her head on my bicep. "See. I knew there was nothing to worry about."

The drive home is quick with less traffic on the roads. When I turn onto my street and spot the white SUV not far in the distance, I bring the car to a halt. Even from half a block away, I know who is parked in front of my house. The woman who just won't give up.

Shelly straightens in her seat. "What's wrong?" When I don't answer, she follows my line of sight. "Is that?"

"My mother?" My knuckles whiten on the steering wheel. "Yep."

"Turn around."

"What?" I twist in my seat to look at Shelly.

"Turn around and go to my apartment. She doesn't know where I live." Shelly lifts a hand to my cheek. "I don't want her to ruin our night."

I pull into the closest driveway, back out, and exit the neighborhood the way we came. The entire drive to Shelly's place, I mull over why my mother is so damn persistent with keeping me in her life if I am such a bother. The only answer I come up with is that she needs someone to step on so she can feel higher and mightier. So she has more people at her feet to kiss them.

In the last two weeks, so much has changed. Once you step out of the shadow of someone else's light, you see the world differently. Once that person no longer has the ability to squash you under their thumb, they come back with more persistence.

After hours of online research since I pushed her away, I concluded my mother is most definitely a narcissist. To what degree? I don't know, nor do I have the time or energy to figure it out. But the further I fell down the dark online hole, the deeper it sank into my bones. The more I realized that people like her will never be happy unless they have someone to belittle or trample.

I don't want to be that person for her. I can't be.

So if I want to break the cycle, if I want to have a healthy life and relationship with Shelly, I have to cut her off. Cut all direct ties. No matter the cost. No matter who I lose in the process. Because from what I've learned, if I don't make a clean break, my mother will slowly and intentionally ruin everything I love. Everything I hold close to my heart. As long as she comes out feeling mighty in the end, she won't care who she crushes along the way.

And I refuse to let her rob me of happiness.

TWENTY-FIVE

SHELLY

Everyone is on edge.

Any day now, Autumn is due to deliver. Jonas started paternity leave days ago, in case Autumn went into labor early. Clementine hasn't allowed Autumn to do a thing on her own except use the bathroom. Even then, she hovers close by.

Although Autumn and Jonas aren't her children, Elizabeth is geared up for the next baby in our group to arrive. We won't be closing Petal and Vine like we did when Cora went into labor, but she is prepped and ready to let me leave the shop and deliver bundles of flowers.

More than ever, Devlyn is holed up in his studio. When I arrive at his house after work, more often than not, he is upstairs. Music echoes throughout the house while he works on commissioned pieces. I don't go up uninvited, not because he doesn't want me up there, but because I assume he needs the time to himself.

Since the unannounced visit from his mother and then

seeing her car out front days later, Devlyn has turned inward slightly. He doesn't shut me out, but is selective with what he shares. His reservation doesn't hurt—I have always known Devlyn's reticent nature—but it has me ready to go into protection mode. Not to protect me, but to safeguard him and his heart.

Art is how Devlyn processes life. How he expresses himself and unleashes what inhabits his thoughts. The good and the ugly. Whichever consumes him, he needs the time to get it out without guilt or interruption or influence.

Most nights, once I start cooking, he comes down. His warm arms band around my waist as he kisses my shoulder, as I melt into his frame and sigh. I love our new routine. Love how easily both of us have fallen into this way of life, without effort or hardship.

"Still no word?" Elizabeth asks as I fill the loose stems at the front of the shop.

I pull my phone from my pocket, tap the screen and find no new messages. "Nope." Just as I pocket my phone, it pings with a text.

Group text from Jonas: It's time!

I spin my phone around and show the message to Elizabeth. The biggest smile plumps her cheeks as she brings her hands to prayer at her lips. Then my phone blows up.

Penny: On my way!

Reznor: We'll head over when the shop closes.

Gavin: Holy shit, man! Congrats!

Cora: As soon as we drop off Clara, we'll be there.

Rex: Congrats, bro! Can't wait to meet the newest family member.

Micah: Peyton and I will swing by in the morning. Congrats, man!

Erin: Ahhh! Turning around now!

My fingers race over the keyboard in response.

Shelly: Aunt Shelly is on the way! Can't wait to meet him or her.

Then, I flip to my text history with Devlyn and type a quick message.

Shelly: Autumn's in labor. Headed to the hospital.

The small gray bubble dances at the bottom left of the screen a moment before Devlyn's response appears.

Devlyn: Just left the park. Be there in a few and we can go together.

Since the incident with his mother, Devlyn spends most of his days at the park and evenings in the studio. Not sure if he draws or paints while at the park, but he appears calmer on the days he visits. As if he needs to sit on our bench while working. As if he needs the energy and serenity of the trees and air and wildlife. As if he needs to be in the same space we shared so many times before.

I fear the reason he leaves the house is on the off chance his mother will stop by unannounced, attempting to stir up more toxic drama. The thought rakes my nerves. No one should fear being home, in their personal space.

On the days a shadow glints Devlyn's gaze, he chauffeurs me to the shop. I don't question his heart or motives. Small as it may seem, I grant him this minute assurance, this form of armor. A way he can shield me from hurt, from his mother.

Shelly: Yeah, that's perfect.

Devlyn: Shouldn't be long.

I fill a few more bins before ditching my shop apron and shouldering my purse. Elizabeth gives me a hug and tells me to send tons of pictures. I bolt out the back door with a small bouquet and hop in Devlyn's SUV, then we are off.

We arrive at the hospital and park in the visitor's lot. After weaving through the main lobby, we step inside the elevator and ascend to labor and delivery. The car comes to a stop and the doors whoosh open. The air hits my face as we step out and my stomach rolls a little at the scent of lemon-scented bleach. I take a deep breath, hold it to the count of ten then release it.

"Hey." Devlyn gives my hand a squeeze. "You okay?"

"Yeah," I say with a nod. "Never been a fan of bleach and it smelled especially strong when the elevator opened."

"Huh."

We steer into the waiting area for the floor, and I look to Devlyn. "What?"

He shrugs. "I barely smelled it is all. Maybe it's because of the cleaning agents I use for my brushes. My nose is desensitized to the strong stuff."

The subject gets dropped when Penny, Cora, and Gavin approach. Cora wraps her arms around me and squeals a little too loudly in my ear. Gavin smiles brightly and says hello to Devlyn.

"How is everyone? Do we know if she's delivered

yet?" I ask Cora, wanting to hold my next niece or nephew sooner rather than later.

"Jonas's mom came out just before you got here. They were going to have Autumn start pushing any minute."

I clap my fingers excitedly and smile so hard my cheeks sting. We settle into the chairs and place bets on if it is a boy or girl. It's three to two for a boy when Erin strolls in and evens the score. Before we get into a face-off about why each of our opinions is fact, Jonas's mom, Irene, walks out with a megawatt smile. The room goes quiet as we all rise and step closer.

"It's a boy!"

The room erupts in cheers. Irene tells us she will come get us once we are allowed to see Autumn, Jonas, and the baby. She disappears down the hall and it isn't long before she returns and invites us back to meet our newest family member.

One by one, we file into the hospital suite. The first thing I notice is how radiant Jonas is. Without question, he will be the best father. That man has the biggest heart and I have never seen it so full.

Like our last trip to the hospital when Cora had Clara, baby Ryker gets passed around for everyone to hold and coo. When I sit with him in the rocking chair, I tell him how lucky he is to have such wonderful parents and the best big sister in the world. And also the world's best aunt.

Baby Ryker has Autumn's dark hair and Jonas's hazel eyes. One thing is certain, this boy will break hearts over the years. Jonas and Autumn may have their hands full with Clementine, but Ryker will be right behind her.

I pass Ryker to Penny and squeeze between Devlyn and Cora.

"Guess you're next," Cora says with a laugh.

It's a joke. I know it is a joke. But I freeze. Not because I fear pregnancy or motherhood or permanency. I freeze because my romantic relationship with Devlyn is little more than a month old. Cora said the words in the moment because she recently had a baby. She'd probably say the same to Peyton if she and Micah hadn't openly told everyone they have no plans to have kids.

But there is another reason I freeze. Another reason my mind tailspins.

When was my last period? Think, Reed. THINK.

I search my mental calendar for my last period. It was before Christmas. A week before. Maybe two. I need my planner. Where the hell is my planner? *Oh god. Oh. God. No. No, no, no, no, no.* This cannot be happening. There is no possible chance I am… pregnant.

"Shelly?" Devlyn's lips are at my ear. "What's wrong? You're shaking. And you look… gray."

Oh god. I think I'm going to be sick. As the thought crosses my mind, my stomach rolls.

I drop Devlyn's hand, slap mine to my mouth, and dash out of the room. In the hall, a nurse smiles then frowns. A hand to the mouth is obviously the universal sign for "I'm going to puke" because the nurse rests a hand on my back and rushes me down the hall to the restrooms.

Bolting into the bathroom, I run for the stall, slam the door and lock it, then drop to my knees and expel the contents of my stomach. When my body finally relaxes, I ease up from the floor, flush the toilet, and step out of the stall. Erin stands next to the sink with concern marring her expression.

"Shell, are you okay? Jesus. You scared us all."

I turn on the faucet, splash my face with cold water and rinse out my mouth. "Yeah. Must've eaten something bad at lunch." The lie rolls off my tongue with too much ease.

She gives me a hug. "Long as you're okay." She releases me and hands me a wad of paper towels. "Devlyn's outside." She points to the door.

"Thanks. Will you tell him I'll be out in a minute?"

With a nod, she says, "No problem. Sure you're okay if I leave?"

I smile at my friend. "Promise I'm good." After another hug, she exits the bathroom.

Staring at myself in the mirror, I brace my hands on the sink and take several deep breaths. For the next minute, I have a heart-to-heart with myself.

I didn't eat anything bad in the last few hours—lunch was more than five hours ago. But the nausea could be from a number of things. The chemical smell of the hospital mixed with the adrenaline rush of being here plus not having much in my system. That has to be it.

"There's no way I'm pregnant," I whisper to my reflection. "We used protection. Every time."

But what do I know about condom usage? Other than the sex ed classes in school—more than fifteen years ago —I haven't had much experience or education in the department. Sure, I know they aren't one-hundred-percent effective, but Devlyn would have said something if the condom broke.

Regardless, I need to exit the bathroom before Devlyn panics and waltzes in. After one last deep breath, I push off the sink and head for the door. Soon as I step out, Devlyn is inches from me, his hands framing my face, eyes studying every detail.

"Are you okay?" he asks, voice low and shaky.

Tears sting the backs of my eyes because I have no clue. For all I know, I could have a virus. It is the time of year for that. I shrug. "Yes. I think." He hugs me to him and I fist the back of his shirt.

A moment later, the same nurse who guided me to the bathroom steps up. "Sorry to intrude, sweetheart. Just wanted to check on you." Her smile is bright and warm.

"Might be a bug," I tell her.

"Why don't you come with me and we can have you checked out? Shouldn't take but a few minutes, if you'd like."

Might as well since I'm here. *Will they also test to see if I'm pregnant?* "Thank you. I appreciate the help."

She walks us to the elevator then takes us to another floor, this one more clinical and cold. Coughs and sneezes and grumbles echo from every direction. The bleach scent is ten times worse and I force myself to breathe through my mouth rather than my nose.

"Hey, Suzanne," a man says from behind the desk. "How can I help?"

"Paul, this young lady…" The nurse looks my direction.

"Shelly," I say.

"Shelly wasn't feeling well upstairs. Would you please run a virus panel?"

He smiles at Nurse Suzanne and nods. "Sure thing." Then he looks in my direction. "I'll just need identification, Shelly, and some forms filled out."

I dig through my purse and hand over my identification. He hands me a clipboard and points to a group of chairs along the wall. While I fill out basic personal and health information, Devlyn wraps an arm around my shoulders and rubs small circles on my skin.

As I sign my name on the consent to treat line, Paul calls me to the counter and says he is ready. He escorts us to a small room with white walls and generic framed art across from the patient chair.

"We'll do a cheek swab and draw blood." He glances at his watch. "Results won't be available for another twelve or so hours. Will you still be in the hospital?"

I shake my head. "No. We're visiting a friend who had a baby."

He nods as he wraps and ties the tourniquet around my distal bicep. "Make a fist." He jiggles his gloved fingers over the veins at my elbow. "Nice veins." His smile makes me want to smile, but I can't muster the strength. "I'd recommend you don't return to see your friend until we know what this is. Don't want to expose the newborn."

Just before the needle pricks my skin, I look up at

Devlyn. He lets me squeeze his hand while I breathe erratically.

"Almost done," he mouths.

The phlebotomist unties the elastic on my arms before easing the needle from my vein and bandaging me up. Next, he removes a long Q-Tip from a sealed tube, asks me to open my mouth and runs the cotton over the inside of my cheek. He places it back in the tube, seals it with a new sticker, then sets it next to the blood vials.

"All set," he says, peeling his gloves away and washing his hands. "Take your time getting up."

Back at the desk, he returns my identification and verifies my telephone number. "We'll give you a call in the morning. Is there a time that works better for you?"

"Any time is good. Thank you, Paul."

"You're welcome. Go home and get some rest. We'll talk in the morning."

And with that, Devlyn and I amble out of the hospital. Devlyn thinking I may have some sort of cold and me considering the possibility of being pregnant.

Devlyn just went through so much with his mother. I don't know if he is in the right headspace to discuss the likelihood of something other than the common cold. During the drive home, I keep the details of my late period to myself. More than pregnancy causes cycle disruption. Stress, diet, a change in sleep habits, physical exertion. No need to ratchet up his anxiety too.

It isn't long before Devlyn parks in his driveway, guides me inside, and tends to me like the most adoring boyfriend. He cooks and feeds me, helps me with a bath, then curls up behind me under the covers.

As my eyes grow heavy, he kisses my shoulder then whispers, "Love you, Shelly."

I tighten his grip around my belly, tears stinging the backs of my eyes. "I love you too."

TWENTY-SIX

DEVLYN

WE STARTLE AWAKE TO SHELLY'S PHONE RINGING ON the nightstand.

"Hello," she answers, voice thick with sleep. "This is Shelly Reed." She goes quiet while the person on the other end speaks. I toy with her hair and wait for her to tell me the news. "Yes, I heard you. Thank you for the update."

Shelly ends the call and stares at the ceiling with glassy eyes. Something twists in my gut. Something that says this isn't just a cold. Maybe it's something much worse. Cancer. Something with her heart. My mind races with various ailments I have heard of. Diseases that appear like common colds but are much worse.

I hate how quiet she is. I hate how scared she looks. More than anything, I hate that she won't look me in the eye. As if I won't like what she has to say.

Unable to deal with the silence any longer, I brush my knuckles over her cheek and swallow down my nerves.

"You're scaring me," I mumble. A tear rolls down her temple. "Please talk to me, Shelly."

"I don't understand," she whispers to the ceiling. "How?"

"How what?" God, I want to shake the information from her brain and soothe away her fears.

Finally, she turns to meet my gaze. "I'm scared." Another tear spills and I am ready to crawl out of my skin.

"I can't help unless you tell me what's wrong."

"Please don't hate me."

This has me confused. Why would I hate Shelly for being sick? "No matter what it is, we'll get through this." I drop my lips to hers to seal the vow. "I love you, Shelly."

She closes her eyes, takes a deep breath, then opens them. "I don't have a viral infection."

Well, that is good news. I breathe easy for only a moment. Wait? Does that mean it is something worse? My mind automatically goes back to cancer or some inherited immune disorder her family doesn't know about.

"I don't know how, but I'm pregnant."

I inch back from her and take in her wince. "What?" My voice comes out louder than I intend it to.

"Oh god."

She pulls away from me, slides out of bed on the opposite side, and fumbles for her clothes. Meanwhile, I can't move. My body weighted with a ton of bricks. My limbs in a state of paralysis.

How?

Before I get another word in, before I get off the bed,

she darts for the bathroom with her purse and starts opening cabinets and drawers. As she dashes out and heads for the closet, I finally snap out of my haze and dress.

"What are you doing?" She yanks shirts from hangers and shoves them in her bag. She attempts to push past me, but I grab her elbow. "Shelly, talk to me. Where are you going?"

"You're freaking out." She sniffles and wipes her cheeks with the back of her hand. "I see it in your eyes."

"Well, I'm in shock." I take a deep breath and speak as calmly as possible. "Please, don't go."

"Did you not hear what I said?" She hangs her head. "I'm pregnant." Her sobs grow louder and I pull her into my arms. She fights it at first, but caves. Then hollow laughter spills from her lips.

"Why are you laughing?" Nothing about this situation is funny. If anything, her laugh has the hairs on the back of my neck standing straight.

She leans back and looks me in the eye. "I heard your mother say I'd ruin your life. Never thought she'd be right."

My eyes go wide and I freeze for the second time in minutes. *Why would Shelly say something like that? Why would she believe a word that comes out of my mother's mouth?*

Shelly slips from my arms. The air around me grows thick and heavy and encapsulates me. Pulls me into a fog. My pulse soars in my ears and drowns out every noise in the house. Until I hear the front door slam. I shake my head and snap back to reality. Run for the door, burst outside and chase after her car as it backs out of the driveway.

"Shelly, no!" I scream after her, desperate for her to come back. For her to park in the driveway, get out of the car, and come back in the house so we can talk about this.

But she doesn't stop. She just keeps driving. Away from me. Away from us. Away from love. With our baby in her belly.

You promised me. You promised that you'd stay.

My knees buckle, and I fall to the pavement. Sharp pain radiates through my legs, and I accept every treacherous stab as I curl into a ball. In the middle of my driveway. For all to see.

A chill that has nothing to do with the January temperature blankets me head to toe. Seeps into my bones as numbness begins to wash over me. A numbness I know all too well.

Shelly, please don't go. Please. You promised you'd never leave. Please… I need you.

Up Next in the Series

Abstract Passion is the final novel in the series and I can't wait for you to read the epic conclusion.

One word makes him freeze. And with his silence, I walk away.

Leave it to me, the unintentional abstinence queen, to get pregnant after my first time. Nothing hurts more than walking away from Devlyn after I share the news. The decision is impulsive and painful… and I regret it instantly.

Not long ago, I envied my friends. Envied their lives, their relationships, their opportunity to move forward. I wanted what they have. Now, it is my turn.

But loving Devlyn Templar isn't that simple. Sharing a life with him comes with its own challenges—heavy baggage and severe insecurity. Every day, we navigate those obstacles together.

And just as we find our groove, another complication gets hurled in our direction. One that refuses to be ignored.

More By Persephone Autumn

The Click Duet

High school sweethearts torn apart. When fate gives them a second chance, one doesn't trust they won't be hurt again. Through the Lens (Click Duet #1) and Time Exposure (Click Duet #2) is an angsty, second chance, friends to lovers romance with all the feels.

The Inked Duet

A man with a broken heart and a woman scared to put herself out there. Love is never easy. Sometimes love rips you apart. Fine Line (Inked Duet #1) and Love Buzz (Inked Duet #2) is a second chance at love, single parent romance with a pinch of angst and dash of suspense.

The Insomniac Duet

He was her high school bully. She was the outcast that secretly crushed on him. More than ten years later, he's her boss, completely oblivious to their shared past, and wants no one but her. More importantly, he doesn't understand her animosity toward him.

Transcendental

A musician in search of his muse and a woman grieving the loss of her husband. Two weeks at an exclusive retreat and their connection rivals all others. Until she leaves early without notice. But he refuses to give up until he finds her again.

Distorted Devotion

Swept off her feet by love, life takes a dark, unexpected turn. Now the love of her life may be the cause of her death. Check out this gripping, romantic suspense.

Depths Awakened

A small town romance which captivates you from the start. Two broken souls have sworn off love. Vowed to never lose anyone else. But their undeniable attraction brings them together and refuses to let go.

Broken Metronome

When the music of the heart dies…

Broken Metronome is an angsty poetry collection full of heartache and the possibility of what may have been.

Slipping From Existence

Would it be so bad to slip from existence? Would it be so bad to give in to the darkness?

Slipping From Existence is a dark poetry collection centered around depression and coping while maintaining a brave face.

Thank You!

Thank you so much for reading **Blank Canvas,** book one in the **Artist Duet**. If you wouldn't mind taking a moment to leave a review on the retailer site where you made your purchase, Goodreads and/or BookBub, it would mean the world to me.

Reviews help other readers find and enjoy the book as well.

Much love,
 Persephone

Here are some of the songs from the **Artist Duet** playlist. You can listen to the entire playlist on Spotify!

Loveless | PVRIS
Touch | Sleeping At Last
Heart | Sleeping At Last
I'll Be Good | Jaymes Young
Fear | Sleeping At Last
Anger | Sleeping At Last
Big Love, Small Moments | JJ Heller
Hearing | Sleeping At Last
Power | Isak Danielson
The First Glance | Anna Yarbrough
Life | Sleeping At Last

Connect with Persephone

Connect with Persephone
www.persephoneautumn.com

Subscribe to Persephone's Newsletter
www.persephoneautumn.com/newsletter

Join Persephone's Reader Group
Persephone's Playground

Follow Persephone Online

instagram.com/persephoneautumn

facebook.com/persephoneautumnwrites

tiktok.com/@persephoneautumn

goodreads.com/persephoneautumn

bookbub.com/authors/persephone-autumn

amazon.com/author/persephoneautumn

pinterest.com/persephoneautumn

twitter.com/PersephoneAutum

Acknowledgments

To my family and friends... I never thought I'd make it through this year. My schedule has been pure chaos. But thanks to you, I am still breathing. Thank you for always being my biggest fans and being proud. I love you more than ever!

To Ellie McLove and Rosa Sharon... Thanks for always performing magic when I hand you my word babies. Commas are the devil. Forgetting words seems to happen more as I lose my mind. But you both make my stories pretty. And thanks for always putting love notes in the margins. xoxo

To Kat Savage... Thank you for making my books pretty on the outside. You helped me gain the courage to put people on my covers and have made this series so perfect. And thanks for being my friend and talking about random shit with me. Love you!

To my author friends... All the hugs! This author thing isn't all rainbows and sunshine, but having you in my circle and corner makes each day better. Love you all!

To the readers and bloggers who read my words... sending you all virtual hugs. Every time I read one of your amazing reviews or see your posts about my books, I cry.

Spilling pieces of yourself on paper isn't easy, but your kindness makes it so worth it each time I start a new book. A million thank yous to each of you!

And if this is your first Persephone Autumn book... thank you for taking a chance on my words. I hope you loved Micah and Peyton, and the future books to come.

About the Author

Persephone Autumn lives in Florida with her wife, crazy dog, and two lover-boy cats. A proud mom with a cuckoo grandpup. An ethnic food enthusiast who has fun discovering ways to vegan-ize her favorite non-vegan foods. If given the opportunity, she would intentionally get lost in nature.

For years, Persephone did some form of writing; mostly journaling or poetry. After pairing her poetry with images and posting them online, she began the journey of writing her first novel.

She mainly writes romance, but on occasion dips her toes in other works. Look for her poetry publications and a psychological horror under P. Autumn.

www.ingramcontent.com/pod-product-compliance
Lightning Source LLC
Chambersburg PA
CBHW061058190726
48286CB00006B/1799